PREACHER FAKES A MIRACLE

PRAISE FOR THE EVAN WYCLIFF MYSTERIES

Kudos for Preacher Finds a Corpse (#1)
2020 Independent Press Awards Distinguished Favorite in Mystery
2020 Eric Hoffer Award Finalist in Mystery

Praise for This Book (Preacher #2):

As anyone who's spent time in a small town the American Midwest knows, there's a lot more going on behind the scenes than you'd expect. Or suspect. And there are plenty of suspects in the latest Evan Wycliff mystery by Gerald Everett Jones. *Preacher Fakes a Miracle* haunted my dreams as I read it, in the way that a good story about a bad situation should. I'm looking forward to reading the next installment of the Evan Wycliff mystery series.

— PAMELA JAYE SMITH, *MYTHWORKS*, AWARD-WINNING WRITER-DIRECTOR-PRODUCER

This is not your mother's preacher. Gerald Jones has created a character who can discover a corpse, kiss a girl, solve a crime, and get back to his trailer in time to say grace over Sunday dinner.

— DAVID DRUM, AUTHOR OF *HEATHCLIFF: THE LOST YEARS*

This time the Preacher digs even deeper, faster, and funnier than his prize-winning debut. It's just what you'd expect, except everything you expect is wrong because the Preacher, in the very talented hands of Gerald Jones, is always at least a step ahead in this very satisfying second time out of the gate.

A fast-moving mystery with twists and surprises that take you in unexpected directions. Jones is adept at creating unique and fascinating characters. His mystery sleuth is a part-timer with lots of heart who splits his time between religion, skip tracing and sometimes the metaphysical. The hero's search for a missing girl and his interactions with various eccentric individuals in the small town make him both sympathetic and compelling. A bit of a shock to learn what's really going on with the abducted young unwed mother... and amazing how it relates to real stories in the news today.

Praise for Preacher #1:

This is literature masquerading as a mystery. Carefully yet powerfully, Gerald Jones creates a small, stunning world in a tiny midwestern town, infusing each character with not just life but wit, charm, and occasionally menace. This is the kind of writing one expects from John Irving or Jane Smiley.

This is an excellent read. Such an engaging storyteller! It really sucked me in. That last page did cause a triple-take, quadruple-take, and whatever comes after, up to about eight. Jones is definitely one of my favorite authors.

— JOHN RACHEL, AUTHOR OF *BLINDERS KEEPERS* AND *THE MAN WHO LOVED TOO MUCH*

A smart, thoroughly entertaining, and suspenseful mystery novel, which is not so much a who-done-it as a how-and-why. The characters are universally well-drawn and quirky, and the relationship between Evan and Naomi is fresh and romantic.

I loved it.

— ROBERTA EDGAR, COAUTHOR OF *THE PERFECT PLAY: THE DAY WE BROKE THE BANK IN ATLANTIC CITY*

The constant shifts in trust and tidbits of new information kept me guessing until the end who was friend or foe and the 'need' to find out kept the pages turning.

Many of the common stigmas, questions, and feelings suicide deaths leave in their wake were also addressed in a responsible way, which will help the conversation around suicide in general.

— RUTH GOLDEN, WRITER-PRODUCER, *THE SILENT GOLDENS: A DOCUMENTARY ABOUT SUICIDE* AND *TALKING ABOUT SUICIDE WITH MARIETTE HARTLEY*

Preacher Finds a Corpse is an absolute pleasure to read. Reminiscent of Charlaine Harris's mysteries and Barbara Kingsolver's early novels like *Animal Dreams* and *The Bean Trees*, it's full of quirky characters who animate the small town in which they live. Evan Wycliff is a complex and compelling protagonist, conflicted and lost in his own life but nevertheless fiercely dedicated to uncovering the truth about his friend Bob Taggart's death.

Jones manages to infuse a deceptively simple story with suspense, angst, and whimsy, as well as surprise. His command of setting, history, and behavior is beyond exceptional. I can't wait for the next book in the series.

— PAULA BERINSTEIN, AUTHOR OF THE
AMANDA LESTER DETECTIVE SERIES AND
HOST OF "THE WRITING SHOW" PODCAST

From the secret contents in a rusty tin fishing box to clues that lead Evan further into danger, Gerald Everett Jones weaves a tense thriller peppered with references to Evan's ongoing relationship to God and prayer.

When the clues boil down to a final surprise, will forgiveness be possible?

Jones does an outstanding job of crafting a murder mystery that romps through a small town's secrets and various lives. His main protagonist is realistic and believable in every step of his investigative actions and setbacks; but so are characters he interacts with; from his boss Zip to a final service which holds some big surprises.

With its roots firmly grounded in an exceptional sense of place and purpose, Jones has created a murder mystery that lingers in the mind long after events have built to an unexpected crescendo.

Murder mystery fans will find it more than a cut above the ordinary.

— D. DONOVAN, *DONOVAN'S BOOKSHELF*

PREACHER FAKES A MIRACLE

AN EVAN WYCLIFF MYSTERY

GERALD EVERETT JONES

Formatted with Vellum

To Benedict Kruse

PROLOGUE

ON TRUMAN LAKE, SUNDAY MORNING

The girl awoke in a fog. She was disoriented, but she didn't panic. It wouldn't be her first hangover, although this one was a doozy. She wanted to scratch her nose, but she quickly realized both of her wrists were bound with soft cloths. And so were her ankles. She could feel bedsheets on her back. So she was prone, her hands and feet lashed to the bedposts.

She'd been tied to a bed before, but it wasn't for sex. Sometimes the nuns or the nurse would restrain her so she couldn't hurt herself. And then there were the clients, who had their own reasons. But if this was a sex game, she wouldn't expect to be wearing much of anything. She could feel the tickle of cloth against her breasts, her stomach, her hips — flannel pajamas! And she wasn't cold. The room was quite warm.

Could it be whoever put her here wanted her to be comfortable?

Her vision was still blurry. The light was dim. A bedroom. Despite what she already knew of her situation, she didn't panic. She'd put up with kinky types before. The comfortable clothing and the warmth of the room made her hope it might all be a game. She had no choice but to go along. Maybe he would get off quickly, then go.

As her eyes began to focus, she felt the bed sway under her. But there was no hot breath on her face, no urgent heaviness hunched over her languid body. And besides feeling she was alone, Melissa noted no accompanying dizziness. This wasn't like any morning-after head she'd ever experienced. The floating sensation could be the drugs wearing off. What had they given her?

She remembered she'd been taken forcefully back to the convent — again — and not being at all happy about it. But perhaps having to live there might be a whole lot more pleasant than whatever was about to go down here. And maybe it was the stress that had brought on another fit. And, yes, the nuns had tied her down to a cot. But the episode had passed, and they'd given her over to that brutish fellow, who claimed to have paperwork.

She wasn't in pain. In her body, a feeling of numbness. Also probably the drugs.

Was this some new kind of drug for her fits? If so, it was something powerful, because she couldn't remember a thing about how she came to be here.

Except — where had they taken her child?

A pang seized her stomach as she remembered how they'd taken him from her. Was that yesterday? She'd have to play their game, give them whatever they needed, and maybe it would all work out.

She had to hold to the belief he'd be safe. Baby Buzz was no good to them dead.

And she convinced herself, which gave her space to worry about her own safety. It wasn't just the threat of being raped. She'd dealt with that before. But what if, now, in this place which must be filled with danger, her body suddenly spasmed?

What if she had another fit? Would they freak out like the nuns had done?

She lifted her head slightly off the pillow — yes, there was an over-stuffed pillow, another deliberate comfort — and she caught a chill as she could make out a shadowy figure seated at the foot of the bed. No facial features for her to study. But he was wearing a dark suit and a white shirt.

He sat very still, with a kind of icy patience.

"Where am I? Who are you?" she asked him.

"In safe hands. And almost home," he said calmly.

It was a mature, confident, deep, resonant voice.

She knew the voice! How could she forget? But after that one time, she never expected to see him again.

"It's *you! Vasili!* Why am I tied up? Is this your idea of —?"

"You never knew my name," he insisted.

"Who are you, then?"

Maybe it was okay after all. Did he have her bound because he thought she'd hurt herself? Without her pills, she could have another fit.

"I am everything to you now. Without me, nothing," he said.

She didn't have the energy to scream. It was more of a plaintive whimper, fraught with sobs. "Where is my baby? What have you done?"

"He is safe, for now. I'll ask the questions. And if you can give me satisfactory answers — *honest* answers — you will do very well — for him and for you."

"He could be yours, you know. We can change his name when I know yours."

"It is of no concern to you now. Listen carefully to what I am asking you."

"So it's a game, right?"

"No, it's quite serious. Your son's life — and yours — could depend on the answers."

She sucked in a deep, panicked breath. Kinky or homicidal, this guy. See where this goes.

"So… ask away."

He waited for a long moment. Then he asked simply, "Why?"

"Why? Why *what?* How am I supposed to know what you're even talking about?"

He took another long moment. The stiff tone of his reply signaled a flash of anger.

She could only submit — what else?

That was how he must want this game played.

"Use your imagination," he snapped.

LORETTA'S TRAILER

THE PREVIOUS FRIDAY MORNING

*M*elissa hoped her sister wouldn't be pissed about her showing up unannounced. But they never stayed mad at each other for very long. All they'd ever had was each other. During the last year, they'd been out of touch for weeks at a time, sometimes months. But when Loretta had moved into this trailer, she'd mailed Melissa her spare key.

It was like an engraved invitation, after all.

The place hadn't been hard to find, even though they were riding in the dark. Loretta had sent her a link on Google Maps, and she'd made Keith stop several times so she could check her phone. The service was spotty out here but not impossible, and the GPS tracked their route. Now she was thankful that the jolting ride on the back of the guy's bike was finally over. Keith was a stranger to her, just some dude who'd plucked her off the side of the road, and she hoped she was done with him. As she hopped off, baby Buzz was wailing in her ear. But she took the trouble to wet her lips and flash the guy a grin and a wink before she turned to go inside, and he sped off.

She was glad to be rid of his rank smell. Maybe she should jump in the shower.

There was no porch light on the trailer, and now that she didn't have the bike headlight to guide her, she had to juggle Buzz as she fished the key from the pocket of her jeans and used the flashlight on her phone to find the lock in the door handle. The place was dark inside, no one was home, and the air felt close and musty. Melissa didn't bother to open a window. She was exhausted, and so was Buzz. The young mother found a blanket, and they were both out cold on the couch as soon as they lay down.

LORETTA HAD GONE off shift at two in the morning, and she was usually home before three. Today, she didn't arrive until half-past five. She'd wanted an apartment over at the marina complex, but Mick Heston, her manager at the club, had said whatever she could afford over here where the rents were lower would have to do for now. (Considering her failed relationship with Mick, she was grateful he bothered to help her at all.) Hence the dinky mobile home. At least she had use of the car and a gas card. She told her coworkers that the Appleton City-Rockville area wasn't sleepy — it was *comatose*. But the commute was just a half-hour's drive east on State Highway B, which was not bad at all unless you got behind one of those enormous double-decker livestock trailers that chugged along at twenty below the limit and stank of manure.

She'd have to ask her landlord, Mr. Zed, for a porch light. (She wasn't sure whether *he* could be trusted, but so far, he hadn't tried anything.) As she let herself in, she gasped as she saw a figure writhing under a blanket on the day bed she used as a couch.

Then the baby started to cry, and Loretta's sister tossed the blanket off as she sat up and rocked her two-month-old son in her arms.

Loretta wasn't upset to see Melissa, but she was startled that the girl and her baby had shown up without warning.

Setting her purse and keys on the dinette, she demanded, "What's going on?"

"Sisters of Mercy sucks," Melissa muttered sullenly as she yawned. "You wouldn't want to keep your dog there."

"I don't have a dog," Loretta huffed, hoping she sounded insistent enough to discourage the idea forever.

But Melissa brightened and giggled. "There's an idea! Now that you got this place, maybe we should get one!"

"*We?*" Loretta realized the answer would likely involve an argument, so she simply asked, "How'd you get here?"

"Ugh, a motorbike. Guy named Keith. Friend of a friend. I didn't have to pay him, but I wouldn't be surprised if he shows back up and, you know, expects something."

"What did you promise him?"

"Nothing in particular," the girl replied with a shrug. "I can't help it if a guy uses his imagination."

Loretta rolled her eyes. Melissa was too pretty for her own good. At least Loretta knew how to turn the gifts nature gave her into a livelihood.

The baby started to cry again.

Melissa added, "Kind of a bumpy ride. Not the best thing for Buzzbomb here. Soft little skulls? He's been upset with us moving around and all."

"Buzz *bomb?*"

"Lighten up! The kid's a poop factory. So some things broke your way, and they didn't for me. You know you're all I've got."

Loretta ignored the familiar plea, saying, "When was the last time you fed him?"

"Still nursing," she said, lifting her T-shirt. "I got plenty. I'm the one who could use a meal. And maybe a breast pump and some salve."

Baby Buzz sucked on a breast and was instantly gratified.

"You can't stay here," Loretta said as she sat in one of the two chairs at the dinette and leaned forward in a gesture she hoped would signal both motherly love and worry.

Melissa looked up, her face screwed into a pout. "So why'd you give me the key?"

"For an *emergency.* You know, like for protection? Like if somebody hit on you?"

"Well, those nuns weren't exactly beating me." Then she mumbled, "But I'm not so sure they wouldn't, and love doing it."

"For one thing, you've got to go to school," Loretta explained. "And there has to be someone to take care of Buzz when you're in class. You both need to eat and someone to prepare nutritious meals. My shift in the evening starts at six. I get home at maybe three. When I get some overtime, like today, I'm still home before the sun is up. I have dinner or breakfast or whatever you'd call it in an hour or so, then I try to relax, watch a movie. I sleep from seven until three in the afternoon, maybe longer. I have to do all the shopping on my one day off. Now, you tell me, when am I going to have time to do whatever for you and Buzz, and just how is this going to work out?"

"Hey, no school. It's summer!"

"So, you finished ninth grade?"

"As *if!* There's all this paperwork to get things the way we want. You'll figure it out. You're good with numbers and money."

Loretta sighed. "Melissa, you're still underage, and you guys need so much more than I can give you. Seriously."

Melissa gave hungry Buzz the other breast, looked up, and smiled sweetly. "Why don't you make us both some eggs, and I'll do the dishes?"

Outside, surveying the house from his jogging path, Evan was just deciding not to knock on their door.

If only he had.

NEAR EVAN'S TRAILER

EARLIER THAT FRIDAY MORNING

*I*f Preacher Evan Wycliff had stopped in to borrow a cup of sugar, this would have been a different story. It was five-thirty in the morning, he'd slept only fitfully, and he was out for his morning jog.

Okay, it's more like a brisk walk.

He'd resolved recently to make healthier choices in his diet and to get more exercise. More vegetables, less animal fat. And he'd cut back on the whiskey — way back, he promised himself — and his permissible vices, at least for the time being, would remain extra-strong coffee with generous spoonfuls of sugar.

The sun wouldn't be up for another hour. The full moon, filtered by a lingering fogbank, basked the woods in a cool, soft glow. He stopped to catch his breath within sight of Loretta Benton's trailer. Hers was on the adjacent lot to the dilapidated box of tin he rented, separated by a thick stand of tall pines. Her privacy was thus assured, not that the preacher would be gawking. She'd moved in recently, and he'd caught sight of her only a couple of times. He had yet to introduce himself, and he knew her name because they had the same landlord — Zip Zed, proprietor of Zed Motors — who also happened to be Evan's weekday boss.

Loretta was a looker, no doubt about it, and, judging by appearances, just twenty-something. Zip had told him with a suggestive chuckle that she worked as a cocktail waitress at the new Twin Dragons Casino and Resort on Truman Lake. Evan's personal code of conduct told him that gambling would be a high-risk activity, especially for him, a man of modest and sporadic income with a presumably respectable reputation. But he did know that his father figure and mentor Reverend Thurston's secret vice was Holdem Poker.

Well, Marcus doesn't touch bourbon, so who's keeping score? He's obviously not. He wouldn't be bugging me to step up as assistant minister if he thought my petty sins made any difference.

Evan shouldn't have been out of breath at that point. Although he had the stature of a football player, he had the lifestyle of a sedentary sportscaster. He was up at least thirty pounds from an acceptable body-mass index. He'd already done about a mile and a half, having made a loop around Zed's properties (which sadly lacked the amenities of a trailer park). He was heading back home now, needing to pee and anticipating the jolt from his second cup of morning coffee-sludge.

The only noises at this hour were the predawn bird chorus and a gentle breeze rustling the leaves in the trees. There were seldom any traffic sounds here, even during the day. This plot was isolated, thickly wooded and lushly green, a half-mile off the sparsely traveled state route about three miles southeast of Appleton City. As Evan hesitated on the edge of the dirt road, there were about fifty yards between him and the young woman's trailer. A recent-model Buick Enclave, a luxury SUV, was parked out front. A light was on inside the trailer, so an approach might be possible.

Nice set of wheels for a barmaid. Boyfriend? An older guy who gives expensive gifts?

Then came the piercing cry of a distressed infant.

Zip didn't say anything about a kid. Or a husband.

Then there were *two* voices. Female voices. Indistinguishable dialogue.

Even though it was an ungodly hour to be calling, Evan had entertained the thought of stopping by, yes, to ask for that cup of sugar. His single-shelf pantry was low on just about everything, and refined dextrose was nearly as essential to his functioning as high-test gas is to a Corvette.

Ever since Naomi's passing from this plane of existence, Evan hadn't allowed himself to think about women. Oh, there was that fleeting moment of flirtation with Edie Taggart. Good thing he'd thought better of hitting on his best friend's widow. But Naomi *had* encouraged him, more than once, to move on. And even though he probably had ten years on this Loretta gal, a matchup wasn't inconceivable. Especially if he was thinking of finally starting a family.

But a readymade *family? And a former cocktail waitress as a minister's wife?*

He wasn't so sure he aspired to a pastoral job, even though Thurston was ready to retire and wanted to shove him in that direction. Anyhow, there was a lot more he'd have to learn about Loretta Benton before he'd go knocking on her door.

LORETTA'S TRAILER

FRIDAY MORNING

Melissa was not exactly forthcoming about her recent whereabouts. Loretta decided not to confront her just now. She could guess her younger sister would be defensive, maybe even snarky as per usual. They both needed rest and calmer nerves before they could get down to making plans.

All Loretta was able to ask her was, "Have you been taking your meds?"

The girl shrugged it off. "I'm fine."

Then Loretta risked asking, "Have there been any… episodes?"

Melissa smirked. "Like I said. I've… been… fine."

After this, Melissa plugged in her earbuds as Buzz slept.

Loretta was feeling groggy. It was more than an hour after her usual bedtime, but the adrenaline from coping with her sister's issues was allowing her to function. She'd get Melissa and herself fed, finally grab some sleep, and then hopefully be clear-headed enough to talk some sense into the girl before leaving again for work in the afternoon. She didn't have a plan yet, but she figured that there wouldn't be any harm in Melissa's staying with her for a few days until they could think of something. The baby was adorable enough, but they'd have to be adults about this.

She was busy at the stove, Buzz was dozing, and Melissa was nodding to the music in her earbuds when three vehicles pulled up outside, followed by door slams and a series of sharp raps on the door.

Loretta shot a fearful look to Melissa and braced herself with a tight grip on the doorknob.

"Who is it?" she called out.

"Family Welfare Agency," came the reply from a deep-throated male.

Loretta hadn't been through this before, but she figured she had a right to ask, "Do you have a warrant?"

"We got the sheriff," came a husky female voice.

Loretta opened the door cautiously. In rushed two men and a woman. The larger man, overweight and white, was in a suit. The younger one, a scrawny red-haired dude, was in a cop uniform. The dark-skinned woman looked almost casual in jeans and a blouse, but her hair was done up and she had pearl earrings.

The man in the suit grabbed Melissa by the arm, and the woman swept in to gather up the baby.

Melissa realized the nuns must have called the cops. She snarled "Bitch!" at the woman as she tried in vain to wrestle free. In the intruder's stoic face, there was no look of recognition. No more words were exchanged, no badges flashed, and the woman was out the door with Buzz and into a car as fast as she could move.

Melissa yelled after them, "Where are you taking my baby?" Then, to Loretta, she pleaded, "They can't *do* this!"

As the big guy muscled Melissa out the door, Loretta challenged him, "She's my *sister!* They live with *me!* Where are you taking them?"

Last of the intruders out the door was the sheriff's deputy, who called back to Loretta as he got into his squad car, "They're *both* children, ma'am."

BATES BANK AND TRUST, RICH HILL

FRIDAY MORNING

*T*he man who had recently wanted Evan dead now sat across the desk from him. Stuart Shackleton, chairman of the bank, top wiz of the local Masonic lodge, and visionary land developer, had at one time simply judged the preacher's existence inconvenient. Just four months ago, Evan had the temerity to investigate — even after Sheriff Otis had closed the case — why his friend Bob Taggart had put a gun to his chest and blown a hole in his generous heart.

And then, of course, there was the small matter that Shackleton coveted Bob's family farmland for reasons it would take a real estate speculator to understand.

The question was, "Who benefits?" And the answer was Bob's widow Edie and her lover, this slick money man. They had plans for the family farm that didn't involve its current tenants. But in the end, Evan had to admit no one else but Bob had pulled the trigger.

Driving someone to suicide might not be a crime, but it's certainly a sin.

Now Shackleton was making nice — or pretending to.

The summer heat had come early, and it was a steamy June in the farmland around Rich Hill, Missouri. But Shackleton's climate-controlled office was as cool as the fellow's demeanor. Not knowing the subject of their meeting nor its degree of formality, Evan had worn his only sport coat, a decidedly uncomfortable wool tweed. Shackleton had on what must have been one of his many Italian silk suits, no doubt from a walk-in closet as big as the trailer Evan called home.

"You're wondering why I asked you here today," Shackleton began. Evan had expected the man to pour on the charm, but his earnest sobriety seemed oddly out of character.

His topic, whatever it is, has humbled him. If it's about Bob's estate, it's early to be talking. The probate court doesn't even have it on the docket yet.

"I didn't think you wanted me to pray with you" was all Evan said, assuming the banker would take it as a kindly attempt at humor.

"You might be wrong there," Shackleton muttered, needlessly adjusting the position of the single sheet of paper on his enormous, glossy desk. Evan couldn't help noticing a simple gold wedding band on one of the fellow's manicured hands, a hefty Masonic ring on the other.

"I'm sorry," Evan said, supposing he'd misjudged the situation. "It's your wife, then? Do you want me to see her?"

Shackleton shook his head. "Ann's the same — yesterday, today, and tomorrow. They don't know shit about dementia and even less about sustaining quality of life." His gaze locked on the document as he frowned into it as if staring at it might cause some hidden message to emerge. "No," he swallowed hard, and he didn't look up. "It's my son."

Fearing he'd been slouching disrespectfully, Evan straightened himself in the chintz-upholstered guest chair. "I didn't realize you had —"

"Luke's been in a… special school… for some time now." Shackleton looked uncharacteristically embarrassed as he added softly, "Not a lot of people know."

"Oh my," Evan said. "Your wife, your son. That's a heavy cross to bear."

"Thanks for your sympathy, Reverend, but I'm not religious enough to think in those terms. Bad things happen to good people and vice versa for no good reason. To tell you the truth, I'm not sure where I stand these days."

I'm not ordained, but perhaps now is not the time to correct him on that point.

"So, is there some new concern with your son?"

"Luke. His name is Luke." Again, the man didn't look up. "I'd like you to go see him, if you would."

Evan swallowed hard and simply said, "Sure. Whatever I can do. Anything I should know?"

Shackleton stood and then so did Evan. The banker handed him the paper, which was a formal authorization for his visit to Myerson Clinic. Then Shackleton said, "He's a sweet, sensitive boy. When he was six and he was in public school, he'd get all jumpy in class, and they said ADHD. A few years later, he was moody, and it was bipolar disorder. Now it's supposedly schizophrenia. He says he hears voices."

"I see," Evan said, although he could only guess at the implications, and took the paper.

"And," Shackleton heaved a mournful sigh, "They're saying he's molested some girl."

EVAN HESITATED outside Shackleton's office to read the authorization letter.

Addressed to Doc Wilmer? That quack? Is he in charge of everything?

Besides being the administrator of the Myerson Clinic, the good doctor was also St. Clair County's Medical Examiner. This letter was, in effect, blanket permission to pry into the treatment and welfare of Shackleton's beleaguered son. People always seemed to be handing Evan powers of attorney, even when he hadn't asked for the responsibility and didn't want it. He'd just about worked through the issues surrounding his friend Bob Taggart's suicide. That was a heap of worry he hadn't expected to take on. He'd been hoping for a breather and the prospect of not having to visit Sheriff Chet Otis for anything but a friendly chinwag.

And schizophrenia? No wonder Shackleton is so unhinged. He must be really stressed to come to me for help.

Shackleton's secretary, Dot Meineke, noticed him puzzling over the document. She asked in a soft, polite voice, "Something I can help with, Preacher?"

"I'll get back to you on that," Evan said softly, hoping he didn't sound rude, and walked out.

In the parking lot, Evan headed back to his practical, if distinctive, loaner vehicle. It was the robin's-egg-blue Fiat Cinquecento that Zip had loaned him after Evan had traded away a battered but serviceable gray Taurus in what he thought was a win-win swap for a candy-colored, tricked-out Mustang. The owner of record had been three months behind on her payments, and after Evan's inspired workout deal, Zip had owed *her* money. But Evan's boss had honored the deal, secretly baffled at how cleverly the preacher had done the math.

I don't know which line of work gets me into more trouble — counseling sinners or chasing deadbeats. And somehow tracking down debtors makes people think I'm a detective? Problem is, I'm just good enough at it to be dangerous — especially to myself!

And now I'm cup-bearer for Stu Shackleton? How did that *irony come about?*

But how do you say no when your gut tells you the angels might be trying to lead you somewhere?

Back when Zip had given him the car to use, Evan had thought twice about the deal and then hid the car away. At the time, a person or persons unknown had had it in for him, including possibly Shackleton, and driving around in an outsized Easter egg was not exactly low-profile. But now the Taggart case had been mostly put to bed (or, more accurately, parked in the courts). And Evan didn't fear for the safety of his person anymore. So he had fetched the secreted vehicle from its cache in old Arthur Redwine's barn. And Evan was now proud for the locals to associate its distinctive appearance with his comings and goings. He'd been tempted to name the little car *Ms. Naomi*, after his dear-departed fiancé. But he judged he should reserve that honored name for a classier vehicle — if he ever owned one. Driving the petrol-sipping puddle-jumper was a kind of testimony to his role as crusader

— like the Batmobile — but for an unassuming man of the cloth who wouldn't mind at all if people laughed when they saw him coming.

Forgiveness, prayers, and reminders of godliness. We deliver! Just because I get those guest preacher gigs, some people want to see me as their pastor. Sure, visiting the sick and the dying is expected of a minister. But I never took the job!

The almost-but-not-quite-ordained minister supplemented his token guest-preacher income by working as skip tracer for Zed Motors, the local Ford car and tractor dealership. His itinerant gigs in the pulpit didn't pay all that much, but Evan could point to local fame as a confessor and sage advisor in compensation. It also didn't hurt that, when trying to collect on a car loan, the debtor was intimidated by having to deal with a presumed messenger from On High. For the most part, people in these parts took their religion seriously, even if some didn't practice it with any regularity.

And, for sure, none of those farmers was about to be caught dead in an Italian kiddie-car. Evan would probably have the use of the Fiat until its wheels fell off.

EVAN WAS HARDLY surprised to find Naomi sitting demurely in the passenger seat of the Italian subcompact. The fact that her soul had left this earthly plane three years ago hadn't stopped her from appearing at odd times, doling out advice, often being downright argumentative. But Evan hated to admit most times she'd eventually been proven right.

"So, what is it now?" she asked impertinently as if she didn't know. (As a manifestation of Evan's longing, she knew everything he knew, but not much more.)

Evan tossed his wool coat in the back seat as he got in, slammed the driver's-side door, loosened his collar and his tie, and started the engine. Before he replied, he cranked down the window because the day was getting hot and the cooling system in the little bug was hardly up to it.

"Shackleton's kid, a teenager. Says he hears voices."

Go ahead. You're going to tell me I'm just as crazy.

Instead, she went off on Shackleton. "Well," she mused, "all that psychosis had to come from somewhere. Don't tell me you're going to go and forgive the man."

Before he put the car in gear, Evan took a moment to reflect. Then he said, "You know, if I don't, who will?"

But to say I forgive him doesn't mean I trust him now.

"This boy is going to be trouble," she said flatly. "And it won't be just him. He lives in a world of hurt." Then before she dematerialized, she added cryptically, "You only have a day or two."

MYERSON CLINIC, APPLETON CITY

FRIDAY MID-MORNING

*L*uke Shackleton was seventeen. He was sitting on the edge of his bed with his back to the door, his head bent down. Evan thought he might be praying. But when Evan stepped cautiously around to get a look, he could see Luke's wrists were resting on his knees, his hands holding a water glass full of amber liquid. Luke was staring into it as if it were a magical elixir.

"Apple juice?" Evan offered with a smile.

Luke shook his head morosely but did not look up.

Then Evan caught a whiff of urine.

Before Evan could think of what to say next, an orderly entered officiously and stepped past the preacher to confront Luke. The guy's head was shaved and he was built like a wrestler.

Jesse Ventura, but probably without the politician's electable charm.

"This has got to stop," the muscular guy commanded. He reached down to grab the glass, but Luke jerked it away, splashing urine all over his black T-shirt and the bed linens.

"There you've gone and pissed the bed again, haven't you?" the big fellow growled. Then, ignoring Evan, he added, "You'll get a timeout for this one," and, clutching the empty glass, he urged his way past Evan and made for the door.

In the doorway, the orderly turned back and snapped at Evan, "You're not to stay long. And the administrator wants to see you." Then he was gone.

Evan sat in the guest chair and took a long breath. "What's a time-out?" he asked Luke, who hadn't moved and looked even more sullen now.

Still gazing at his hands, Luke answered, "They lock you in an empty room. Nothing on the walls. Nothing on the floor. No place to sit. No place to *piss.*"

"For how long?"

"It can't be forever. They won't let them do that. But you lose track of time. So it *feels* like forever."

"Doesn't seem worth it," Evan suggested softly.

For the first time, Luke looked up at him. His eyes were wet. "I can't let them have it," he sniffed.

The boy looked scrawny and pallid, your stereotypical geek. He had a nervous tick and a fleeting, embarrassed smile. Without any evidence at all, Evan sensed right away this kid shouldn't be a threat to anybody.

Molested a girl? I'll bet that's a story within a story.

"I heard you have a girlfriend," Evan ventured.

Luke answered softly, "Melissa."

"Melissa," Evan repeated and waited for more information.

"They took her away. Medics in an ambulance. Back to the convent. April, I think it was," Luke said. He looked up and added, "To have her baby."

"I see," Evan said as if he already knew the story.

Did he get her pregnant? How could that happen in here — with everybody watching them so closely?

Evan decided not to get into that just now and asked, "So you haven't seen her since?"

"No. No. They won't let her in here now. I don't know where she is. But I know she's in a bad way."

"You're in touch with her?"

Luke nodded and informed Evan, "I can feel her heartbeat. Maybe I don't know what she's doing, but I always know what she's feeling."

Luke couldn't pick up on where Melissa was exactly, nor could he know that she and Buzz had been separated. He could only tune into feelings, and he knew she was hurting awfully. For him, it had begun this morning with a disturbance throbbing in his head, and it built to a wrenching pain in his gut. He didn't tell Evan how he knew this, nor did he want to admit that he would always know — for certain — Melissa's state of mind, in this life or in the next.

Not asking about the girl would turn out to be a mistake, but Evan was more concerned about the welfare of this boy in the here and now. The baby was indeed a complication. Shackleton must know about it but had left that minor detail out of the briefing. Luke might have a motive in a young man's horniness, but Evan had trouble imagining Luke would have had the boldness — much less, the opportunity in this lockup — to cause the pregnancy.

Why did Shackleton avoid telling me that part of the story? Does he really think this girl Melissa is an unimportant player in all this? Or does he want me to think her involvement with Luke is old news and of no concern to any of us now? I'm going to bet Luke still cares about her. Maybe, a lot.

For the moment, Evan was more concerned about the problem he'd just witnessed. He asked Luke, "And the urine? Why do you need to save it?"

Luke studied Evan's face as if to determine whether this stranger could understand the answer. Or perhaps the boy was baffled that an older and wiser person wouldn't know the answer already. Then he said simply, "Because it's all I have left to give."

As the kindly man left Luke alone, the voice came to the boy immediately:

Your sweetheart is mine now. If you pursue her, it will only bring you pain.

Melissa had been gone from the clinic for more than two months, but Luke still thought about her constantly, especially as he was trying to fall asleep. But what could he do? Why was the voice still pestering him about it? It's not like he could go try to rescue her. Then the voice came back:

Your friend's searches are pointless. He worships only himself. If he tries to interfere with me, he will die.

By now, Luke didn't trust anything the voice said. In fact, he took this last warning to be a testimony to Evan's powers, which must be formidable to invite the wrath of demons.

Luke wondered when they'd be putting him in timeout.

He wanted to watch TV in the community room. But these days all they'd let him see was baseball. He'd overheard Richards telling Clint he wasn't allowed to watch the news because "the kid's so suggestible." What did that mean? Did they think he was going to blow up some school?

Okay, he'd just have to turn on the TV in his head. He projected himself up above the clinic, ascending straight over the roof, then hovering there, looking down. Greenery everywhere. Bright yellow sun. He hesitated a moment, listened for Melissa's heartbeat. Although she was miles away, he could feel the throb of her. He knew she was panting. Crying!

And his heart began to beat in time with hers.

He sent his spirit shooting off to hover near her.

EVAN HAD EXCUSED himself from Luke, left the boy's room, and sought out the orderly. He hadn't yet introduced himself to anyone but the receptionist, but he figured he'd better hear what the administrator had to say before he got involved any further. It was pretty clear during this cursory meeting that the boy was seriously disturbed.

Okay, maybe I'm way out of my depth here. They're supposed to be treating him, but is he also being abused?

The orderly, whose name according to his badge was Clint Everly, showed Evan to a sparsely furnished waiting room. This space lacked the luxuriously upholstered furniture of the visitors' lobby. Instead there was a long cafeteria table and several metal chairs. The cinder-block walls were painted a glossy yellow, a scrubbable coating that would resist food stains and graffiti. Clint indicated for Evan to sit and promptly left him alone.

Evan guessed they'd hold client and parent conferences in here. Perhaps it was also meant to be a no-nonsense space where child-clients could receive counseling, instruction, or reprimand.

A well-dressed, middle-aged African-American woman came in. She wore a beige twinset with a black velvet collar, an ivory-silk blouse with a foulard twist at the neck, and a single strand of pearls. Her lizard pumps probably matched a handbag somewhere. She sat down opposite Evan and pushed her business card across the table:

Bernice Richards, MSW C-ASWCM
Psychiatric Social Worker

She arched a tweezed eyebrow slightly and asked, "And who might you be?"

"I'm Evan Wycliff," he replied and handed her the letter from Shackleton.

Reading it at a glance and handing it back, she sighed, "Clint — he's the practical nurse who showed you in — he keeps calling me the administrator, but I'm only a contract consultant. Between you and me, Wilmer isn't much of a doctor, but he's the man they pay to run the place. That letter should go in his file, but I'm not so sure he has any files."

"Well, as long as we're being honest, I'm not ordained. Not officially. More like guest preacher some places. And, as for Wilmer, I've had the pleasure."

"He's your physician?" she asked as if to say, *Are you a fool?*

"He was for a very short time. When I was admitted here. Over on the clinic side."

"I've only been here a month," she explained. "You were in treatment?"

"Yes and no," Evan admitted. "I took a nasty blow to the head from a cop who thought I was stealing drugs. This was last winter, hazardous road conditions that night, and the sheriff told me later they brought me here because the ER was overbooked with traffic-accident victims. But then they kept me for observation for days, as if they believed I really was some strung-out junkie. A case of mistaken identity, I assure you."

"Wilmer wouldn't know the difference," she said with the hint of a smile. "I trust you won't try to get me fired for saying as much. I'm just getting my bearings, and a lot of things in this place need... shall we say... closer attention?"

Evan shook his head. "My only concern is Luke's welfare."

"You're the Shackletons' pastor?"

"More like a friend of the family," Evan replied.

That might not be an outright lie, but it's a good-sized fib.

His recently having prevailed against Shackleton's devious plot against the Taggart estate might have won him respect, but he doubted he had any claim on the banker's friendship.

"We're not set up to handle young people who are as disturbed as Luke seems to be," she said.

"Because, what, they're saying he molested somebody? Was it Melissa? If so, how can I get in touch with her? I understand she's not here anymore."

"Melissa Benton is in foster care. Or will be soon."

"She had a child?"

"A seventeen-year-old girl is an unfit mother, by any standard."

"You mean, they've *separated* her from her baby?"

She nodded. "There are qualified adoptive parents waiting."

Whoa. I've blundered into another snake pit.

Evan wasn't aware in the moment that *snake pit* is a term older generations used to describe a mental hospital. No doubt he'd heard people say it when he was growing up. The farm culture of yesteryear was rife with superstition. And some — including presumably enlightened clerics — still believe the mentally ill are possessed by demons, condemned to live out a horrific earthly punishment they must deserve for some retched transgression, past or future.

"You've got a lot to handle in this new job," Evan offered, hoping he sounded sympathetic but fearing he was dealing with the Queen of Mean.

She ignored the opportunity to be more candid and simply stated, "If Luke is a danger to himself or to others, that's an immediate problem and a reason for him not to be here. But I'm afraid I don't have the facts, and the incident you mention is a matter of hearsay. We'll be watching him closely."

"Hearsay?"

Richards nodded. "The girl. The staff. There are several versions of the story, including the boy's. It was all before I came here. Obviously, the Benton girl was compromised, but the children are sometimes allowed home leave, which we don't supervise. So, you see, almost anything is possible. If I were you, I'd stay out of it."

"Maybe I'd better," Evan agreed.

Maybe it's not a lie if I wished it were true.

She got more comfortable when she promised, "I'm trying to get him a complete workup so at least we have a formal diagnosis. We get an ICD code, maybe I can get him a more appropriate placement. As of now, I don't have a diagnosis."

So you can get rid of him?

"What's this code?" Evan asked.

"ICD-10-CM. International Classification of Diseases, Tenth Revision, Clinical Modification. It's how the providers and the insurance companies identify cases and authorized treatment protocols. Without a diagnostic code, we're just guessing at managing symptoms and behaviors."

"Like saving his urine in jars?"

"That would be *hoarding complex,* an obsessive-compulsive disorder. It could be wads of paper or soiled clothes or feces. Anything. The more disgusting the better. It's a symptom of extreme anxiety, possibly paranoid delusions. He thinks people are stealing I-don't-know-what from him."

"His father told me Luke is schizophrenic."

"We try not to use that term. *Schizophrenic* in everyday language has come to mean *split personality.* Clinical schizophrenia is a spectrum of disorders, but none of those mean the *dissociative identity disorders* exhibited by people who present multiple personalities." She sniffed. "That's why we have the codes."

"So I take it he's not like those people?"

"No, he's the same depressed kid from one day to the next. He says he hears voices. Auditory hallucinations could be a symptom of schizophrenia. Or drug abuse. Or some kind of cognitive disorder that misinterprets external stimuli. Or he could be a talented little actor who is trying to manipulate the people who are trying to help him. Which I don't mind telling you would be my theory-du-jour unless tests prove otherwise. But he's started to wet the bed at night, which is unusual in an older boy and seems more like a cry for attention than a symptom of psychosis. Luke is clever enough, he might be deliberately pissing himself."

"Do *you* think he's faking it?"

She sniffed again. Evan began to see that the short intake of air accompanied by a bad-smell wince was her nervous tic. She said, "It wouldn't be the first time I've seen it."

"He told me he doesn't want to give his urine away. Maybe he's trying to hold it in during the day? Or when he's on timeout?"

"Perhaps." She shot him a look but didn't take the bait.

I'm not supposed to know the t-word. *Outsiders probably aren't told about those confinements.*

She went on breezily, "I have to get a workup for that too. We have to rule out neurological causes. There could be some disruption in the nerve reflex arc in the lower spinal area. A tumor, say. We had a neuro guy in here yesterday who took a spinal tap from him, and we're waiting for the results. I doubt we're going to find anything, but best practice says we have to rule out the more treatable causes first."

"And a tumor is more treatable than mental illness?"

Are you hoping *he has cancer?*

She nodded. "If you go by the book, yes. Not only more treatable, but also more accepted by the healthcare system as a medical condition that can be cured. Or at least treated."

Evan decided to press the point: "I heard Clint threaten him with a timeout."

She shrugged it off. "Like I said, I haven't been here all that long. Some of the procedures will have to be reviewed. This isn't a prison."

Evan thought for a moment.

Could've fooled me. Sedative drugs instead of bars? The effect is the same.

Then he asked her, "What did you tell Luke about that procedure?"

She shrugged again. "Just that we were going to do a test, put a needle in his lower back. We said it might be uncomfortable but promised it would be over in a wink. Surprisingly, he was very cooperative."

"I could be way out of line here, but does he know whether you took something out or put something in with that needle?"

She looked surprised. "Frankly, he didn't ask and we didn't say."

"What if you told him the neurologist gave him an *injection?* A recently approved drug that is sure to cure him?"

Richards suddenly looked uncomfortable as if some bug had wriggled up her leg. She adjusted her posture and sat up straight as she gave her skirt a modest tug. "Lying to a client would be unethical. Possibly even grounds for malpractice."

"Mind if *I* tell him? I don't have a license to lose, after all. And you don't have to admit we discussed it."

She hesitated a moment, then said, "We'd be taking a chance on the placebo effect, which is not entirely out of the question. They don't tell the patients in a drug trial which ones are getting sugar pills. But they *are* informed it's a possibility, and they *agree*. I don't know whether there's a distinction to be made here. How about parental consent?"

Evan studied his letter from Shackleton. "I'm reading between the lines here, and I'd say we already have it." Then he gave her his best winning smile and added, "You could say it's faith healing, but I promise you I won't be advertising it if it works."

～

"Luke, I'm Preacher Evan Wycliff. Your father asked me to give you a message."

Luke roused himself. He was back in his body after his soul's flight, but he wasn't about to tell this guy about it, however friendly the fellow might seem. He thought about telling the preacher how Melissa was suffering, but he decided not to take the risk.

The boy tried to look interested. "Oh, yeah?"

"It's confidential, you see."

"Okay."

The boy hadn't moved from the spot where he sat stiffly on the bed. No one had yet cleaned up the mess, and the room reeked of urine.

Perhaps they're deliberately letting him stew in it. I want to make sure they don't lock him up.

"Your father loves you very much. And he's very worried about you. He went to great expense, and he paid a lot of money for a new drug they developed in Switzerland. Had it flown over on a private jet. It's just come out of clinical trials, very successful, but almost no one outside of Europe has been treated with it. It's just so expensive, you see. But when the doctor came to you yesterday and put that needle in your spine, he injected you with that drug. *Lorem ipsum dolor.*"

Sounds like Latin, anyway. I hope he hasn't read any books on typography.

Evan studied Luke. The boy's eyes were clear, his focus steady, and his look penetrating. There was curiosity, but no suspicion. "Okay," the boy repeated.

He's awfully trusting for a kid who should be old enough to know better.

"The result is, you're going to be fine. Absolutely fine. You won't wet the bed tonight, for sure. Or any night. You'll be able to use the restroom like anyone else, just as easily as can be, and you won't have to worry about it ever again. And you'll find there isn't a need anymore to save your urine. You will just flush it down. It's the waste products from your body, full of the stuff your body doesn't want and can't use. That's what this drug is doing, do you see? Flushing all the poisons out of your body."

"I see," Luke said. Then he asked, "This drug — can other people get it now?"

"Yes," Evan smiled. "Now that it's worked on you, anyone suffering that way can have it. Thanks for being so brave."

Luke shrugged and gave him a weak smile. "I guess."

Why do I get the feeling he's humoring me? If this works, will it be because Richards is right and he thinks we see through his act?

Evan smiled. "So, then, may I come back to visit? Maybe we can talk some more?"

"I guess," the boy said. His smile might have meant conspiratorial agreement. Or he might simply have been grateful for some kind attention. "Sure."

Evan was about to leave when the boy said quietly, "Melissa's in pain."

The preacher turned back quickly to ask, "How do you know? What can you tell me?"

Luke just shrugged and gave Evan a blank stare. He stated a fact, "If you don't get to her soon, she'll be hurt. Bad. And soon."

"Give me more, Luke!"

The boy shook his head. "I'm sorry. I feel her, but I can't see her." And he started to sob.

NATHAN'S SCHOOL OF FASHION DESIGN, OSCEOLA

TWO YEARS AGO

*E*very year, Jack Nathan fretted he wouldn't be ready in time. The locals loved his annual fashion show. More importantly, the publicity and the brand promotion for the school helped keep enrollment up and the cash flowing. And, for the institutions that sent their girls to him, a successful show proved he could make silk purses out of sows ears. Because if it weren't for his dressmaking skills and fashion sense, along with his savvy from his years in the industry, these newbie runway models would be raising prize hogs in 4-H or selling cookies for church or thrusting out their budding breasts on the cheerleading squad at the high school.

It was Friday night, it was getting late, and the show was tomorrow afternoon. And some of his students were still having trouble walking in high heels. Why some of them insisted on wearing five-inch stilettos, he'd never understand. Well, yes, he understood, but he knew at this age they only catch half of what you say, and they end up doing almost none of it.

The guys at the Masonic Lodge in Osceola had always given him a break on the room rental. Some of them had pitched in to build the runway, and they'd kept it in storage for him, even providing a crew to haul it out and set it up each year. The surface was one-inch plywood with two-by-six joists, sturdy as an apartment roof. He'd had it covered with carpet to deaden the noise of those clopping heels. But the stage gave a little with each step, and Jack had to admit navigating it gracefully in those high-fashion heels would challenge even experienced performers. But he had a budget, and Osceola isn't Hollywood.

Abigail Sharkey was standing nervously on the edge of the proscenium, ready for the nod from him that would signal the start of her run. (Like first-time skiers down a slope! He knew they were terrified.)

Jack beckoned, and Abby started to walk. She was wearing a red-satin A-line, with a Fifties-era flare at the waist and a softball-sized fabric rose on the shoulder strap. She enhanced the classic movie-star look with bright-red lip gloss and tight pin curls at the temples of her page-boy-cut, raven-black hair.

She was managing well enough in her pumps, but she was walking too slowly, even cautiously.

"Stop!" Jack yelled. "*Prance,* don't slink!" He gestured with an outstretched hand like a conductor beating out a march cadence: "Prance-prance-*prance!* Then *stop.* Sharp turn *right.* Big *smile.* Back to *front.* Welcome *gesture.* Sharp turn *left.* Big *smile,* and back to *front.* Then an even *bigger* smile. *Sell it!* Then one more sequence — *prance-prance-prance!* — and it's back to the barn."

She started to move again from where he'd stopped her, but he waved her back. "Again! From your entrance. And, if you measure your steps, you won't have to look down, and you won't *fall off the end* of the runway!"

This time she more or less followed directions. Her walk had energy. Her steps and her turns were precise. Most of them couldn't get that. But her lips trembled when she smiled!

She was at the end of the runway now, looking down at Jack where he sat and yearning for approval. In a low tone, Jack told her, trying to sound sincere as he always did, "Lovely, sweetheart. Practice at home tonight, in the heels. Chin up, you're gonna do great!"

He gestured with a wind-up motion for her to turn all the way around, and she pranced back to the proscenium and then offstage.

Abby's performance was C plus, but "Easy Jack" would give her a B minus. Her run was next to last, and he was already thinking about a bourbon and branch. A double. No, maybe on the rocks, no branch water.

The schoolmaster's biggest challenge was turnover. So many of his students lacked talent, but that wasn't the worry. No, their parents or their sponsors, having paid in advance for a semester, usually couldn't be convinced to reinvest in careers that were going nowhere. Girls got pregnant and had to drop out. Some of them gained weight — and still might have made decent dressmakers — but they'd get discouraged when they realized they no longer had the figure to show off their own work. And the pretty ones — omigod the pretties! — they were his treasure to lose! In every class, some were gorgeous. But few of them were slender enough (never mind, graceful enough!) to actually aspire to modeling as a profession.

Besides, he'd have to send the most alluring of them to work for Mick Heston at the casino. That was the deal.

Jack would get finder's fees as handsome as the girls were pretty. But he wanted that money to stay in his pocket. He needed the tuition fees to cover his operating expenses. Which was why he was sweating this show.

Last in the lineup, here came Melissa Benton. Omigod.

HEADQUARTERS OF ACH
ENTERTAINMENT, NASHVILLE

TWO YEARS AGO

*D*mitri Churpov was not a man to suffer fools. In fact, his unwavering approach to discipline in his organization was to make fools suffer. If he suspected that anyone had lied to him, cheated him, or even evaded one of his pointed questions, the consequences would be quick and severe. Churpov never wanted to know the details of how his retributions were delivered. It sufficed for him to be sure that a crippling punishment had been meted out. But essential to organizational discipline would be the resulting swarm of unsubstantiated but plausible rumor: For example, the music critic's review of the performer had been not only disappointing but potentially damaging to a multimillion-dollar world tour. Some would say the pinkie finger on his left hand was severed, but such a visible deformity would arouse suspicion from outsiders. No, other wags would correct the story: The *tendons* of his pinky had been cut surgically. He used to be a crack touch typist and an accomplished guitarist. In service of deniability, others would say both of those versions of the story were wrong and the fellow simply had a stroke that paralyzed his hand.

The initials of the organization stood for *Armenian Consolidated Holdings.* However, not a single member of the organization was actually Armenian, except perhaps on a far-flung branch of the family tree.

All were Russian by birth and citizenship, but pretending to be former inhabitants of a region considered historically friendly to their new host country was judged to be better for public relations. Also for the sake of appearances, the rank and file conducted all business, including their personal conversations, in English. Although their careful recruitment guaranteed their competency in the language of their hosts, even some of the best-educated could not speak without an accent — except, that is, for Churpov himself. Even though English was his second language, he had perfect pitch when it came to dialect. He spoke with a flat, Midwestern plainness. Combined with his fastidious taste in fine tailoring and his impeccable manners, his resonant (and charming, if need be) voice made perfect his protective coloration. Fortunately for the less talented in his cohort, no American they'd ever met, including some of genuine Armenian descent, remarked on the difference between Russian and Armenian inflections.

Oleg Olachek had asked to see the boss first thing today. He carried only the thinnest manila folder, which contained three glossy photographs. He stood beside the boss, cleared his throat, and silently presented the file. When Churpov flipped it open on his desk, he growled, "Ollie, this is the digital age. Why do you give me glossies like I am some sleazy casting director?"

In a hushed tone, the burly man with the thick beard answered obsequiously, "Camera is optical. Analog images on film. Negatives taped to inside back cover. These are the only prints. Nothing to be intercepted or compromised. No one on the planet besides myself will know of your interest in this matter."

Until this moment, Churpov had only glanced at the top photo on the thin stack. He started to say, "I fail to see —" and then he got a good first look. He grimaced, then gasped, sucking in a great gout of air, which panicked Olachek. This was hardly the reaction he'd been expecting. Then the boss choked and clutched his chest, caught in the vise-grip of a severely constricted bronchial asthma attack.

As Churpov leaned back in his overstuffed executive chair, Olachek deftly reached into the vest pocket of the man's suitcoat, retrieved an inhaler, and handed it back to him.

Churpov shoved the inhaler in his mouth, dispensed a dose, and inhaled deeply. As the tightness in his chest began to subside and he thought he was out of immediate danger, he glared at Olachek and whispered, "This is a cruel joke. That can't be her!"

The photos were a long shot, a closeup, and an extreme closeup of a pretty model who was wearing a flashy, low-cut gown as she grinned broadly and pranced proudly down the runway in a fashion show.

The subordinate hastened to admit, "No. No, it's not. This girl is fifteen. And hardly Russian. She is what some unkind people call a *cracker*. From Southern Missouri."

"Tatyana would be twenty-five by now," Churpov sighed. Now that he realized he wasn't seeing a ghost, he was beginning to relax. "Still, the resemblance is remarkable. Amazing."

"Yes," Olachek agreed cautiously. "Remarkable."

"And why do you presume I would be interested?"

"You could do... whatever you like... to her. Call it *closure.*"

"Pleasure? Punishment? What are you talking about?"

Olachek shrugged. "Anything. Everything." Then he added. "The girl is an orphan. They seek foster family for her. But I believe suitable foster *parent* with sufficient resources would qualify."

C'MON INN, APPLETON CITY

FRIDAY NOON

*C*ora poured Evan his fourth cup from her steaming Pyrex carafe of Farmer Brothers. He promptly opened two foil packets of Folgers instant and stirred it in, along with two heaping teaspoons of cane sugar.

"That's not coffee," she said. "It's syrup."

"And how long have I been doing this, right under your ever-watchful eyes?"

"How long since you showed up from Back East? A year? Long enough it should have killed you by now."

Cora had not known Evan before he'd left for college in Boston. When his plans for divinity school and then theoretical physics had gone astray and then his love affair with the gorgeous Naomi Weiss had been abruptly terminated by a weapon of war, he'd returned to his roots here in Appleton City. Even now, he hadn't come to terms with why his fiancé had been so eager to accept that civilian assignment in Lebanon. Since his return to Southern Missouri, the C'mon Inn diner had been his home away from home.

After his morning visit to Myerson, he was having breakfast for lunch — his favorite, biscuits and gravy — as he sat in his usual place at the counter, delighted to be served by the attentive — and he now had to admit, comely — Coralie Angelides.

"And you know I'm happy to sell it to you," she went on, "but it's ninety-some friggin' degrees today, and you're still chowing down the grease like it's freezing out there. How about a damn salad? We got Niçoise, Club, or Chicken Caesar. Fresh lettuce, even. And not just iceberg. Romaine, red-leaf, bib, and arugula, just like in the places with those white-linen tablecloths."

Salad is on my list. Just not today.

"You're jerking my chain," he said as he took a noisy sip. "What did I ever do to you?"

"It's what you *didn't* do," she shot back with a lascivious cackle, and she walked away to chat up the next customer down the line, a trucker-type Evan didn't recognize, who was having steak and eggs with a cold Hamms.

True, Evan had not yet made a move on Cora — even after Naomi's ghost had encouraged — no, she'd *insisted* — he do so.

When Cora came around again, he startled her by getting suddenly serious. "Ann Shackleton. Stu's wife. You said you knew her. How long ago did she... lose it?"

"I didn't *know* her," Cora corrected, dropping her voice. "Years ago, they'd come in here together. Not regular, but every now and then. Sunday supper after church, that kind of thing. She was absent-minded even then. She'd eat her salad, I'd clear the plates, and she'd order it again like she never had it. Or she'd be talking to friends who weren't there."

"And what about their boy?"

"He must've been nine or ten. Jumpy as all get-out. It got worse with him too. I heard he's in a home somewhere."

"The Myerson Clinic. I visited him this morning."

"You don't say. Maybe you're the real thing after all." And she smiled. "They're saying you heal the sick!"

As a minister's wife, you'd be up on all the gossip. And you'd be fussing over the ladies on the Loving Embrace committee, telling them they need more mustard in the egg salad. But — who do you know at the clinic? A guy can't get away with anything in this town! Are people already assuming Luke won't wet the bed anymore?

Cora had walked away again before he had a chance to ask how she'd heard the gossip about his pastoral visit to Luke. Evan was deciding whether to have grated cheddar, vanilla ice cream, or Cool Whip on top of the famous C'mon You Gotta fresh-baked apple pie when the jangle of the cowbell on the door behind him and the *clack-clack-clack* of high heels signaled someone's hurried entrance.

He looked back over his right shoulder to glimpse a gorgeous young woman he'd so far only seen from a distance. It was Loretta Benton, and she was panting with excitement.

Or panic.

He got a whiff of musky perfume that almost made him faint.

Her eyes were accented with heavy black eyeliner and rose glitter on the lids. Her raven hair fell in satiny tresses past the tops of her bare arms. She wore a semi-sheer knit kimono, tied at the waist, which hid almost nothing underneath. The hostess outfit she was wearing was obviously not the uniform of a humble diner. It was made of glistening red satin and about the size of a skimpy, one-piece bathing suit. The robe might have been intended for modesty but would barely have sufficed on a public beach. She'd left the neckline open in the heat, and evidence of her bulging cleavage was decidedly immodest under the circumstances. Fish-net stockings set off the look.

Loretta locked eyes with Cora, who had turned from her ministrations to another guest at the counter, but at the same time the sensational intruder was pointing a shiny, lacquered fingernail at Evan.

"This the guy?" Loretta huffed.

Cora nodded.

Only then did Loretta look down at Evan from her haughty perch atop those designer pumps and demand, "You're coming with me."

Cora's cautionary look told Evan he'd best obey and not worry just now about paying the bill.

LORETTA'S CAR

FRIDAY NOON

*L*oretta's Buick was parked at the curb. She unlocked the car with the remote, quickly got behind the wheel, and started it up. Evan figured he was expected to go along for the ride, wherever to. He got in the passenger seat and closed the door.

Naugahyde or leather? Still has the new-car smell.

He was about to buckle up then saw she hadn't.

She pressed a button to roll up the windows and flipped the air on max. Then she blew out a puff of breath and announced, "I'm on my way to work, so this can't take long. I hope you don't mind the air, but I can't be sweating up a storm in here."

"Sure," Evan said. "You wanna… just… take a breath?"

"You're the preacher works miracles, right?"

Wow, a person could get a reputation. The whole town must think just because I spoke the word to Luke that all will be well. He might not piss the bed tonight, but both he and I know he'll be the same disturbed child tomorrow.

Evan began, "Well, I am a preacher, but I'm not ordained —"

She cut him off and finally turned to face him. Her big, brown eyes were filling with tears and her mascara was beginning to run. Even though crisp air was circulating, the smell of her perfume in the small space was overpowering.

"I need you to find my sister. Melissa Benton. And baby Buzz. They came and took them from my place this morning."

"They?"

"Family Welfare Agency. In separate cars. A big guy in a suit, a kid sheriff, and some mean-ass black lady."

I'm guessing I know two out of the three. How would both Griggs and Richards be involved in this?

Evan began, "Look, this isn't exactly my —"

"Reverend... ?"

"*Mister.* Evan. Evan Wycliff. Or Preacher, if you prefer."

"Mr. Wycliff, I can't go to the cops, for a lot of reasons. I'm Loretta Benton. I think we're neighbors? My little sister is Melissa. She's an unwed mother. She was at Sisters of Mercy for a while, then at the Myerson Clinic, then back at the convent. And while she was with the nuns, before she had a breakdown, they got her a job in the laundry at the Twin Dragons Resort. For her, that didn't last. I work in the casino there."

Evan thought for a moment. "If child welfare grabbed her, of all those places, where is she *supposed* to be?"

"She was living at the convent when she had her baby back in April. But she ran away from there day before yesterday. She and Buzz showed up at my place."

"Seems like the nuns would be responsible for her," Evan said. "And if she ran away, the authorities would take her back there. But if you're next of kin —"

"No one will talk to me. And I don't know those people who grabbed her. I'm sure you can find out. They won't tell me shit. Excuse me. I've been phoning everybody I can think of all morning. Maybe they'll give you some respect. Will you at least try?"

"The boy — Luke Shackleton — was your sister somehow involved with him?"

She sighed. "People at the hospital thought they messed around. Even that maybe Buzz is Luke's kid. But I don't know about that.

Melissa always thought Luke was some kind of saint. Melissa certainly isn't. She said he could see into her soul. Like they have some bond."

Evan remembered, "When I saw him this morning, he told me he knows she's hurting."

She asked eagerly, "Does he know where she is?"

Evan shrugged. "I don't think so. All he would say was he knows she's hurting, fears she's in trouble. I'm sorry, I didn't know she was missing. Maybe I'd have pressed him harder. I mean, I don't know how Luke senses these things, but I'm not ready to say it's all in his imagination."

"If she's back with the nuns, I don't see how they can keep her. Melissa won't exactly be cooperative. Especially if they won't tell her what they've done with Buzz."

"The place is in Osceola, right?"

"Yes," Loretta said. The town was an hour and a half to the northeast on Route 65. Evan had never been to the convent.

I don't even know what to ask, much less promise. Do I dare play the Reverend card with Catholics? But if the girl is there, what do we have to lose?

"Look," Evan said. "Sheriff Otis is a friend of mine. At least he is on most days if I'm careful to show some respect. Maybe I can ask him without letting on I know you. Or that I even know about Melissa's being gone. Like I want to know how to deal with the child welfare people. I'm sure he has some answers. Maybe he could help us get things done."

"Please," Loretta insisted. "No cops. If they were on my side at all, they wouldn't have pulled my sister and her baby out of my home." She hesitated, then said, "I have an arrest record. I told you I work at the casino. I could lose my job if they find out, and if by some miracle she and Buzz can ever come live with me, it's the only way I have to support us."

In fact, Loretta had no arrest record. And if she had, the casino's background check would have been sure to find it. Her fear was that she didn't want her boss at the casino thinking she was telling tales to the authorities. She knew Evan couldn't begin to appreciate the implications. And, she'd have to admit, she wasn't all that sure what was going on.

In her embarrassed pause, she picked up her phone from the console, asked him for his number, and called it.

"I'm Loretta Benton." She insisted, waving the phone, "And you're my new best friend."

Evan looked down and tapped his phone to add the caller. "Sure" was all he could say.

She checked her face in the sun-visor mirror, smeared the tear tracks from her cheeks with a tissue, and sniffed, "You need a lift?"

"Uh, no," he said, finally realizing they wouldn't be going anywhere.

"You find out anything… the *tiniest* thing… *call* me!"

"Are you sure you don't want me talking to the sheriff?"

"I don't trust the law. I don't trust the nuns. And I don't trust my employers to be understanding about any of this."

Otis has more than one deputy, but 'kid sheriff' is sounding like someone I know all too well.

In Evan's obsessive mind, he was already connecting the dots. "This deputy, did he have red hair?"

She looked surprised. "Yeah. Yeah, he did."

Yep, Deputy Malcolm Griggs! Nickname Mal — and he doesn't object! I guess I'm not done with him. He doesn't have to know I'm helping Loretta, though.

Loretta closed her eyes and held them shut like an Olympian who was preparing to dive off the high board. "There's something else you need to know," she said softly.

"I try to be a good listener," he said, fearing she was about to admit something scandalous.

Hearing confessions could be a full-time job.

She turned to him, her eyes filled with tears. The mascara was running down her cheeks again. "Melissa suffers from epilepsy."

It took a moment for this revelation and its consequences to sink in. Then he asked, "Is she on medication?"

"That's just the thing," Loretta said as she took a drugstore vial from the console. "She didn't have a chance to take these with her."

"And what happens if she doesn't take them?"

"She could have a fit anytime. The main worry is she could get injured falling down." She gasped, then went on, "But it's what people *think*. What they might do to her. Or *not* do."

"I don't follow."

"When she was at the hospital, they could help her maintain, monitor her, manage the dosage. But at the convent she didn't get much support. Just the opposite. You'd think these days people would be more enlightened, especially in a childcare facility. But to some of those nuns, along with their faith they hold onto some old superstitions."

Evan nodded. "They think she's possessed?"

"Possessed and cursed. Rejecting God, controlled by Satan."

Evan gently took the pill bottle from her quaking fingers.

She thinks I've got more miracles up my sleeve.

He tried to sound confident when he smiled reassuringly and said, "I'll call you this afternoon." He got out, closed the passenger door, and she backed out and drove off east on Main Street.

STILL STANDING on the curb before he went back into the diner, Evan called the Sisters of Mercy Children's Home at the convent. When he asked after Melissa Benton, he was put through to Reverend Mother Bernadette.

"I'm Reverend Wycliff of First Baptist," he told the nun, "a friend of the Benton family. Perhaps you know Melissa and her baby were taken forcefully from their home this morning."

The mother superior's voice was kindly but feigned ignorance, not of the child but of her whereabouts. "Bless your concern, Reverend," the nun replied. "But if I did know more about it, the matter would still be confidential. All I can say is this institution is no longer responsible for that poor girl's care."

Assuming a devout Carmelite would have trouble telling a deliberate lie, Evan surmised that, if the girl had been taken there, she was no longer in their custody.

I had no right to expect this would be easy. If the abbess is lying, Melissa is probably safe — unless she starts having fits. But if she's had an episode — or if they're worried she will — maybe they shipped her back to Myerson? She'd get her meds at the clinic, but would the nuns make sure she's medicated?

He took a chance blurting out, "You know she suffers from epilepsy. I have her pills. At the very least, we need to find a way to make sure she can stay on her meds. The label says twice a day, so I worry she might be at risk."

"Bless you for your concern, Reverend," Mother Bernadette said. "All I can do is refer you to Father Coyle. He manages our business affairs."

The recorded message on the priest's extension allowed Evan to leave voicemail. He identified himself in his official role, fibbing as he had done to the Mother Superior, and requested an urgent meeting without saying why.

Okay, no cops. But I can smell Griggs on this. If I can't go asking Chet straight-out for help, maybe I should find out who those other two were who staged the intervention. This much I know — that deputy isn't exactly an original thinker. He was following orders from somebody.

Now that the sun was up over the town's buildings, the day was getting hot. Evan began to sweat through his clothes, and he didn't have much that was clean at home. He had a hunch. His next call was to Bernice Richards. The "mean-ass" social worker might not have been Bernice, but Evan would soon find out whether he was right. The connection between her and the deputy would be the puzzler.

I'd better stop short of accusing her of anything.

When she answered the call, he led off with, "I made some notes after our visit. I believe you said the girl Luke might have... interfered with... was Melissa Benton?"

"I didn't say anything of the sort" came the cautious reply. "You got your nerve, Reverend. How is this any business of yours?"

"She and her sister attended our church. A pastoral visit wouldn't be an unreasonable request."

"First Luke and now Melissa? Are you gonna start messing with all my clients?"

"So Melissa *is* a client? Where is she now?"

"No, not *my* client. Not now. All I know is what I've read in the case file," she said. "That girl was discharged before I took the job, and I learned enough to be thankful I don't have to be dealing with her. She was discharged back in April to Sisters of Mercy Children's Home." Richards sniffed, "She was pregnant at the time."

"Are you saying Melissa Benton is not with you now?"

"Now, why wouldn't she be with the nuns?"

"And what about baby Buzz?"

"Same answer. I'm not the one you should be asking about this."

I've said too much. She's wondering how I know what I know.

Before he gave up, Evan decided to ask, "So you must know that Luke was accused of being the father?"

Richards must have figured she was off the hook for the time being. Perhaps by speaking more freely, she wanted to give Evan the impression she had nothing to hide. "Now, don't go putting words into my mouth. She gave birth back in April, I believe, right after she left us. Before my time, as I said. So how would I know? Our teenage clients are permitted to have platonic relationships. And, like I told you before, those kids can earn home leave, a privilege that gets revoked if they don't behave." She took a breath. "Look, I'm not saying he did, and I'm not saying he didn't. I'm not sure what difference it makes now unless someone insists on opening that can of worms."

Something tells me I'd better not let on that I think this woman is the one who snatched Buzz. Or that I'm Loretta's new best friend.

"Could you put me in touch with Melissa? I'd like to get her side of the story. Informally, you know. If Luke cares about her at all, he deserves to know how she and her baby are doing."

An innocent question, right?

"Again, how is this my problem? Ask those nuns. Besides, all that's confidential information. These are minor children. Their case files are sealed. Even parents and guardians don't get to know everything."

Evan tried to sound offhand when he asked, "Can't you tell me where she is?"

The woman's tone became even more officious. "I'll say it again. I have to believe she's at the convent. But I'm sure they don't just give out information any more than we do."

"So who controls her custody now? Who decides who can see her?"

"They're not going to go telling me either. I'm on the outside, just like you."

"Let me ask you, Bernice, and you know this is a totally hypothetical question…"

"Which of course it isn't."

"If Mr. Shackleton were to engage an attorney to assist in our understanding of the facts, would that make a difference?"

Now she was indignant. "Are you gonna go and lawyer-up on me?"

"On *you?* I didn't say anything of the sort. You just said you were out of it."

She took a long moment, then said quietly, "You get a lawyer, there's a process."

"What process?"

She chuckled, "Now, that's what you *pay* the lawyer to tell you, hon."

EVAN's next call was to Sheriff Chet Otis. Not to the office but to his personal phone. Evan had won the officer's respect when the preacher refused to accept Bob Taggart's suicide as the simple act of a distressed man.

"Hey, Chet."

"Reverend."

"I said you can stop calling me that."

"And I told you to lay off all the greasy food."

"Like you're eating salad now? Are we still on good terms? I mean, unofficially?"

"Why? You got some unofficial shit you need buried? Some unofficial documents you need to hide? Now, if you've got unofficial gossip, I'm all ears."

Sheriff Otis is teasing me about Bob's last will and testament. I don't know which of us owes the other a favor now.

"Do you know where Deputy Griggs was this morning — at the beginning of his shift?"

"You think I don't know every little piece of diddly shit falls into my own backyard?"

"Well, what was he up to?"

"Said he had to accompany a process server, make sure the guy didn't get roughed up. Somewhere out near your place, I think. Was it one of your deadbeats skipped on some payments?"

Now, why did Griggs have to lie about where he was going? Why is that guy always playing both sides against the middle?

"If it's one of mine, I didn't ask him in on it," Evan said. "But I'm never the only one chasing them. Do you know where Griggs went after that?"

"Reported in. Half-hour late with my crullers. Do you need to talk to him? Your guy skip or something?"

"No, nothing like that." Evan had enough to confirm his suspicion that Griggs had been in on the morning raid at Loretta's.

No use burning Griggs now. If I have this to hold over him, maybe I can get him to tell me what really happened.

Evan wrapped it up with, "Thanks, Chet. For now, as far as Griggs is concerned, I didn't ask, okay? I promise I'll fill you in when and if you want to know."

"Somebody threatens you, I want to know about it. I got too much worry already invested in you. I might need a favor now and again from someone who don't wear a badge."

"You got my back?"

The sheriff laughed. "You can't shake me loose, son. I'm on your back. Hell, I'm right there on your *ass!* You fuck with me, what do you think's gonna happen to you immediately if not sooner?"

"Do you mind if I have a word with Griggs?"

"I won't be in the office rest of the day," the sheriff said. "Tell you what. We're fresh outta Folgers. You drop by, if the deputy is in one of his better moods, he might brew up some for you."

C'MON INN

FRIDAY NOON

*R*eentering the diner, Evan resumed his place at the counter. It had already been cleared. Somehow he wasn't ready to reward himself with pie. He left a twenty, which included his usual five-dollar tip. He didn't want Cora to think he was the slightest bit bothered by her teasing.

"Nice tip," she said, glancing down as she sidled over. "Thanks. You know I live to serve. Short trip?"

"What did you tell her about me?"

Cora leaned across to confide, "My friend Clint works at that place. Says you waltzed in there this morning and spoke the word to Shackleton's kid. Straightened him right up."

"He *might* stop wetting the bed. It's hardly a miracle."

"Anyhow, Loretta gets nails and hair done across the way, and girls talk. So I guess she thinks of me as a friend. I don't know what kind of trouble she's in, but she called crack of dawn today all spun up and said she needed help and no cops. So a damsel in distress needs a soldier of fortune. Who else do I know?"

"Do you know her sister? Melissa?"

Cora muttered, "Now, there's trouble," and wouldn't say more.

"Come on," Evan begged her. "What else you got?"

"Years ago, during the time you were away, I'd see those girls in Sunday School at First Baptist. Seemed like they were orphans even then. Pastor Thurston might be able to tell you more."

Evan didn't want to make a trip to the store, and besides he was short of cash because he'd tipped Cora so generously. He wheedled a can of Farmer Brothers out of her so he wouldn't be showing up at the sheriff's empty-handed.

~

EVAN HAD no doubt he'd be seeking Rev. Marcus Thurston's advice. He remembered there was a function at the church tonight. Meanwhile, he was losing patience with making phone calls. He had to confront Deputy Griggs, and then he'd make the trip to Osceola and barge in the front door of Sisters of Mercy. He'd deliver Melissa's pills, and maybe he could find out if she was there and if she was okay — or as well off as she could be without her son.

As Evan was getting into his car, its new ringtone sang.

It was Stu Shackleton.

"I don't know what you did," the banker said with uncharacteristic deference, "but I owe you."

Evan was quick to correct him. "I may have helped Luke stop wetting the bed. But I only saw him this morning, and somehow already the word on the street is I'm a healer. Now, I believe in the power of prayer, but I don't think anything I can do will cure schizophrenia overnight."

"All the same…"

"I didn't have much of a chance to talk with him. I'll be going back."

Shackleton wasn't sure what to say next. "About that… about the… girl…"

"Perhaps you don't know, but Melissa Benton and her baby were taken into custody by child welfare this morning."

He sighed. It sounded like relief. "Well, then. It's out of our hands."

Kind of convenient for him?

Evan was quick to add, "Her sister Loretta has asked for my help. She says Melissa suffers from epilepsy. And the girl must be out of pills, because I have them."

Shackleton paused, then said, "If the state agency took her, I'm sure she's in capable hands. And if she needs care, she'll get it. In my view, it will be best if Luke has nothing more to do with her. Which means — I'd advise you to stay out of it."

"Loretta doesn't think anyone will help her, but she's hoping they'll talk to me."

Shackleton was growing impatient. And irritated. "I don't know what she thinks you can do. Sounds like it's up to the authorities now."

Evan needed to ask, "Is that baby Luke's?"

Shackleton's reply was cautious and quick. "Has anybody said it is?"

Evan had to say, "No."

"Then it isn't."

Wow. This could be the end of the Shackleton dynasty, and he doesn't care. He's decided Luke can never be a banker or a father. Then again, maybe he's convinced the baby isn't his blood.

Evan pressed the question, "Is it at all possible Melissa was pregnant before she was admitted to the clinic? Maybe even why she got sent there?"

"And why would either of us care?"

"Because, if that baby *is* Luke's, then he will care, and so should you!"

"I really don't see why —"

"Because they've *taken the baby away* from her! Loretta is in a panic, over the top. And frankly your son's emotions and state of mind might depend on whether he knows his girlfriend and her baby — okay, *his* baby — are safe."

Shackleton's tone regained its usual swagger. "Trust me, there's nothing more to be done. The girl's an orphan. Do you understand? You have to figure she and her kid are wards of the state. And no doubt in the care of professionals, as Luke is. I don't mind your comforting him. I don't mind at all. I respect what you did… what you do." Then he added, "Look, there's no way to know who the father of that child is without a DNA test. And why ever would I be the one to go and insist on such a thing? I'm sure you'll agree it's best you forget all about the Benton girl."

"I do understand," Evan said.

I'm not necessarily complying with an order but simply affirming I've received his version of the facts.

As he ended the call, Evan reflected on his recent choice of ringtone, George Beverly Shea's resonant rendition of the hymn "How Great Thou Art." Evan had been tempted to choose Roy Orbison's "Pretty Woman," which always made him think of Naomi. But he knew advertising his lust for a dead woman would be sending the wrong message to anyone on the street who overheard. As it was, the hymn was doubly ironic. Praising God might be the expected clarion call for a preacher. But just as often Evan felt *he* was being summoned, and it bucked up his self-esteem.

How great am I? Am I selfish — or just self-absorbed? I pray God appreciates the joke. I refuse to believe that Jesus ever said anything about people being filthy rags in the sight of the Father. Some medieval priest must have thought that one up right before he did a number on his naked back with a scourge of nails.

Not taking every word of the Bible literally was a consequence of Evan's liberal education in divinity school. Above all, he believed loving oneself affirms God's love and opens the heart to love others, even though Evan found that difficult to do much of the time. And preaching self-love to this community of conservative Christians was a stretch, if not a joke, and they didn't joke about such things.

The ringtone reminds me to lighten up.

Now that Luke was no longer in trouble for pissing in the wrong places and everyone except Loretta was telling him it was no use fretting about Melissa, Evan understood Shackleton would prefer he didn't meddle any further. But he'd nominated himself as one of Luke's caregivers. And in his role of professional skip tracer, he now regarded the distressed Loretta Benton as a new client.

And, from the vague warnings he'd received from Naomi and then from Luke, if he didn't act quickly, Melissa might soon come to serious harm.

SHERIFF'S OFFICE, APPLETON CITY

FRIDAY, EARLY AFTERNOON

*E*van entered the sheriff's office to find Mal Griggs seated behind the boss's big desk and the other officers, including Chet Otis, absent. Facing the deputy alone meant Evan didn't have to wink at the sheriff to hint why he needed to have a confidential word or two with the junior man.

Evan set the can of coffee down on the desk as he took a seat confidently in a guest chair.

"The sheriff's at a training with Frank and Nolan," Griggs explained. Then, eyeing the coffee, he added, "But I guess you knew that. They'll get lunch on the county, and I'm stuck on the desk. Something I can do for you?"

Evan palmed the bottle of pills in his pocket. His face lost its pleasant expression when he said, "You grabbed a girl and her baby from their home this morning, but you forgot *this.*" And he held up the pills. "We're talking medic alert. The girl has epilepsy. Now, are you going to tell me where you took her, or do we call Chet out of his meeting?"

Griggs looked miffed. "So am I to understand you didn't tell him already?"

Evan shook his head. "He asked me to run the coffee over here.

But don't bother, I've had too much already. And, yes, he doesn't know why I've come to see you. I wanted to hear your description of events first."

Griggs swallowed hard, but then he shrugged innocently. "She ran away from Sisters of Mercy, and we took her back. I'm sure those folks can give her whatever she needs. But if it'll keep us friends, I'll call over there, and if necessary I'll deliver the medicine myself."

"I just got off the phone from Reverend Mother Bernadette. She refused to give me details, but she tried to make me think they don't have Melissa anymore. 'No longer our responsibility' was how she put it. Then she passed me to Father Coyle, and I got voicemail."

"News to me," the deputy said. He smiled. "You waltzed in here, I thought you wanted to kiss and make up."

"I'll settle for a promise you won't hit me on the head again."

Griggs sniggered. "Now I thought I'd explained all that. A misunderstanding! Thought you were some drugged-up burglar."

We were both looking for the same thing in that basement, you weasel — the only valid copy of Bob Taggart's will. Your problem was I got there before you did.

"I didn't hear an apology in there," Evan said.

Griggs' eyes narrowed. "Frankly, I'm not sure one is called for. Mighty suspicious you being in the basement of that drugstore at that hour in that storm when decent folks should be home. And later you said yourself you had a thing for the opioids. But I'm genuinely sorry you got hurt." He smirked and shrugged as he added, "So. You have my apologies. Sorry that we're fresh outta donuts."

Evan leaned forward slightly and shot Griggs his best menacing look. "I know where you were this morning, and I know Chet didn't, and I also know you didn't have a warrant. Who sent you there and where are the girl and her baby would be my questions."

Griggs sat up straight and cleared his throat. He looked down at the desk blotter as he said quietly, "And tell me again why this would be any business of yours?"

Evan pulled the letter from his hip pocket, unfolded it slowly, and pushed it across the desk. "Firstly," he began, "because Mr. Shackleton gave me this letter of authorization to look after the welfare of his boy, who is suffering emotional trauma because he's a close friend of the girl you abducted."

"Now, *abducted* is a strong —"

"And *secondly*, because Chet wanted to know this morning if I'd asked you along to help me serve papers on a skip. Which was obviously not the case."

Griggs' not having a warrant was a scientific wild-assed guess on Evan's part. If Melissa had just shown up unexpectedly at her sister's, her presence there would be a presumption by the authorities, and there wouldn't have been time to present the facts to a judge. But from the look on the deputy's face, Evan's surmise about the deputy's faking it was true.

Maybe I should go along with Thurston the next time he heads over to Cape Girardeau for one of those Holdem Poker meetups. I believe he said there'd be a judge or two at the table.

Griggs swallowed hard and handed the paper back. "What did you tell Chet? I mean, about whether I was working with you?"

"I didn't confirm or deny. He didn't seem worried. But I suppose if I were to decide to clarify things for him…"

"Okay, I get it," Griggs huffed. "You got me in a box." Then he caught himself. "Bad choice of words."

"Are you speaking of the tin box I was searching for the night you conked me? I know who sent you there and why. You were after it too. I didn't enjoy my stay in the hospital, but I didn't die, and the guy who wished me harm is now thanking me for helping his son. So here we are. Maybe if you confess your sins now I'll put in a good word for you — down here and *up there*." Evan rolled his eyes skyward.

Maybe he won't get the joke. Or know I'm kidding.

Griggs became matter-of-fact. "The fee for one of our guys serving process is fifty bucks paid to the department. I guess you never availed yourself, but you're always welcome. Depending on how busy we are, there could be a wait, maybe a few days. None of us gets any of the fee for making the run. But if it's — shall we call it — a side deal? We do it the same day, before our shift or during a lunch, and we pocket the fifty. We all do it, Chet looks the other way, and everybody's happy."

"So what about today? Who set it up?"

"Bernice Richards from Myerson calls and says she needs to go in there with Chuck Holloman from child welfare. Loretta Benton's trailer. They didn't expect trouble, but if there's some surprise boyfriend in there swinging an iron skillet, they want some cover. And it was double the fee because it was two extractions — the girl *and* her kid."

"So where did you take them?"

Griggs looked at Evan like the answer was obvious. "Like I told you. Sisters of Mercy. Don't need a warrant to take a runaway back home."

"Not to drive her back, maybe. But to push your way into her sister's house and grab her, I think you might."

"I didn't lay a hand on anybody, and none of them rode with me. I was more or less an escort. Security detail. Chuck put her in his car, actually. She wasn't even cuffed. I rode along behind just to make sure she didn't do something stupid like, I dunno, try to jump out. Chuck marched her into the convent and Father Coyle signed for her. Chuck had his paperwork in order, I had my hundred in cash from Bernice, and the both of us drove on to our places of business."

"You didn't mention the baby."

"Bernice took it. She said she'd meet us at the home, but she didn't. Maybe she took it to the doctor's first to make sure no hoof and mouth? Damned if I know, but she never caught up with us."

"Have you known Bernice long?"

Griggs shrugged. "She had a business card that matched her ID. Are we done?"

No use asking Bernice where she took the baby. She'll go 'What baby?'

Griggs also had a business card for Charles Holloman at Family Welfare Agency, and he gave it to Evan.

WHILE EVAN WAS SITTING with Griggs, Bernice was on the phone to Father Coyle. She wanted to wash her hands of this situation as quickly as possible. Before the end of the day, she wanted nothing to do with either the young mother or her chubby baby. She strongly suspected it wouldn't take the preacher long to figure out where they'd taken Melissa. And she was equally sure he'd take it upon himself to track the girl down.

"You got trouble headed your way," she told the priest.

His reply sounded mildly amused, "We strive to see grievances as opportunities, openings for miracles. What is it this time?"

"Reverend Evan Wycliff. Stuart Shackleton sent him into the clinic to check on his son yesterday."

"A pastoral visit might do the boy some good."

"Nossir. This guy is out of control. He doesn't just say a prayer and leave. He's telling Luke he's been cured some kind of way, and then he sits down with me and wants to know the whole case history of Melissa Benton and her baby. You know I wasn't on the job back then. I'm just doing evaluations to get these kids placed in better circumstances. His father wants Luke stabilized, and he wants the girl out of the boy's life. You don't want her either. Without a clinical diagnosis for her epilepsy, what were you gonna do? Use demonic possession as your excuse to keep her locked up somewhere? I want Luke out of the clinic as soon as I can get a code for appropriate placement. We're a drug rehab, not a mental hospital."

"Are you trying to say this minister will be paying me a visit?"

"You better believe it."

"Ms. Richards, let me assure you. We've found appropriate circumstances for both the young mother and her baby. The girl is hardly capable of caring for her son. She needs professional therapy and maintenance medication. Her foster father can afford to give her the very best. As will the baby's adoptive parents. You told me you concurred with the placements."

"I do, and I took the baby over there myself today. I'll be dropping the paperwork in registered mail to you. What about Melissa? Is she still at the convent?"

"Bernice, I think it's best you don't involve yourself in the details," Coyle replied carefully. "A gentleman with the foster parent's power of attorney is on his way here, and the girl will be leaving with him."

Bernice couldn't believe it. "Without a *fuss?*"

The priest's tone was placid, supremely confident, when he said, "She's under light sedation. And she'll be leaving with our prayers."

Bernice gave out a sardonic chuckle. "You must've snuck up on her with that one." Then she added coldly, "You know I can guess where she's going. The guy must be smitten to put up with her. He's no angel, that's for sure. You got yourself a donation, of course."

"I'm sorry," Coyle sighed, "I haven't heard anything you've said. You don't know where she is, and you don't know where she's going or with whom." Then he added more pleasantly, "On Earth, God's work must truly be our own. Send me an invoice for your writeups and expenses, and we'll be prompt."

"There will also be a finder's fee for the adoption. Separate invoice, different account."

He assured her, "Whatever is customary."

BEFORE HE SET out for Osceola, Evan tracked down Charles Holloman at Family Welfare Agency, the guy Griggs said had taken Melissa. Evan reached him at his desk phone at the agency. When Evan informed him he was the Bentons' pastor and had Melissa's pills, Holloman freely admitted he'd taken the girl back to Sisters of Mercy. Asked about the baby, he flatly stated that child adoptions were not his department. Asked about his association with Bernice Richards, the fellow warned Evan the matter was none of his business and abruptly ended the call.

They all keep saying it's none of my business. Just what do they think my business is?

Evan was out of options. Driving over to Sisters of Mercy and confronting Coyle or anyone who would listen was all he could think to do.

ABOARD THE YACHT NAMOUNA, TRUMAN LAKE

FRIDAY EARLY AFTERNOON

*S*tuart Shackleton might not yet have gotten his way with his nefarious plans for taking the Emmett farm, but at least one of his ambitions had been fulfilled: He was proud to have perhaps the largest luxury motor yacht on Truman Lake. Truman is the mirror-image of the other artificial lake in the state's midsection, Lake of the Ozarks. In satellite views, their twisting watercourses and shorelines spiked with inlets resemble two coiled dragons. Indeed, the locals call the Lake of the Ozarks *The Magic Dragon*.

Truman is primarily home to freshwater fishermen, for whom two-person rowboats powered by a small Evinrude or Yamaha are numerous out on the water, despite being harassed and swamped occasionally by the churning wakes of overpowered cigarette boats favored by both skiers and hardcore party animals.

Shackleton enjoyed his expensive toys. And — these days with his wife in assisted living, his boy in a clinic, and his girlfriend stormed off in a huff — he didn't have much else to care for. He had previously ordered a custom-made, luxury automobile, a Mercedes-AMG S65 sport sedan, and he was even more meticulous when he acquired his yacht. He'd wanted an elegant sailboat, and he'd had his heart set on a built-to-spec, 140-foot single-masted sloop, the kind of salt-water craft he'd coveted ever since he and Ann had vacationed in St. Tropez years ago. But his research soon told him there was no way to transport a boat that size from the broker in Sarasota to the inland Missouri lake. Yes, it was possible to sail from the Gulf of Mexico, up the Mississippi, then into the mouth of the Missouri. But then you'd be stopped at the eastern end of Lake of the Ozarks by Bagnell Dam, and at the other end of that body of water by Truman Dam. So a boat bound for either lake must be put ashore at Jefferson City, where a crane would load it onto a long trailer. But checking the Department of Transportation regulations, Shackleton was dismayed to learn that the longest boat transporter legal on a Missouri highway is 75 feet, with an overhang of 3 feet in front, 4 feet in the rear.

So Shackleton finally decided on a 75-foot Horizon V68 motor yacht. At 19.5 feet, its beam exceeded the permissible 16 on the highway, but a friend in Springfield managed to finagle the permit for a hefty fee. It rankled the banker that the manufacturer described this model, which was modest in size compared to the other private ocean-going vessels in its line, to be "designed as an entry-level motor yacht with superyacht attitude." Shackleton didn't want to own a "starter" anything, but he was pacified to learn that the largest motor yacht on the more fashionable Lake of the Ozarks was a 68-foot Sunseeker Predator named *Miller Time*. Truman Lake had a few eye-catching motor yachts, but nothing like this!

Nevertheless, Stuart Shackleton was no sailor, never would be. Even with an experienced skipper and a crew of two, he used the lovely *Namouna* as little more than a high-class, ridiculously overpriced houseboat. And every time he had to fill her up with diesel fuel at the marina, he still hankered after a yacht that could slip quietly through the silvery water, catching the wind in her sails.

His burly guest today was both a landlubber and a foreigner. A helpful clerk at an upscale, urban men's store had probably advised this fellow how to dress. He was wearing a garishly floral Rayne Spooner Hawaiian shirt with an immaculate pair of crisp, white ducks that hugged his ample belly and generous backside. He wore Bass Weejun deck shoes with no socks, exposing his hairy ankles. There was an ostentatiously large Rolex Oyster on his wrist, which drew attention to the Cyrillic tattoo on his forearm. Were it not for the ink, he looked like a well-to-do American tourist, dressed perhaps more appropriately for a vacation in Cabo or St. Thomas. But here on sleepy Truman Lake, he was decidedly out of place. A T-shirt from one of the Branson music halls and a pair of faded jeans with a pair of beaten-up Vanns, socks optional, would have been perfectly acceptable. A ball cap, preferably advertising the Cards or the Royals, that didn't appear too new would be the expected headgear. Or a monogrammed golf shirt from Pebble Beach or St. Andrews and a pair of chinos with gum-sole Tom Fords would have marked him perhaps as a prosperous client of the bank who was no sailor and a day-guest on the boat.

The day-guest part was true enough. This guy might get a queasy stomach even on this placid water. In any case, his dark, thick beard was too well barbered and his accent was much too thick, even though his English vocabulary was more than adequate to deliver the message he was carrying.

His chuckle was lascivious, as if he traded in dirty jokes. "Why you want some big boat? You like to fish?"

The burly fellow, whom Shackleton knew as *Oleg* with no surname, was relaxing with his pudgy legs crossed on the port-side bench of the flybridge. The banker sat across from him in the captain's chair. The boat was at anchor in the marina, so there was no risk Shackleton would run aground. He had on a faded navy Ralph Lauren golf shirt and distressed designer jeans. His deck shoes were Sperry Gold Cup and well-worn. He'd planned to relax by himself on the boat today, perhaps doing some minor chores that nevertheless polished his pride of ownership, when he got the call asking for this unscheduled mandatory meeting.

"It's quiet," explained Shackleton. "A kind of quiet you can't get anywhere else."

"It's a write-off, isn't it? Clients want to fish?"

"My clients who want to fish have their own boats. But if they're the kind who would rent a boat, well, they wouldn't be my clients."

The guest looked around as if appraising the sale price. "Nice boat for party." Then he wheezed, "Maybe a few girls and a *very* good client."

"It's a leaseback. You should know. You guys hold the paper. I'll do a half-dozen guests on an afternoon and evening. But overnight, it's usually just me and the crew. Sun, wind, a dip, and sound sleep. Maybe a cocktail at sunset and a good meal from the galley."

"What kind of host are you? You're not going to let me sleep in my own bed?"

"You said a meeting, not a sleepover. And I don't have those kinds of parties. Or, if I do, it's only one guest." He tried to make a joke to lighten the mood when he said, "And you're not near pretty enough."

"Nice, private conversation out here. You put our phones in the safe, maybe? Lined with lead?"

"You know I did. What do you have to say that we had to do it out here?"

"Your son, Luke."

The banker was expecting that Oleg was sent for a bottom-line status report, which hopefully would only be temporarily disappointing to their accountants. He had the numbers to back up that claim, nothing written down. But the personal approach came as a shock.

Shackleton didn't dare offend. He depended on their laundered cash, not only to keep his bank solvent by underwriting his loans but also to fund the development deals he was planning. And he wasn't exactly an unwitting party in their hotel and casino operations.

Shackleton drew a deep breath and spoke rapidly, delivering a speech he'd rehearsed for some worst-case showdown. "Look. I draw a line. If you're going to threaten me, it won't work. Okay, I live in the gray area. I never know enough to put myself on the other side of the law. There are powerful people in the government who live in this gray area with me. That's why I'm useful. They don't want to know anything about anything, same as me. But I could tell them more than they'd ever want to know about your side of the deals, and then they'd have to do something about it. You don't want me as an enemy." Shackleton stared the other fellow down as he added what he desperately hoped was the clincher: "And I have those contingencies in place if anything should happen to me. Or to my family."

The banker removed his hand from the chair arm, hoping his guest didn't notice its slight tremor.

The bearded fellow actually laughed. "No, no, my friend. We would assume as much. Prudent protection for a man in your position. We wish no harm to come to your son. Or anyone dear to you. This is not how we wish to do business. We simply have a request."

Shackleton didn't think before he blurted out, "I'm done with your requests! You're already overdrawn! I leaned on Wilmer to put the girl in the clinic — against my better judgment, I might add. Now I believe she's back with the nuns, and as far as I'm concerned, that's where she should stay — that is, until she's of age or they find her a foster home."

"Your son was involved with this girl." It was not a question.

"No, *no.* Not at all," the banker insisted. "That was just a rumor. He might have had a crush on her. And I believe there was some kind of misunderstanding. In his condition, when he's not properly medicated, he has almost no impulse control. His actions must have been misinterpreted."

"There is a baby," Oleg said simply.

"Yes," Shackleton said. "Back in April. Father Coyle called to tell me there were no complications, mother and child healthy. But he needn't have bothered. It's no business of mine. I helped you put her into treatment — *why?* Because I take it she is a favorite of your boss. More than that, I don't know — I don't *want* to know. I do remember her. A couple of years back, she was in the fashion show at the lodge. We help the trade school put it on every year. Yeah, she's a looker, I can understand the attraction. But now she's nowhere near Luke, so don't ask me to worry about what happens to her."

"Or the baby?"

"None of my concern, I assure you."

"Could be your son is the father of this boy."

"No. *No!* I told you I don't believe that for a minute." In fact, Shackleton wasn't so sure, but he wasn't about to give Oleg ideas. Thinking he cared about what happened to either Melissa or Buzz would be one more thing they could hold over him. In his world, leverage always had a dollar value.

To Shackleton's surprise, Oleg actually looked relieved. "Your son must have nothing more to do with this girl," he said.

Relieved that this warning and his panicked reaction seemed unnecessary, Shackleton said, "He won't. How could he? As far as he knows, she's gone."

"Which also means, this investigator, whoever he is, must not go nosing around. Consider this girl… disappeared. A nonperson. Do you understand?"

"Are you talking about the preacher? He's hardly an investigator." After all, the girl was a stranger to him, and he'd already told Evan where to draw the line. Shackleton knew Melissa's name, and he'd seen her once when he'd visited the clinic to see Luke. "Let me be clear," he said firmly, "I want her far away from my son. We can agree on that. Where she ends up is not my worry."

Oleg came close and jabbed a thick finger into Shackleton's chest. It was the kind of theatrical gesture a goon would deliver on a bad cop show. In a low growl, the thug bullied the subordinate, "You have one more obligation."

Now anger welled up. Shackleton was not a man who easily tolerated being told what to do — by anyone. He struggled to remain calm, even though he could feel the blood rising to his face. "So," he replied, "like I said, why should I care? We didn't need all this drama for you to tell me this."

"You should be the one to tell this church guy to stop running around, asking questions, causing trouble."

"He's counseling my son," Shackleton insisted. "It's a personal matter and nothing you or your organization need to be concerned about. The doctors and the priest, they're worse than useless. This guy has been a help, and it's on me to make sure he doesn't go prying into our mutual interests."

"Are you saying you won't tell this fellow to back off?"

"I'm saying it's not your concern." Shackleton saw Oleg's brow twitch with irritation. "But somehow I sense that you haven't said all you came to say."

Oleg took a breath, then said, "If we know we have your cooperation, there is a service you must perform."

"Now we're getting to it."

"This boat. You use it as a… pied à terre?"

Shackleton could think of much less expensive venues for that kind of entertainment. "You think I spent all this money on a *fuck pad?*"

Oleg couldn't help himself and smiled. "Charming expression. I had not heard. Nevertheless, this usage is also something we desire. Not for long. But on demand, this one time."

Shackleton clenched his teeth. "Why bring her here? You guys own the marina. Are you telling me you can't find some vacant condo for this?"

The burly fellow held up a placating hand. "As I say, not for long. Days, not weeks."

"Do you plan to sail somewhere? Get out in the open water where no one will hear? What does he plan to do to her? I can't be a party to this! On *my* boat?"

"No. No excursion. Just like houseboat, nothing more. Nice linens, good food. Quiet. Nice time for everybody."

"She's a child! Underage! You're making me an accessory to statutory rape — and God knows what else!"

Shackleton's hand was clenched so hard the veins in his forearm were standing out.

Oleg persisted, "It is a matter of security. You grant us this, we ask nothing more, we go away, you never knew us." Then he added, "We can't leave until paperwork is done. The boss, foster father. Then, everything legal, we go."

It would be up to Wilmer, since the girl was still his ward, to sign off on the new guardianship. That aspect of this deal, if he dared call it a deal, was hardly a surprise. But, the banker couldn't believe the rest. He demanded of Oleg, "You're pulling out?" He gestured toward the luxury buildings surrounding the marina. "What about your stake in all this?"

Oleg shrugged. "Money is invested, sunk cost. Last phase construction, done. We don't need to mind the store."

"So you're going back to Nashville?"

"No. Back home."

Shackleton had to admit, not having to deal with these guys would be a relief — as long as they didn't go pulling their capital from his deals. He asked, "Can you give me at least an approximate timeframe?"

"Tonight." Oleg hesitated, then added sheepishly, "And there will be some necessary, shall we say, upgrades."

The suddenness was downright rude, but at least it would all be over with soon. Shackleton ran his relaxed hand along the gleaming dash panel, encouraging his visitor to appreciate the meticulous craftsmanship of this world-class vessel. "All needs are met. What can we possibly lack?"

Oleg's voice grew soft as if even out here in open water they might be overheard. "Intrusion detection and countermeasures."

The banker was offended. "Sonar, radar, radio, emergency gear? We've got it all."

"Military-grade. Our expense. Our team. You are not required onboard. After I leave, you go, you don't come back until I let you know. After our guests leave."

"*Weapons?* Are you bringing heavy hardware onto my boat?"

Oleg sneered as if to say no explanation was necessary. "Wherever the boss goes, security goes with him. It's only natural." Then he added, "What we bring, we take with. Like we were never here."

Shackleton paused again. These new factors wouldn't plug into a simple equation. It would take a whole whiteboard to work this all out so he could figure just where and how he might gain or lose. It still perplexed him that these guys were pulling out. It might not be a good sign. Were they leaving him holding the bag?

He faked a wry smile. "Do I have a choice?"

Oleg eagerly took the clue as a positive and laughed heartily, nudging Shackleton's shoulder. "Now, Stuart. You are too smart a fellow to go making enemies of your friends."

SHOOTING RANGE, EL DORADO SPRINGS

FRIDAY AFTERNOON

*E*ach kick of the Sig Sauer pistol was exhilarating, like throwing his head back and laughing. Stu Shackleton usually preferred the tension and the thrill of shooting at combat or crime video simulations, but today he was firing a rapid series of rounds at the dark silhouette on a stationary paper target. He just wanted the release of blasting away.

The first time he'd fired the weapon, four years ago, after his Ann was institutionalized, the shock of the recoil had been fearsome. But he soon found it awesome. The gun had taught him that he could turn his fear into anger, his anger into rage. He came to realize that rage is the wellspring of the warrior's courage, the fierce determination to defy death.

He used to think his likely enemies wouldn't be coming at him with firearms. They'd send auditors or lawyers in suits. And their masters would be gangsters or politicians or gangster-politicians — a gangster like Oleg's boss, a mystery man Shackleton had never met. Oleg had referred to him as Vasili once. No surname. He must be a high-powered thug if he needed to surround himself with all that protective hardware. Who were they to kick him off his own boat? And for what? So the guy could abuse an underage girl — out on the water where no one could hear her screams? That's high risk — and for what crucial gain?

And all over a girl who might be the mother of his own grandson?

But what if the Russian were the father? Maybe that's why he was obsessed with having this girl and no other. But Churpov didn't seem to want the baby. Usually so sure of himself, in this situation the banker wasn't sure of anything. The only certainty was that he was being manipulated, and it infuriated him.

He was supposed to meet Griggs here this morning. It was a good place for them to confer in secret. The deputy had the excuse of needing range time for his sidearm certification. And Shackleton actually paid him for lessons in tactics and situational awareness. A home invasion wasn't out of the question these days.

Their meetings were certain to be confidential. The assistant manager on the counter today — who handled bookings, rented guns, and sold ammo — was conveniently deaf.

Griggs was late. It aggravated the banker that he was forced to put his trust in a man who was not a hundred-percent reliable.

Then here he came. Shackleton let his gun hand drop to his side, and the men stared at each other through their safety goggles.

"You're late," Shackleton snapped. "Taking a long lunch?"

"A bag of peanuts from the machine, as it happens," Griggs explained. "Had to hold the fort all by my lonesome this morning." Then he chuckled. "I'm sure you didn't mind getting your gun off by yourself for a while."

The banker didn't appreciate the joke. He came back, "You screwed up the transfer. This girl's a distressed property. I have to unload her, and here comes a willing buyer. She's not supposed to stay with Coyle. He's just the middleman."

"How do you figure I got it wrong? Everybody got where they were supposed to go."

"Coyle is yelling at me. Says the girl isn't being cooperative. Says you weren't the one to bring her in. You were supposed to make sure she wouldn't be a problem."

"Hey, Chuck had all the paperwork. I was just an escort. What'd you think? I'd rough her up?"

"Coyle is saying she's having fits. I'm not sure whether he meant just tantrums or for-real seizures. I'm sure they had to give her something to calm her down. He threatened to wash his hands of it and send her back to Myerson. But I won't have her going back to the clinic. Now the preacher is in there sniffing around, trying to put pieces together. And I don't trust Bernice."

"That guy is a danger to himself, let me tell you. That's why I was late. He came to see me, and he barged in there like he had Chet's blessing. Maybe he did, but he doesn't know enough to tell anybody anything."

Shackleton warned, "And now Loretta Benton has got him all spun up. Wants him to help her find Melissa."

Griggs looked amused. "Yeah, I know. He won't get far. By the time he figures out where she is, she's supposed to be somewhere else, right?"

Shackleton looked worried. "Somebody was holding it up. Coyle, Bernice, Wilmer? Like one of them is stalling, holding out — for what? They're pulling the girl from the convent as we speak, and after that, neither of us wants to know where they'll be taking her."

Griggs chuckled, "Things are always more complicated when you try to do it all legal-like."

Shackleton had another thought. "Wycliff was asking whether Melissa was already pregnant before she was admitted to Myerson. He didn't say it, but it's like he suspects someone put her and Luke together deliberately. It wasn't something I wanted to happen."

"Shove those kids together? What the hell for?"

"Maybe after they knew someone *else* had already knocked her up. Muddy the waters? Blackmail. Maybe to hold it over *me!*"

"Get outta here. Now you're the one who's paranoid." Griggs chuckled and added, "Get off a few more rounds, and you'll feel better."

But Shackleton wouldn't be sidetracked, insisting, "Today I got a whiff, that faint odor of deals about to go bad. They'll be trying to get leverage over me some way, maybe to shut me up just in case I might be tempted to, you know, write a book or something. The big bad wolf wants Melissa. Fine. We helped that happen, so maybe we've got some leverage the other way. We don't know if he wants the kid. If he decides the girl's a keeper, he'll have to decide about the baby."

Griggs knew precisely what the banker was implying. "Those guys don't make it a habit to play nice. Why don't you stay out of it? I'll have a chat with Wilmer. If he's been dragging his feet, maybe he can help things along."

"That's the first intelligent thing you've said. And if you need to twist his arm, go right ahead." Before Griggs turned to go, Shackleton asked him, "Deer season's a ways off, but I'm going to need a new rifle. Any ideas?"

The deputy answered, "I like the semi-automatics, I guess it's the soldier in me. I have a Remington Seven Hundred I bought from a friend. But it doesn't have scope mount, and I suppose you're gonna want that. For accuracy and range, maybe the Ruger American Three-Aught-Eight? Bolt action, but it's not like you're gonna kill the whole herd. Now, get some practice in, y'hear? And align that scope. Don't hesitate to ask." He thought a moment, then said, "Self-defense would be a pistol at close range. You shoot somebody, make sure you drag them back into the house. And don't call *me.*"

SHOULDER OF STATE ROUTE 13

FRIDAY AFTERNOON

*G*riggs didn't want to confront Wilmer at the clinic. He waited for the doctor to drive out of the parking lot in his new Elantra sedan, then followed at a distance in the squad car. When they were on an open stretch, the deputy pulled up close behind, switched on the emergency lights, and pulled the car over.

"Mal, what the hell!" Wilmer exclaimed as he recognized Griggs and rolled down the window. "Are you trying to give me a heart attack? My blood pressure is high enough these days."

"This doesn't have to take long. And it's one way to have a meeting without drawing attention."

"Okay, out with it!"

"Shackleton is wondering whether Melissa Benton might have been pregnant before you guys admitted her."

"And this history lesson is because *why?*"

"As it is, if everybody thinks Luke is the father, maybe the real perp dodges a rape charge. I mean, the fact of a baby means somebody did something. And Shackleton is left not knowing what's what, having to deal with it. Maybe even worried the whole thing will blow back on him."

"Naw, that girl's gonna be in high clover. She won't go blaming anybody. Now, I wouldn't be surprised if some people want to go putting pressure on Shackleton. If he gets involved in these high-flying deals, it should be no concern of mine — or yours."

"I think you know who her new sugar-daddy is. Shackleton needs that guy to stay happy, get whatever he wants, you hear?"

Wilmer admitted, "I don't know his name. And I doubt the voice on the phone is his. Some guy with a rough accent. Documents by courier. I signed the guardian paperwork, but I didn't get it until today, then I sent it by courier over to Stu's office. The application had a name, but I'm not so sure it was the one this fellow was born with. There's also a birth certificate and custody for the baby. Stu may want to change those names, or not."

"The guy who wants the girl controls businesses where Shackleton is involved. Establishments in these parts you'd recognize."

"Things we both know enough to stay clear of. So what's the concern?"

"If there's evidence this boss was the one who knocked her up, maybe the leverage could go the other way."

"I've got nothing," Wilmer insisted. "You can't trust the names on any of the documents, and I'm not about to ask questions. I'm glad to have that girl off my hands, and, to tell you the truth, I'd just as soon get Luke placed somewhere else. Myerson isn't the right facility for him, but I can understand Stu wants to manage the situation. For now, I have to live with it, but he knows I'm not happy about it."

"Shackleton says Father Coyle had to sedate her so they could get the transfer done. He almost sent her back to you."

"Transfer? Is that what they're calling it? Well, it's not kidnapping if they've got the paperwork. Coyle should have done his part with that. The state sanctioned it, and Bernice pushed it through. The clinic won't take Melissa back, and Coyle knows it."

Griggs started to go, then turned back and asked, "You wouldn't be fool enough to hold this over Mr. Shackleton, would you?"

"Mal, this job is gonna give me a comfortable retirement. Then I don't plan to stick around here. I'm gonna raise white-face cattle in Calgary and fish for Walleye in Minnesota and forget that I ever knew any of you."

Griggs flashed a phony grin and touched the brim of his hat, "You go safe now. And mind your back."

Wilmer was trying to make a joke when he said, "No ticket, then?"

The smile disappeared from the deputy's face, but the reply sounded courteous: "Call it a warning this time."

TWIN DRAGONS CASINO AND RESORT, OSCEOLA

A YEAR AGO

$\mathcal{N}$atasha was both house mother and trainer. During Melissa's first week after she'd been transferred upstairs from the laundry, the severe-looking woman schooled the girl in the basics of massage therapy.

Melissa was to keep her nails cut back. She must always use a massage table, never the bed, and she must let security set up and remove the table from the guest room for each session.

Natasha was middle-aged, and she always looked tired. Her Eastern European accent was as severe as her lined face. Melissa thought the woman creepy, like a character in some vampire movie. "Begin by ask what they want," Natasha coached her. (All of her instructions sounded like scolding.) "Style of massage: You do Swedish, you do deep tissue. They want hot rocks, okay, not so much problem. I show you how long to heat and where to put. You burn a client, you're done. But needles, anything crazy, you don't do. Deep tissue, and here is most important: When you press down hard, use elbow or knuckle as much as possible. When you use thumbs, stand on your toes. Body weight gives the pressure. You don't do, your hands so sore end of day, you won't last."

Most of the training wasn't hands-on. It was more like schoolwork.

Melissa had to study diagrams of the human body, memorizing the locations of muscles and pressure points. The soles of the feet are particularly complicated. She was told the art and craft of it are Chinese and ancient. She practiced deep tissue on Natasha herself and then on other girls. A big lesson was how much pressure to use and where, which varied by client. Melissa quickly came to realize that, given enough knowledge and experience, a therapist hitting a precise spot and going too deep could inflict searing pain. Maybe even torture. But Natasha explained that, even so, some clients wanted it that way.

Melissa expected to be coached on where to draw the line on sexual activity. She wasn't naïve. At least she thought she knew the risks. But she wasn't sure about the obligations of the job. Still, anything was better than sweating through your clothes down in the steaming laundry, not to mention the long hours, the backaches, and the sucky food, along with various kinds of verbal and physical abuse from the housekeeping supervisors — even from the janitors and the maids. She figured this new gig wouldn't be harmless, but she did expect to be told how to handle herself if any situations got ugly.

But Natasha's only advice was: "This remember, and I tell you once and once only: No matter what you do, *the client* must be the one to ask for it. You don't ask, you don't know anything to offer, you explain nothing. They must be clear. And you don't take money. We give you everything, more than your wildest dreams we give. Someone try to hurt you, I want to know. Our gorillas go have friendly talk. Maybe we tell client don't come back."

"But what if it's something I don't want to do?"

Natasha hissed, "I *told* you, they want to hurt you, you get out, come tell me quick. You can't get out, you use call button, security comes. Anything else, you don't mind, you decide and you tell me nothing."

They'd given her a small electronic device, a kind of key fob. This was her panic button, and she was only to use it as a last resort. She got the message that embarrassing a client would get her dismissed, even if they told the guy to pay up and check out.

Natasha also gave Melissa a phone, something she hadn't been permitted to have at the convent. She rightly guessed the phone would be Natasha's way of summoning her and issuing directions, especially work assignments in the hotel.

She learned later there that the hotel had further safeguards. Massage times were typically booked as one-hour sessions, sometimes ninety minutes. At times during the session, and always after an hour had elapsed, Natasha or one of the big men on the security detail would go to the guest room. They wouldn't knock. They'd just stand outside the door and listen. If they heard any kind of ruckus, they'd call the guest on the house phone. If whatever was going on inside was not consensual, most guests would get the idea they were being discreetly observed and would quietly send the therapist away. In an extreme situation, security would enter with a passkey and politely inform the client that the therapist was late for her next booking.

Melissa was still not clear what she was and wasn't expected to do. She asked her mentor, "But what if they insist?"

"You decide! Like any job, you don't want to go to work someday — it's your choice."

"But what happens if I turn them down?"

"You came from the convent, right?"

"Yes."

"You don't want to work someday, you go back." And she laughed. "Free country!"

MELISSA USED her new phone to call Loretta, who was overjoyed to hear from her. However, even though they were now working for the same employer, they had no opportunities to see each other. Loretta worked crazy hours as a cocktail waitress at the casino, and Melissa's jobs — both in the laundry and at the spa, were at the hotel. The hotel was physically separate, built on a plot across an inlet from the casino on Truman Lake. Surrounding the two facilities and spanning a bridge across the inlet was a complex of luxury condominiums bearing the Twin Dragons signage. A marina on the inlet provided controlled access to the property for renters of boat slips and yachtie hotel guests.

The supervisors had warned on Melissa's first day as an intern at the casino that the private apartments, the dock, and the boats were strictly off-limits to hotel staff at all times.

Understandably, when they talked on the phone, Loretta was full of questions. They hadn't spoken since last visitation day at the convent, almost a month ago.

"They had me in the laundry," Melissa explained. "Ugh. But some of us got moved up. We're getting trained to work in the spa." She avoided mentioning the work was massage therapy, fearing her sister would draw the obvious conclusions.

Loretta wanted to know when they could see each other, and Melissa put her off. "They're telling us hotel staff can't be caught anywhere near the casino. Are they saying you can't come here? Best stay away. I'm in a dorm. It's nothing to complain about. You remember Abby. She's my roommate now. So all around it's pretty much okay. We're just glad to get out of housekeeping."

"When can I see you?" Loretta laughed and exclaimed, "Hell, I don't even know if you're fat or thin anymore!"

"I'll have to let you know" was all Melissa said.

"Melissa! What about days off? You can't be a prisoner over there. They have to let you take a break, come home sometime."

Melissa sniffed, "This is home now." In fact, she hadn't asked about breaks or time off. Weekends were busiest, after all, and because they ate in the staff cafeteria, she didn't need to run errands. She and her roommate Abigail Sharkey bought their toiletries and other necessities at the hotel gift shop, where staff got a discount.

Abby had been Melissa's roommate since their days at the convent. Both had gone through Jack Nathan's fashion school, and now they'd both been placed at the spa.

Loretta was angered but held it in. From experience she knew that lecturing her little sister would do no good. "Well, can you promise me you're taking your meds?"

"Sure," Melissa said. "Don't worry about it. And I've got plenty."

Throughout their childhoods, Loretta had been both Miss Nosey and Mother Hen to Melissa. Now that the younger one had a real job and a chance to make her way, she wasn't about to follow directions or suck up.

Loretta didn't want to press, but she had to try. "I'm going to leave a key to my place for you at hotel reception. You get a break, you need anything, just come."

"Sure thing, sis," Melissa said, vowing to herself it was the last thing she'd do.

But Melissa would come to wish that someone as caring as Loretta were still in charge.

MELISSA'S early clients were not staying in the luxurious suites on the higher floors. They were mostly women, mostly old. None of them asked for extras. But just about all of them wanted to talk. That is, they wanted her to listen, and their chatter ran nonstop through the session. These ladies were one type or the other: The first complained that their husbands or companions were obsessive about gambling, usually cards, and wondered how to pull them away. The others were addicted themselves, playing the slots at all hours. To these guests, a break for a massage was more important than eating. And while they were hovering over the whirling machines, the wait staff would keep the free booze and snacks coming anywhere they happened to be on the floor.

Melissa also assumed that Natasha would keep checking up on her. There must be some way for the hotel to keep track of customer satisfaction. She also wondered, although she never had any confirmation of it, whether her performance ratings would somehow get back to Mother Bernadette and Father Coyle. Did the nuns think she was still working in the laundry? How would her employer's evaluations be reported to them, if at all?

Melissa got a modest paycheck, which was automatically deposited to a personal bank account, from which the hotel took deductions for her lodging, meals, uniforms, and laundry. What little she had left she could draw from an ATM in the hotel lobby, which was as close as she ever got to a bank, but she had nothing to spend it on.

~

MELISSA's first male client was checked into an Executive Suite on the next-to-highest floor of the hotel. He was a thickset man, and when he spoke, his voice was surly and deep. He spoke with an accent similar to Natasha's, but his command of English was better.

"You like job?" he asked her as he lay on his belly and she kneaded his back.

"I'm learning," she said, "but, yeah, I think so."

She had to keep his back oiled up lest her long strokes tug at the guy's dense body hair. She did most of her work on his pressure points, but she had to bear down extra hard through the thick layer of fat he wore like a heavy coat.

He didn't say much. He grunted a lot.

At one point, he fell asleep and began to snore.

When he roused, he asked her drowsily, "Whassyer name?"

"I'm Melissa," she said proudly. Natasha had told her she could use any name she wanted, but Melissa didn't see the point. She liked her name, and she hoped repeat clients would remember it so they could ask for her.

She held the sheet up for his modesty as she asked him to roll over on his back, and he did, with effort, emitting another series of grunts.

"I'm Oleg," he said. "I will be your good friend."

She'd been waiting for whatever special requests this man would have, and she figured now was the moment. She hoped he wouldn't want anything too weird. Or too gross. His looks were crude but not repulsive. And he was clean. He must have showered right before she came because he smelled of the hotel's signature sandalwood soap.

"You do favors for guests?" he asked softly.

She hesitated, then answered cautiously, "I try to please."

He surprised her by saying, "I have a friend. Good friend. Very rich, very powerful man. Handsome fellow. My boss, actually. He will like you. I tell him you like to party."

She had no idea where this was going, but she said, "Okay." Then she asked him, "So, are we done for today?"

"Not yet," he chuckled as she deftly covered his lap with the sheet and he struggled to sit up. "Call this final exam. For my friend."

She was wearing the spa uniform, Chinese-style silk pajamas with entwined Twin Dragons on the breast pocket. He politely instructed her to take it off, and she did. He asked her to turn around slowly, and she did as he admired her with approving grunts. Then he asked her to lie down on the bed, which she did. He was naked himself as he let the sheet drop and lowered his bulk into a chair next to her. He handed her the bottle of massage oil and told her to pleasure herself. (It was a skill she'd practiced late nights in the convent dorm, she and Abigail sweating in unison so that, if the house mother barged in and they got caught, both of them would have to do penance.)

Oleg stroked his own stubby self heatedly, never taking his eyes off of her. It took her longer than it did him, but he didn't seem to mind.

As she put her uniform back on, he pulled a hundred-dollar bill from the nightstand and held it out to her.

She shook her head. "No, I can't accept that. House rules. But thank you."

He chuckled again. "Maybe I tell Natasha buy you pretty dress."

Now she couldn't help a smile. "I don't see why not."

Oleg grew serious. "My friend, his name is Vasili. He ask for you, you... be flexible? Okay? Me, I don't touch you. Him, he's like movie star. Does what he wants."

MELISSA DIDN'T HAVE to tell Natasha about Oleg. Somehow the house mother knew. And she eventually gave Melissa not one but a half-dozen dresses. The first one was a size two cocktail dress with a short skirt, to be worn with sheer stockings. Melissa had the long legs for it. The dress was stunning but must have been a hand-me-down from another girl on staff. The bodice was too small for Melissa's ample breasts. So one Saturday morning, a hotel driver chauffeured her and Natasha, heading down U.S. 13, on a trip to Branson. It took almost two hours to get there.

Melissa was surprised that Natasha hadn't driven her in the staff van. The two women had the back seat to themselves. Natasha wouldn't engage in small talk and was preoccupied with her phone. She made no calls, but she busied herself with texts, some of them bringing a frown to her face and that exasperated puff of air.

They dropped a ton of money at a shop called Grand Glitz on Highway 76, including not only evening dresses, but also tourist hotel daywear and alluring lingerie. Natasha picked out flashy costume jewelry for her, which, while not encrusted with precious stones, was not exactly cheap.

On the way back, Melissa thanked Natasha for her good fortune. She guessed that this Vasili, whoever he was, would be footing the bill. Natasha wouldn't confirm. Melissa remarked that everything they'd bought that day was simply gorgeous, but she wondered out loud why they didn't go to Jack Nathan for custom-made. Natasha sneered at the mention of his name and added curtly that these purchases were not to be considered Melissa's personal property.

Nevertheless, on their return to the hotel, Natasha informed Melissa that staff had already moved her things into a private room. It wasn't a luxurious suite, but it was considerably upscale from the dorm room she'd been sharing with Abigail. Melissa's association with other spa workers might have been another source of on-the-job training, but Natasha had warned them all that gossip — and particularly any discussion of their work with clients — would be grounds for dismissal.

To Melissa's delight, she found the rack inside her closet had been stocked with designer shoes. Most of them were stiletto heels, but thankfully there were two pairs of comfortable trainers, one in pink and one in black. She'd wear those with her daywear shorts and slacks.

Melissa began to fantasize about this guy she named Prince Vasili, and she anticipated his arrival with both eagerness and dread. With all this bother, would she be exclusive to him? What would she be expected to do when he was not in residence? While she waited, she expected Natasha would once again assign her to rubbing down old ladies on the lower floors.

But there was absolutely nothing for Melissa to do. The spa assignments never came. Now that she had her own room, she was not allowed to take her meals in the cafeteria. Natasha instructed her to dress in her new daywear, dine in the hotel restaurants, and to all appearances conduct herself like a guest. But she could not drink in the bars or at poolside, and she was to abruptly turn down any personal approaches or propositions from guests.

Natasha came to check on her now and then — never on any predictable schedule. She took appraising looks at her, asked after her health, and posed a series of questions intended to make sure the rules were being followed (although Melissa had no doubt her answers simply confirmed what the woman and her spies on the security detail had already observed). On the first of such inspections, Melissa asked about what she was waiting for and when it would happen, and all she got in return was a sneer, which was mean enough to discourage her from asking again.

Since she'd come to work at the hotel, Melissa had not been particularly friendly with the other interns who worked in the laundry. But she still regarded her former roommate Abigail as a friend. At the convent, they'd shared late-night stories, complaints about past boyfriends, and confessions of crushes and nonexistent relationships. And they shared their disgust about the refectory, along with the food cravings they could never satisfy. And, as Melissa had done, after they'd done duty in the laundry, Abby had been trained in massage therapy by Natasha.

Now in her new role as kept-woman-in-waiting, Melissa assumed Abby had been likewise promoted. But when she was lounging poolside one day, she saw her friend prance by in her spa uniform, followed by Stan, a security guard, who was carrying her massage table.

Melissa called out, "Abby!"

But all she got from the girl was a quick head turn and a mocking look as she walked briskly by.

That's when Melissa realized her new status was special, and, spited for rising above her station, she apparently would have no friends. In this new world of hers, she wasn't staff and she wasn't truly a guest. She was someone else's property, stored away until ordered to serve — *when?* This realization came with new worries, which were the same as the old ones, but with consequences likely more severe: What would they expect of her? And if she didn't know what they wanted, how could she make sure she wouldn't screw up? What if they threw her back into the laundry — and she didn't even know what she'd done — or hadn't done — to deserve it?

It wasn't long before she was bored out of her mind. The TV in her room got hundreds of cable channels, and, if there were charges for pay-per-view, she didn't see them. So in the afternoons, especially if it was too hot at poolside, she'd binge-watch movies. Her favorites were fantasy warrior-princess tales and romantic comedies. She remembered that Oleg had called Vasili a movie star, and she began to wonder whether the guy might actually *be* some famous actor. So she used her phone to search movie credits on the Web, hoping she'd find a leading man with the name. She found a few character actors in foreign films, but none of them met her imaginary model of Prince Vasili. Then she searched country artists, thinking he might play Branson, but no luck. After all that, she suspected Vasili might just be a code, a cover for someone so well-known even his stage name couldn't be disclosed.

For a time when she was spending hours glued to the screen, she'd get the munchies. Natasha had placed no restrictions on her food. She could order whatever she wanted. But after she'd gained a few pounds, she realized here was another way she could get bumped back to folding sheets and towels. So she resolved to balance her viewing hours with time spent on the exercise equipment in the guest gym.

After weeks, still no Prince Vasili. That's when Melissa entered a manic phase. She held fast to the belief that her prince was a celebrity, and this blind faith fed her own swelling opinion of herself and her ambitions. Hadn't Jack Nathan singled her out as a star pupil, heaped her with praise, featured her on the runway? She could see now that placing her in the laundry was just an excuse to get her working at the casino. Natasha had been grooming her — not for prostitution — but for stardom! After all, every few years, Hollywood needed new faces. Even the young hotties she watched in the movies would soon be so yesterday. She was smart, she was pretty, she had the slender figure with curves, and Jack had shown her the grace. She'd need acting lessons, but her prince would see to it. Her protector and sponsor would demand the studio bosses do whatever was necessary to lift her up the rest of the way — up there with him! And she used to think Branson was so fashionable!

Natasha had made sure that Melissa had a supply of birth-control pills, along with refills of the prescription pills the convent had given her, a treatment that seemed to be working. She'd had no episodes since the convent.

She wondered how much Natasha knew, if anything, about her epilepsy. It was never discussed. Perhaps the convent hadn't told them why she needed the pills, fearing her condition might jeopardize her employment. They seemed to want to push girls out of there, after all. Especially Melissa, the poor unfortunate whose demons their prayers hadn't been able to cast out!

What was noticeably missing from Melissa's supplies were condoms. She guessed correctly that the guests strongly preferred not to use them. No one gave her any advice on the subject, but a further guess was that disappointing clients by dulling their experience would be another reason to throw her out. It was a risk that came with the job, and especially now that Melissa could glimpse where her life was going, she was more than willing to cooperate. After all, it wasn't like she'd be screwing the field. She'd been promised to Vasili, and, if he valued her — as she *knew* he would — he'd make sure she was protected and taken care of in every way. And didn't she have ample evidence of his devotion already?

At the peak of this manic phase, Melissa had herself convinced she was on a rocket ride to stardom. She could do no wrong because the invisible people and forces that had brought her this far would surely push her the rest of the way.

But the birth-control pills made her breasts tender. And the epilepsy meds gave her dizzy spells, especially in the morning.

So she stopped taking all of them.

SISTERS OF MERCY CHILDREN'S HOME, OSCEOLA

FRIDAY AFTERNOON

*T*hey'd locked Melissa into a room by herself. It was a small space in back of the nurse's station where they lashed her to a canvas cot. Such restraints are generally against the law in an institution, but Nurse Crandall had never had to deal with a case of epilepsy before, and she was improvising. She'd stuck a clean, wadded-up athletic sock in the girl's mouth, thinking that it was necessary to prevent her from swallowing her tongue. In fact — and Melissa could have told her this if she wasn't gagged — it's impossible for a person to swallow their tongue. But biting it during a seizure is a risk — along with drooling and possibly choking — so the nurse's precaution wasn't entirely unnecessary. Melissa was already prone on the cot when the attack took hold, so the greater danger of being injured from falling or thrashing about wasn't a risk.

Melissa had been screaming, then sobbing, and all the while she was physically agitated, gritting her teeth and clawing at her bare arms. The gross injustice of grabbing Buzz away from her made her furious. It was unbearable! No doubt it was the stress that brought on the seizure.

They'd phoned Dr. Wilmer at the clinic, and he'd prescribed

phenobarbital, an outdated but not ineffective remedy. Father Coyle had directed Sister Margaret to fetch it on her trip into town.

The girl's convulsions had subsided, perhaps because the nurse had given her an injection of a tranquilizer, diazepam. Melissa hadn't seen the needle coming, or perhaps she'd have fought back. Then she didn't have the strength or the will to fight.

Melissa slept. Her dreams may have been wild and anguished, but her body lay still. When she awoke, she was calm but exhausted. Now, standing in the open doorway to the little room were three people — the Reverend Mother in her severe habit, the nurse in her starched uniform, and a heavyset fellow in a tailored gray suit that almost flattered his ugly body. They were talking among themselves in excited, hushed tones.

As the girl lifted her head and squinted, her focus improved. She recognized the burly fellow.

It was Oleg!

Nurse Crandall and the Reverend Mother were arguing, but quietly, as though careful she wouldn't overhear. Something about needing her medicine before she could be allowed to leave. While they continued to talk as they stood in the doorway, Oleg excused himself from them, stepped inside, pulled up a chair next to the cot, and sat. He leaned forward, bending his huge head over her, and she could smell his aura of cigar smoke, sweat, and musky cologne.

"Melissa," he cooed softly. "You remember me? Your friend Oleg?"

The muscles in her neck recoiled from him, and she winced. But she didn't have the strength to answer. Her reaction was enough to say she recognized him, and not fondly.

"You going to be just fine," he said. "Better than fine! Sister Margaret getting your medicine now. She bring, we go. You and me, we go to Vasili."

On hearing the name, Melissa began to whimper, but Oleg pressed a finger to her lips with a firm, insistent pressure.

"You behave now," he hissed. "Quiet, sweet. Good girl."

She wanted to cry. She wanted to scream, but she couldn't summon the strength. And she was too scared.

In the semi-darkness of the windowless room, she saw the flash of his yellowed teeth as his fat lips drew back in a sadistic grin.

"Quiet now," he soothed. "You good girl, you see your baby again."

That shut her up.

EVAN PULLED his Fiat into the circular drive in front of the children's home. It was a grand, Depression-era red-brick building that had once served as a state-run sanitarium. Broad concrete steps led up to a Federalist-style portal with a row of whitewashed Corinthian columns.

He assumed the silver Genesis G90 luxury sedan parked in front of him didn't belong to anyone inside. Perhaps some attorney? Evan figured it would be okay to leave his car out front. He didn't plan to stay long, and neither his car nor the sedan was blocking the exit of a private-service ambulance, which was also parked at the curb.

Is it unusual for a Jesuit priest to be the business manager of a children's home in a convent run by nuns and caring only for female orphans and unwed mothers? Those nuns of the Carmelite order must see themselves as reclusive caregivers.

Their policy was to delegate inquiries to this fellow who supervised the budgets of all Catholic charities in Southern Missouri.

The reception desk was unattended, and there was no one in the lobby. A gilt-lettered sign over an open walnut door on the right indicated the priest's office, from which he administered Flat Branch Catholic Charities. Peering in, Evan could see it was unoccupied, a handsomely furnished suite paneled with the same ponderous, dark walnut.

No one prevented Evan from taking a tour around the perimeter of the lobby. The ground floor housed the refectory, classrooms, and a small auditorium. All were empty. A long wooden stairway led up to the second floor. Some distant bustling noises and muffled voices wafted down from up there, where Evan guessed there would be the nuns' cells and the girls' dormitories.

Evan walked out a rear exit and encountered Father Coyle in the courtyard. The priest was wearing an apron over his cassock as he trimmed bushes full of blood-red rose blooms.

"Reverend Wycliff, First Baptist," Evan announced, hoping his smile looked innocent.

Coyle seemed distracted. "I'm sorry, did we have a meeting? The Reverend Mother didn't say."

"I spoke with her on the phone this morning," Evan said, implying she knew more than she did. "And I left you a message." Then he added, "There was no one at reception."

"Sister Margaret took them into town on a field trip. Baseball game at the high school." Then the priest muttered, "I'm sure you'd prefer to be there."

Evan wanted to sound cheerful, even eager. "It's about an interfaith marriage ceremony. I expect to be the officiant."

If I ask about Melissa right away, I'm sure I'll get nowhere. Maybe I can engage him as a colleague?

"There's always the question of how to raise the child," Evan continued as he spread his hands in a gesture of implied inclusiveness.

Marcus Thurston is also proud of his roses. Maybe this guy is a kindred spirit after all.

The priest was tall and slender. His black robe hung loosely on his gaunt frame as if it were still on the tailor's rack. A widow's peak set off his thinning gray hair, which he combed straight back, pasted with thick pomade over his large ears, from which shocks of small hairs grew like insect antennae. The fellow's face was likewise long and thin, with sunken eyes and cheekbones. Wire-rimmed glasses were perched on his slender nose. He had the heavily stained teeth of a chain smoker, but there was no evidence of spent smokes on the ground in this garden.

Maybe he's vowed to quit?

Coyle's voice was deep and resonant. "I presume you know the answer, Reverend. The parent who is Catholic can't stay in the Church unless the child is baptized in our faith. It's a matter for prudent premarital counseling. And if the couple is not in accord on the matter, I'd suggest postponing the nuptials until they are. If you'd be inclined to refer them to me, I'd happily take the responsibility. Are these your congregants? I presume one is a Baptist."

Evan admitted, "We have a situation where the baby has already been born out of wedlock. And whether the groom is the father is an open question."

"I see," Coyle intoned as he nodded soberly and resumed his work with a pair of shears, letting the cuttings fall to be swept up later. He was probably already wishing he'd refused the meeting. Bernice had warned him, but he saw no need to let on. He wouldn't answer questions not asked, and then, if necessary, he'd stonewall, citing his custodial responsibilities and the wards' rights of privacy.

"Another complication is that the mother is an underage orphan, a ward of the state. I'm not at all sure whether permission for her to marry will be forthcoming, regardless of the couple's religious preferences."

"I see," the priest said again and pressed a fingertip to his mouth. He thought a moment, then asked, "And the mother? I presume she's Catholic?"

"No," Evan said. "She is — or was — a member of our congregation in Appleton City. The groom grew up in a Catholic home but so far has not expressed his intentions in this regard."

Coyle straightened up, stared straight into Evan's eyes, and said reluctantly, "In my experience, the mother's wanting to raise the child in the Church after persuading the father to acquiesce — perhaps later considering to convert — is apt to be the more successful situation. The father persuading the mother? I've not seen it work."

"I should add that currently the father is facing some mental health challenges."

The frown on Coyle's face created a deep cleft in the center of his hirsute monobrow. Surely this fellow couldn't be serious. "My dear fellow," he began, "with all due respect, I'm beginning to think this marriage unwise. Time and prayer may heal all wounds, but there is the more urgent welfare of the baby to consider in the near term. I'm wondering if the obstacles are just too great. Perhaps giving it up for adoption might be the most prudent — if regrettably painful for the parents — course of action?"

Of course that's what you'd recommend. You've already done it.

"I have to admit," Evan said, "as of now, the impending marriage is only hypothetical. The biological facts are a given, but the future path for these two young people is undecided."

"I am sure you expected to come in confidence, but is there a chance I know them?"

"Very possibly." As innocently as Evan could manage, he stated, "Melissa Benton and Luke Shackleton."

It should have been a clue to Evan that the priest did not seem surprised. He cooed, "I can't imagine who sent you to me or for what purpose, but your line of inquiry is misdirected, misguided, and frankly rude in its dishonesty."

"I believe she was brought to the convent this morning — forcibly? And separated from her baby? How is that possible or advisable?"

"This meeting. False pretenses. Ugly motives," Coyle muttered. He started to turn away as he snapped, "I must ask you to leave."

"On the phone, Reverend Mother Bernadette said that Melissa is no longer in your care. Is that true? Her sister wants her back. She wants to make a home for her. And — at the very least — we need to make sure she's taking her medication." He produced the prescription vial and waved it at Coyle. "But she wasn't given a chance to take them with her this morning. She hasn't had another episode, has she?"

The priest didn't seem to want to take the bottle from him. It was a subtle move, but it reinforced Evan's assumption that the girl was already gone.

"We are ever watchful of our wards, body and soul" was all the priest would say. "I should have called Loretta to tell her that Melissa is safe. It was a stressful morning, and I was hoping time in the garden would provide some solace for me."

As he'd done with Richards and later with Griggs, Evan produced the banker's letter as he gestured for the priest to indulge him.

"I'm inquiring into this matter on behalf of Mr. Stuart Shackleton, who, among other distinctions, I believe has made significant donations to your organization. He and I are deeply concerned about the emotional welfare of his son, which seems somehow connected to the health and well-being of Miss Benton and her child."

The priest looked amused. "I inferred from your remarks you were here on behalf of the lovely Loretta."

"That's right," Evan realized. "You would have known her too."

"I trust she's doing well — that is, other than the unfortunate anxiety these custodial issues may be causing her? Believe me, it's all for the best. Although she might not see it right away."

Evan ignored the priest's dismissal and let him know, "My clients, if I can take the liberty of referring to them as such, are engaging the services of Jeremy Bailey of Butler, an attorney who specializes in family law. Among other facts in evidence, I believe the sheriff's deputy who facilitated the intervention this morning was acting outside the scope of his assigned duties and without a valid warrant."

"What do you want from me?" came the terse reply.

"Where are they?"

"The baby boy is in the custody of qualified and loving adoptive parents. Miss Benton is on her way to join an eminently capable foster father. I assure you, they are both in the most fortunate possible circumstances." He gestured to indicate the pill bottle Evan was gripping too tightly in his fist. "And I have not the slightest doubt her every need is being met. Good of you to bring the pills, but there was no need. That's really all I can tell you."

"Names? Locations?"

"That's really all I can tell you. Now, if you don't mind." And he waved to indicate the way out.

When Evan started to speak, Coyle raised a hand and stopped him with, "Our lawyers are in court every day. If we meet again, it will be there."

As Evan was getting into his car, a bus pulled up behind him. A dozen teenage girls, all in their school uniforms, climbed out noisily, followed by the driver, a young nun dressed in her habit. She carried a simple black purse and a small paper bag. A thickset man in a suit emerged from the building, greeted the nun, took the bag, and smiled his thanks. As the nun and her wards went inside, the man got into the Genesis and drove off, following closely behind the ambulance. Perhaps because the van's emergency lights weren't on, Evan might have assumed it had been dropping off rather than picking up.

Even though he prided himself on his perceptiveness and reasoning, he didn't make the connection. From what the Reverend Mother and Father Coyle had told him, he'd assumed that Melissa was already gone. After all, Bernadette had said the girl was no longer their responsibility. Father Coyle had said the baby was with adoptive parents, and Melissa would be joining her foster father. While both statements were true, neither gave any information about the girl's present location.

LORETTA HAD BEEN PINGING Evan with anxious texts, which he hadn't answered. Before he started the car, he phoned her. She was just waking up to begin her Friday-night workday.

He didn't tell her he was still at the children's home. All he said was, "I'm told they're with responsible foster parents. But in separate situations."

"You have to know that's unacceptable."

"I know," he said. "We're going to try to fix that. But it's not like she's on the street. I tried to give Father Coyle the pills, but he wouldn't take them. He insisted she's already been placed in a foster family. So there's no reason to think they're in any kind of danger, even if we could hope things could be different. It's a legal matter now, I'm thinking."

He quickly assured her he would be consulting with an attorney tomorrow who could help them demand more information. She was concerned about the expense, and he told her not to worry. The guy owed him a favor.

He told Loretta he was doing all he could and promised he'd go see the attorney as soon as he could. He agreed with her that going back to work could help her take her mind off her worries. He ended the call by stressing that her sister and the child were surely safe and in responsible hands.

Okay, white lie.

On the way back from Osceola, Evan planned to look in on Luke at the clinic.

Maybe the boy knows something I've missed.

MYERSON CLINIC

FRIDAY, EARLY EVENING

*A*ll during the drive back from Sisters of Mercy, Evan couldn't shake the feeling of failure. He thought about calling Sheriff Otis despite Loretta's warning, but what would he say? What help could he expect? Other than the question of whether Griggs had acted without a warrant, the preacher didn't have any evidence laws had been broken. Going to Griggs had been risky in itself, but the deputy would have his own reasons not to involve the sheriff. Evan had to rely on the hazy admission from Coyle that Melissa would be in a new situation — a foster family, one that the priest must surely have vetted. And Griggs was right — returning a runaway to her guardians wouldn't be illegal. Rough treatment might be alleged, and there could be valid objections to separating mother and child without a hearing. But those questions were in the gray area he intended to explore with legal counsel. For now, it seemed as though Melissa would have to remain wherever she was, and he had to hope that Luke's intuitions about her suffering were no more than vivid fantasies.

Before he entered the clinic, Evan placed a call to Bailey & Associates. When he asked for Jeremy, Marcella informed him the only way to catch up with her husband would be to make the rounds with him on the local golf course tomorrow. Jeremy would be in court all day today, she said. Evan wasn't a golfer, but he didn't press for a dinner meeting this evening. He wanted to get home and do some online research before he met with the attorney.

In truth, Evan had no right to expect Jeremy would even consider taking the case — or any part of it. Before the conversation with Father Coyle, Evan had hoped Stu Shackleton could be persuaded to retain a lawyer to follow whatever process Bernice Richards needed to release Luke's case file, which must contain a writeup of the incident with Melissa. But it was clear to Evan by now that Shackleton had no interest in helping the girl or her baby — and no reason to make it possible for Loretta to get custody.

Besides, having the banker for a client would be a conflict of interest for Jeremy. He was already representing Evan as the executor along with the Taggart farm-tenant beneficiaries against Edie in the probate matter. Presumably, one day they'd be squaring off against Shackleton, whose plan was to grab the land for himself, either by marrying Edie or by purchasing it cheaply from her with promises of a stake in future profits.

Shackleton planned a high-end entertainment development for the land, and the word was he was backed by big offshore money.

Evan needed wise counsel, and not just from Jeremy. He was half expecting Naomi would show up, but she didn't. He said a prayer. He believed the Great Mathematician was listening — indeed, was here and now and had never left. But even after the Amen, Evan still felt alone and friendless.

LUKE WAS STILL where the preacher had left him, sitting calmly on the edge of his narrow bed, his back to the door. He was staring at the blank wall as if it had secret writing on it. Evan asked gently as he approached, "Luke, when I was here before, you said you're in touch with Melissa. Can you just tell me where she is?"

Do I sound desperate? He seems to know she's hurting, but does he know she's gone missing?

Luke turned calmly as Evan drew up the guest chair and sat down.

The boy's heavy-lidded eyes suggested the staff might have given him a dose of something to mellow him out. He asked drowsily, "What are you, some cop?"

They must not have thrown him in timeout for his misbehavior that morning. Bernice was nowhere to be seen, and, from the approving smile of the receptionist on Evan's return, the preacher's new reputation as a miracle worker preceded him. The orderly had simply escorted him to the open door of Luke's room and then promptly went about his business.

Nurse or jailer?

Evan wondered where on that spectrum Clint would fit. After the briefest pause for careful reflection, Evan assured Luke, "No, not a cop. I'm kind of a… counselor. Friend of your father's, like I said."

I probably shouldn't tell him I'm an investigator on the side — and now faith healer, depending on whom you ask, including maybe your baldheaded muscle Clint.

Luke screwed up his face and twisted his head as if he literally had a pain in his neck. "It's not like I know where she is, like I could point to a map." Then his face relaxed. His gaze became clear-eyed, confident. Evan believed the boy was sincere when he stated, "But I'm always with her. I see what she sees. I know what she feels."

Evan leaned in and asked cautiously, "So, what about now, right this minute? What can you tell me?"

"It's kind of personal, you know."

Evan smiled and said, "I can only guess what it would be like getting inside your girlfriend's head. I was close to someone once, and I hardly ever knew what she was really thinking." Then he added seriously, "Luke, you're right to mistrust the cops. An officer and some other people showed up this morning and took Melissa and her baby from Loretta's place. They took the baby in a separate car. I want to know they're safe, but no one will tell me where they are or who they're with. So… whatever you can tell me… ?"

"Why didn't you ask me before?"

"When I saw you, I didn't know they'd taken her," Evan explained. "I didn't even know much about, well, what you two mean to each

95

other. You haven't had a chance to tell me. But I promised your dad and now Loretta that I'll do whatever I can to help you guys."

"You mean me and Melissa? And Buzz?"

"That's the baby? Buzz?"

And you're like, what, a family?

Deciding it wasn't the time to query Luke about the baby's parentage, Evan went on, "Yes, I'll help. Absolutely. I'm sure I'll need help myself, but first I have to figure out which people we can trust. So, how about it?"

"We're not supposed to close the door, but go ahead. And shut off the lights. It's like meditation, you know?"

"Yes," Evan said. "I know about meditation." He got up, closed the door quietly, and flipped the light switch off. The curtains were drawn on the room's one tiny window, which was located high up on the wall, too small for even a scrawny boy to get through. Sunlight shown around the edges, casting the room in half-light.

Dark enough for an afternoon nap. Or a jump through hyperspace.

Evan sat back down as Luke asked softly, "Give me a minute," and closed his eyes. After a moment, he winced. "She's in pain. Her stomach's in knots. She has to piss real bad, but she can't get up. She's lying on her back. Hands and feet tied to the bed."

Tied up? Something a criminal would do. How could law enforcement or child services, even on their worst day, hand a kid off to someone like that? No — floating and bound? It doesn't necessarily imply evil intent. Drugged to calm her nerves? Restrained to keep her from harming herself?

Evan urged him, "Tell me about the pain. Is she hurt? And *where is she?*"

Luke remained calm. But he was stoic, jaw clenched.

Can he actually be feeling her pain?

As though he'd heard Evan's thought, Luke answered, "She isn't hurt like injured. Just confused and angry about Buzz. Worried she won't see him again. Worried he's not okay. She feels like throwing up."

"Can you get anything at all about where she might be?"

"The room there is dark, very dark."

"Can you ask her if she knows the location?"

Luke whispered, "She doesn't know I'm with her. It doesn't work both ways. At least, I haven't tried that with her."

"Can you see anything? Is she alone?"

Luke's eyeballs moved around inside his closed lids, as in REM sleep, as he scanned the scene in his mind's eye. His throat went dry and his voice cracked when he said, "There's some guy watching her."

As Luke spoke, the door was pushed open, and Clint's broad shoulders filled its frame.

"You can't be in here!" he insisted.

Evan started, "I showed Bernice his father's letter —"

Clint lowered his voice. "Bernice left here in a hurry, said she wouldn't be back today. Something's going on. I think you'd better leave."

FIRST BAPTIST CHURCH OF
APPLETON CITY

FRIDAY EVENING

*T*he church's coffers being particularly low this time of year, the banquet was a fundraiser for the Loving Embrace bereavement committee. A dozen chickens were gnawed to the bone along with mounds of mashed potatoes, rivers of gravy, buckets of coleslaw, steaming platters of buttered corn, and generous dollops of collard greens simmered in lard. The evening remained uncomfortably warm and humid, and the doors and windows of the fellowship hall were left wide open. The iced tea was replenished frequently, even though all the ice had melted early on. There were three kinds of fruit pies served with scoops from two frosty canisters of hand-cranked vanilla ice cream. The cost of the groceries was probably more per person than the total of the individual donations, so it was the home cooks who sponsored the evening.

When Evan finally managed a private moment with his mentor, the faithful had all loosened their belts and climbed back into their cars. The Loving Embrace ladies were clearing tables and washing up.

Evan had already declined Thurston's invitation to deliver the sermon on Sunday.

The pastor of First Baptist was not a man who was easily startled. Just a few years from retirement, he figured he'd pretty much seen it all. That's why today's news about his protégé's pretending to heal the sick was troubling. The young man seemed to have a talent for asking too many embarrassing questions.

"What'd you do to Shackleton's boy?" Thurston asked Evan as old Birch, the sexton, swept up around them. "He seems to think you deserve the Nobel Prize. But on the other hand, you've got Michael Coyle all spun up. I had to fib and assure him you're our assistant minister."

Evan shrugged sheepishly. "I might have talked Luke out of wetting the bed."

Thurston smiled as though he were amused, but there was an edge of concern to his question: "Did you pray with him?"

"No," Evan was quick to say. "I got there in the middle of something quite unexpected. He'd been saving his urine in jars, and there was a tussle with an attendant who tried to get it away from him."

"He's seriously ill, I take it."

"Schizophrenia, they're saying. He claims he hears voices. Hoarding the urine could indicate some paranoid fantasy about their wanting to take everything from him. But that's just one possibility. He was lucid, even sweet-tempered, when I saw him."

"So... no... laying on of hands? It was all... talk therapy?"

I know why Marcus is concerned. If people around here start thinking I'm claiming to do faith healing, there will be no end of grief.

Evan took a breath. "I wasn't entirely truthful with him. I suppose you could say I spoke in metaphor and he took it literally. Call it a psychological placebo."

Thurston's smile was genuine now. He knew Evan too well. "So, you told the kid a white lie?"

Evan nodded. "They'd given him a spinal tap, and I told him it was a therapeutic injection."

"Sounds to me like he believed — he had *faith* — in what you told him, and he was *healed.*" Marcus chuckled. "So how is that not faith healing?"

"You know, *white lie* is an odd expression coming from you. In this part of the world, going way back, they might excuse a white man who said he never touched a drop, but they'd come down hard on a slave who claimed she found her master's wallet out in the yard."

"So what would *you* call it?" the black man asked.

"If you want to talk theology, it would be a *heuristic fiction*. A useful lie."

"You're reminding me how silly they can get in divinity school."

"Not at all. Situation ethics. The end in this case justified the means."

"Again with the Kierkegaard… or Karl Marx… or Adolph Hitler?"

Marcus might be liberal for this community, but relativity, in any sense, would not be his thing.

"Look, Marcus," Evan began, "no matter how hard I pray, with hands on or hands off, we both know I'm not going to pretend I can cure schizophrenia."

The older man was more worried than Evan had suspected. "Stuart Shackleton is an educated man," Thurston said. "But I doubt he cares how you got the result. You two were effectively enemies a few months back. You were sure he'd done wrong by Bob Taggart. And now because you've pulled this stunt he's likely to go along with whatever you suggest. Do you think you can make friends with a devil? I don't know him all that well, but I suspect he hasn't changed his stripes or his goals. Forgiveness aside, it might be better if you still regarded him as an adversary."

"I'm sure as a father he wants to know, as I do now, whether Luke is in the right place and he's getting appropriate care. I need to spend more time with him. But what has me worried just now is the welfare of Melissa Benton and her baby."

Marcus now knew Evan had waded into even deeper waters. "Yes, Loretta phoned me, all in a panic about what happened. And she said she'd asked for your help. Her call, coming on the same day you visited the clinic, was what made me worry this faith healing thing could get out of hand."

"I didn't promise her anything, Marcus," Evan insisted. "How could I?"

"There are complications, Evan," Thurston warned. "These government folks don't seem to answer to anyone."

"Both children have been taken into custody. *Separately.* And it seems like Father Coyle is somehow at the center of it. I'm guessing he and Bernice Richards are tight." Then he added, "And it was Malcolm Griggs who showed up with them at the house."

"Mal Griggs," Thurston mused. "You guys can't leave each other alone. You know he's pushing to get on the board of deacons?"

"Frankly, I'm amazed he has the nerve to show his face in church."

Thurston smiled, "There's a pretty young woman on the Loving Embrace committee, Winona Hughes. I'm told he has his eye on her."

"I don't know her," Evan confessed. "But if Griggs hooks up with her, at least she's one you won't be pushing on me."

The pastor smiled again. "Evan, I haven't been able to sell you on the ministry, let alone a wife." He grew serious when he said, "I lost touch with the Benton girls some time ago. I don't have any inside information. It's all so unfortunate."

"I'm worried about Melissa. Loretta says she needs meds for epilepsy, but we can't be sure she has them. I drove all the way over to Osceola to see Father Coyle. He was insisting she'd already been given over to some new foster parent."

"Sorry to say this, Evan. But it seems like it's out of your hands. We can offer up our prayers, but we can't make the people who are supposed to be responsible be… responsible."

"But why would they lie about it? Deputy Griggs, Father Coyle, and Bernice Richards at the clinic — they're all giving me the runaround!"

The Reverend gave Evan a wry smile, "Maybe they don't trust faith healers."

Is he seriously worried about that?

"I'm seeing an attorney tomorrow," Evan said. "Maybe we can get some leverage through the court. For now, I suppose you're right. I've hit a dead end." Then he asked, "You said you knew the Bentons before. They're strangers to me, and here I am fighting city hall on their behalf."

"Years ago, when you were studying Back East, both girls were enrolled in Sunday School here. The stepmother — I didn't even know her parents' names — would drop them off. I mean, are we some kind of babysitting service? The father wasn't around, then all of a sudden the woman wasn't either. Child welfare put the orphaned girls into the Catholic system. I think they were at Sisters of Mercy for at least a couple of years. Loretta is the older one. She seemed to do okay. She kept her grades up, and she was on the cheerleading squad at the high school. But Melissa, she's been what you'd call a troubled teen."

"So how did she end up in a mental-health clinic? Was it her epilepsy?"

"I don't know the particulars. Maybe the onset was later," Thurston said. "I suspect she was in and out of foster care. Some of those folks do it for the income, after all, not because they're particularly good with kids. And being passed back and forth would stress a child. Perhaps then some social worker thought she needed treatment." He took a moment, then added, "Children don't thrive in clinics or in communes. They need close supervision, love, and attention from a parent. Preferably two."

It was Evan's turn to smile. "Two... of either sex?"

Thurston chuckled. "You're not going to catch me on that one. You know I'm a traditionalist. But these days I'd have to say, whatever works."

"Marcus, you amaze me. Will I be hearing sermons on the subject?"

"Not if I retire quick enough. Then *you* can get up there, and, as far as I'm concerned, the rest of the twenty-first century is yours to deal with." He frowned as he said, "I understand you've involved yourself in this, and I'm not going to warn you off. Who am I to question where God leads you?" Then he emphasized, "But I mean it. Be careful around Shackleton."

"And what about the Bentons?"

"Assuming Melissa and her baby are somehow 'in the system,' I have no idea how that works. I'm guessing you're going to find out. I hope you're not sorry you did. If I can be of any help..."

"You know I'd be lost without your advice."

Reverend Thurston rested a hand on Evan's shoulder as he said, "You're always in my prayers."

He's saying I'm on my own for this one.

EVAN'S TRAILER

FRIDAY NIGHT

On the way home from the church banquet, Evan stopped to pick up a bottle of Wild Turkey. So much had happened in just one day. Anxious adults had tasked him with the welfare of disturbed children — and neither of them had any real reason to trust him. He'd run himself in frantic circles seeking answers to questions that should have been freely given. But he'd hit a wall. The stresses of this day called for serious reflection followed by alcoholic anesthesia.

Maybe I have to tell Loretta I've done all I can do. Jeremy can advise her where to go from here, but anything involving the courts takes time. And other than tricking Luke into not wetting his bed, how have I helped?

When he checked his phone, he saw three missed calls from Loretta, along with a dozen texts, simply:

???!

He didn't think he had anything to say that would calm her, but he finally texted back:

> Coyle says she's for a foster family. Won't say where. Neither will Richards. All saying she's safe. Legal route only way. I'm on it.

AND I'M EXHAUSTED!
She replied:

> At work. Call me early morning?

And he sent:

> I won't know any more by then.

She protested:

> Call me!

Ah, well. Why don't I mind taking orders from her?

THE EVENING HAD FINALLY BEGUN to cool. He flipped on the trailer's swamp cooler, changed into a fresh T-shirt and shorts, poured himself a double whiskey over ice, popped open his laptop, and went straight to his YouTube bookmark for *A Black and White Night,* Roy Orbison's 1987 concert at the Cocoanut Grove Lounge of the Ambassador Hotel in Los Angeles. To joyous repetitions of "Dream Baby," Evan chugged his first drink and then sipped a second and a third.

In this song in this fateful place, a celebrity hotel that had hosted an assassination and would eventually be demolished, here was the calm before the storm. This fleeting moment of peace and calm was not unlike the fate of cold, grime-smeared soldiers who were finally getting a hot meal before dawn at Argonne Forest or Okinawa or Da Nang or Kandahar. Or birds singing in the trees on that horrific morning in Hiroshima. Or coffee-stoked traders ascending at high speed in an elevator of the World Trade Center on a bright Monday morning in 2001.

Orbison, the country-and-western singer-songwriter with the natural range of an operatic tenor, struggled with poor health for years. He would be dead a year later from a heart attack at age fifty-two. Joining him on that electric stage was a cohort of superstars — most of whose reputations would soon peak and then burn out or fade away. There was Bruce Springsteen on lead guitar, dressed like a Las Vegas high roller in a tailored silk suit, brocade shirt with a bolo tie, neatly barbered curls, and cowboy boots. About the time his friend Roy's life ended abruptly, Springsteen's own career would tank. He'd reemerge later as The Boss, the workingman's hero, clad in denim with a tousled look, leading the E Street Band. The other musicians in the background could eventually expect to own the spotlight: Tom Waits, Elvis Costello, Jackson Browne, J.D. Souther, and Steven Soles. The gig was produced by the lanky T-Bone Barnett, who also picked up a guitar and played along in the shadows. And perhaps most amazing of all, far off to stage left stood three female background vocalists — k.d. lang, Jennifer Warnes, and Bonnie Raitt. Unaccountably, the sound mixer had cranked their levels down so low they could barely be heard. But they were grinning and jiving, apparently just as thrilled as the others to be in Orbison's entourage.

It wasn't that they were all being paid top dollar. They might have been working for minimums or even gratis. All because Orbison was one of those rare talents in show business — what they call an *attractor*, not the more typical and fearsome star *attacker*. These stunning talents would overrule their angry agents and work for scale or nothing just to sing in this man's shadow.

The blooming of a rose. Exuberant life in its full flowering. A coming together that would never be repeated.

Evan's eyes were wet. Naomi's life had blossomed, and rather than take a normal span to wilt and wither and eventually die, it had been sheared off abruptly at the height of its beauty.

And then here she was sitting cross-legged on the floor beside him.

She was dressed in a sweatsuit, her dark hair pinned back casually with some stray wisps in her eyes, her face damp as if steamed from a workout.

"Yeah, it's about time you showed up," Evan muttered.

"You could stop playing that video," she suggested. "How many of those million Likes are yours?"

Small thing, you can only like a video once from the same account. But I'm not the one who always has to be right!

"It's magic" was all he said. "I won't apologize. Times gone by. Not mine, but theirs."

"It's ancient history," she insisted. "Like my life with you. Don't you see the connection?"

"There aren't many Bible verses can move me like that. Precious few hymns. You want to take away my pathways to visions of the divine?"

"No, I'd say I want to drag you kicking and screaming into the present."

"You were bugging me about Cora. She told me today she's dating Clint Everly. If that's her taste in men, I'm definitely not her type."

"You'd be more any woman's type if you could learn to laugh now and then." Then she asked with an obvious edge, "Loretta Benton — is she your type?"

"I dunno," Evan said, draining his glass. "If her perfume were whiskey, I'd be out cold. Those are some high-powered pheromones. I can't picture her in the parsonage, though."

Naomi let out a long, exasperated sigh.

In a low voice, she pronounced, "I'm going to get you some help."

And she was gone.

~

EVAN DIDN'T SET his alarm. His eyes popped open at six, and even before he had his first cup of coffee, he felt obliged to make that promised call to Loretta.

She answered on the first ring and didn't sound sleepy. "You're a man of your word," she said, not with charm, just stating a fact.

"I live to serve," he said, realizing he was quoting one of Cora's sarcastic cracks.

"You have to follow through," she insisted. "No one else will."

"They all assure me she's safe, and I have no reason to think different."

Except for Luke's fantasies. I'm not about to tell her, even though I don't disbelieve him.

"I know you're just saying that," she said coldly. "But I believe you when you promise you'll stay on it."

"I will," he said.

"She was involved with some nasty people at the casino. She went quiet then, cut me off. And it was all hush-hush. I wanted her out of there, but she wasn't about to listen to me. I worry about those people. I worry she's still somehow mixed up with them."

"What about your management at the casino? Do they know what went on?"

She sighed. "If I even asked, they'd show me the door. I report to a floor supervisor, and the site manager and I used to be close, but we don't talk these days." She softened when she said, "I'll let you go. I'm going to take something to sleep."

"Yes, please try to get some rest" was all he could think to say. "It'll all be okay." Then he said, "I'm holding you all in my prayers, you know."

But she came back with Yoda's humorlessness when she said, "There is no *pray.* Only *do.* "

107

BUTLER COUNTRY CLUB

SATURDAY, EARLY AFTERNOON

*W*hen Evan had called the office yesterday, Marcella told him that Jeremy wouldn't be on the golf course until afternoon, so the preacher spent the morning data-drilling on his laptop, reading whatever he could find on family law and child welfare. He learned enough to fear he should turn back. He began to feel as though he was about to descend into Hell.

The classiest thing about The Butler Country Club might be its name. It's a semi-private community course with nine holes and a par 36. The Missouri Golf Tours reviews rate it 2 out of 5 overall, Course Condition 6.5, Difficulty 7, and Walkability 9. Although modest in features and short on distances, the club rates an impressive 8 in Quality/Cost Ratio: The greens fees will set each player back exactly $18, a buck a hole if you go around twice.

But to the young attorney, who could only aspire to play Big Cedar Lodge in Ridgedale someday without embarrassment, puttering along on the local greens was an affordable and convenient way to relax. Although the summer would be high season for the club, the place was not so oversubscribed that Jeremy couldn't book a time to walk its fairways all by himself, especially if it was, like today, an uncomfortably hot afternoon. (His fellow duffers preferred early-morning golf.)

Jeremy answered Evan's call just before switching off his phone on the first tee. Although Evan swore he didn't know a mashie from a wedge, Jeremy was eager to have him join up on the "back nine," or his second circuit of the executive course, which would give Evan time to drive up from AC. They'd share Jeremy's set of Callaway Men's Strata Ultimate clubs, which his wife had given him for Christmas and had stayed wrapped up in the closet at home until just last week. When Evan protested he didn't own a pair of golf shoes, Jeremy assured him the course rules would permit him to play in sneakers — or even barefoot. Evan was able to play in his new Reeboks, the only sportswear he'd allowed himself to buy in years, purchased expressly for his regimen of morning runs.

Okay, walks.

"Great-looking set of sticks!" Evan cried out as he approached Jeremy at the tee on the eighth hole.

"And you said you didn't know anything about golf," Jeremy chuckled as they shared a comradely handshake.

"Well," Evan confessed. "The terminology is easier to learn than the game." He was trying to keep it light, and he was reluctant to get serious with the lawyer. They had some unfinished business which had left Evan overdrawn at Jeremy's favor bank. But the preacher went on, "Jeremy, I'm going to need some advice…"

Jeremy shot him a look and gripped his club more tightly. "My advice," the lawyer began, "and I can now tell you from experience considering myself a veteran on this course, is that we'll have no need for the woods. The fairways just aren't that long. Use a low-numbered iron at the tee, a wedge to get to the green, and then putt for more strokes than it should take to make it into the hole. And that's the extent of my guidance."

"I'm going to have to get serious. And I'm sorry to do this to you on your day off."

Jeremy chuckled. "No, you're not." Then he asked, "Are you at least willing to play a round? You know how to walk and talk, don't you?"

"And chip and putt," Evan grinned.

"Yes, exactly," Jeremy said. "You *do* know the terms of art. Is it possible you know more than you're admitting and I'm gonna get hustled?"

"Come now. Would a man of the cloth bet on a game?"

"He would if he owed me money," Jeremy teased. "Which I believe you do."

Here was the sensitive point. Jeremy had handled the execution and filing of Bob Taggart's final will and testament — a surreptitiously revised document that had stayed secret until after Bob's untimely death. In a last-minute decision, Bob had named Evan the executor, unbeknownst to the preacher. And, yes, Bailey & Associates was owed their fees. But the money would come out of a trust Bob had set up for the purpose, a provision that was sure to be contested in probate court — by none other than Bob's widow Edie.

Jeremy should know as much. He knows he won't have any trouble getting my signature on a check — when the time comes.

A complication of the Taggart affair was an affair — the one Edie had been carrying on with Stuart Shackleton, even when Bob was alive. She and the banker had been secretly engaged to be married — after Stu's divorce from the sadly demented Ann was final, which had not yet happened. More recently, Edie grew angry that her share of Bob's estate might not be forthcoming for a long while. She'd already broken it off with Stu, another reason the banker seemed less of an enemy to Evan today than he had yesterday, especially since the preacher hoped the fellow was having second thoughts about ending his first marriage. Given Ann's state of mind or lack of same, Stu's decision might make no practical difference. But Evan would give him credit for at least pretending to have a conscience.

As Jeremy was sighting his tee shot, Evan asked him, "Did you know Stu Shackleton has a mentally challenged son?"

"News to me," Jeremy muttered, and swinging decisively with his two iron, he sliced the ball hard to the left. It landed — *plop!* — in the water hazard.

Jeremy blew out a puff of air, then fumed, "Some people call this game *goof*, you know."

"Lawyer theatrics," Evan chuckled as he teed up his ball. "Playing for sympathy from the jury? It's Edie who owes you the money, not me. And good luck collecting your fee until the court orders it paid out of escrow." Evan chose a three iron and hit it high and hard down the center of the fairway, landing about forty yards from the green.

"I used to like you," Jeremy quipped as they walked toward the site of his ball's drowning. He'd have to take a one-stroke penalty and toss a new ball onto the fairway just behind the edge of the water closest to the tee.

It's now or never. I shouldn't be joking around about this.

On the way to the water hazard, Evan stopped and turned to ask, "Jeremy, I need you to help me get a couple of kids out of the child welfare system."

His friend also stopped, and his tall body slumped as if someone had let the air out of him.

"*This* is the new assignment? Evan, is this your weird idea of fun?"

"It's kind of urgent," Evan said sheepishly. "Why I had to chase you down today. They were taken into custody yesterday morning. Taken forcibly. The rightful custodial party should be this sister, and just now she's an emotional mess. I'm just trying to help."

Jeremy looked disgusted. He was already connecting the dots. "And what does all of this have to do with the upstanding Mr. Shackleton?"

"His boy, Luke, was somehow involved with Melissa Benton, the underage girl who's been taken into custody, along with her newborn baby. The girl's supposedly in foster care, and the baby might already be in the hands of adoptive parents."

"How old is Luke? Melissa?"

"They're both seventeen."

"Oh, goody," Jeremy fumed. "If the kid just happens to be Luke's, the way things have gone down just happens to save Shackleton all kinds of embarrassment. The girl and her baby disappear into the system."

"Yeah, I've thought about that."

"And now you're saying Melissa and her baby are not only in custody but already outplaced. Evan, not only is the door closed, but it looks like it's chained and bolted from the other side. How did this unlucky Luke get involved?"

"He and Melissa were both in care at the Myerson Clinic. You know the place?"

Jeremy replied, "You're going to need a briefing, and I'm thinking I suck worse than you at this game."

They agreed to cut the golf game short and adjourn their discussion to the bar at the clubhouse, where Jeremy insisted his advice would come at the cost of several tall vodka tonics.

～

JEREMY WAITED for the barman to deliver their drinks and took a generous gulp before he began, "You've heard about the privatization of prisons?"

Evan decided he'd better try to keep a clear head and ordered a Coke with lots of ice. "Surely Myerson isn't a prison?" he asked, hoping as he poured the fizzy stuff over the cubes he wouldn't be tempted to switch to bourbon.

"No, but it works much the same from the standpoint of government funding."

"What do you mean?"

"I looked into getting into family law. I mean, it's related to divorce, particularly child custody issues. And then there are the disputes over parental rights and child welfare, along with allegations of neglect and abuse. And these days, the state is right in there as the deep-pockets referee. But compared to the estate work I've been doing, the juvenile justice and welfare system is an unholy mess. In fact, I'd say it's about as broken and corrupt as things can get. The messiest divorce I ever handled looks like polite teatime conversation compared to what passes for due process in a child-protection case."

"How does Myerson figure into it?"

"Let's begin at the beginning. The structure of the family has been disintegrating for years, even more rapidly in the farm and rust-belt states. It takes dual-wage incomes to make ends meet. Childcare suffers. Then one or both parents lose their jobs, or the family loses the farm. More stress on the family unit. Some of the more desperate ones turn to using drugs — opioids? Or even making them — meth? Too often, parents are dysfunctional or totally absent. No childcare. Education isn't a priority. Kids get into trouble. And where is the community support? Churches and charities? Not so much in the picture these days. And where is the government in all this?"

"Running the show, I'd suppose. It seems like there's a huge social safety net. And both the voters and the politicians complain about how expensive it is."

"That's where places like Myerson come in. State budgets for all kinds of social services have been shrinking for decades. At the same time, the need — and the demand — for those services have only increased. For the government, paying cash subsidies to private institutions is cheaper than trying to operate facilities. And if they contract for those services, the bureaucrats still have the cushy jobs of *administering* the funds and the programs.

"Take, for example, the child welfare system. There is — and there has always been as far back as anyone can remember — a shortage of foster beds. Not to mention, qualified foster parents. So you get a kid who breaks the law. Or one who is on the street, who seems to have no caregivers at all. The kid breaks some law — say, shoplifting, maybe drugs — and ends up in court. And what does the judge do? No one wants to put the kid in jail. Juvenile detention is just junior prison. Someday they'll graduate as a highly trained criminal with gang loyalties. So the judge — who may be acting out of compassion *or* because there's some kind of political or financial incentive — puts the kid in a private treatment facility at state expense. Sounds nice, doesn't it? A place like Myerson, for example, looks downright upscale. There's a clean bed, hot meals, school curriculum. Problem is, to be certified and qualify for subsidies, it's a private *mental* hospital! And so you have kids who are mainly disciplinary problems housed alongside seriously ill clients. Once those kids are in the facility — *they all look alike to the staff!* The doctors should know different, but the staff doesn't care whether they're psych cases or playground brawlers. They're all given drugs to keep them under control. And they get behavioral consequences if they act out."

Like timeouts. And worse, I'm guessing.

"Don't they get psychiatric evaluations?"

"Yes and no. The shrinks are renta-docs. They might drive by the place a couple of times a month and fill out some forms. If they do a serious evaluation on a kid, their write-up has to err on the side of medical necessity. Maintains the status quo. The funding keeps coming, the kid stays in place, and the caregivers keep their jobs. The same thing can happen on the clinical side — with the drug rehab patients. Rich folks might be paying hefty fees for some family member who is seriously intending to get sober, but those patients are housed alongside subsidized public-assistance cases who have no clue why they're there."

"But aren't most of those people in the best place they can be? And getting professional attention?"

"How do you figure? There's no incentive whatever for them to get better or for the professionals to care whether they do. A mental patient doesn't have a period of commitment — like a prison sentence — of any specific duration. You've got attorneys like me — well, not *like* me — who represent families and children, making more money with every tick of the clock. Also living off the system would be social workers, medical doctors and psychiatrists, schoolteachers, administrative staff, practical caregivers, and, yes, judges and state agencies and their bureaucrats. None of them has a financial interest in letting anyone out of there. Oh, and I forgot the insurance companies, for the lucky ones who have coverage. *They* might want the kid treated and discharged, but there are lawyers like me (again, *not* like me) who will sue them so they keep coughing up."

"But I'm sure kids get outplaced into foster families. Orphans and kids who had abusive parents get adopted. Those are good results, aren't they?"

"Through a series of Congressional grants — over decades, mind you — the Feds have tried to incentivize better-quality care and outcomes. But what they've succeeded in doing is fueling a bloated welfare engine that only feeds on itself and keeps getting bigger."

"I don't quite understand. Give me an example."

"Okay, child adoption. The government in its wisdom decides that a kid is better off with a family, *any* family. On that, maybe we can all agree. But the federal subsidies pay bonuses for each child adopted. Even more for special-needs children, as well as for older children, who are considered almost unadoptable. And you've got laws that incentivize *reports* of suspected abuse by parents — reports based on suspicions and accusations by doctors, by teachers, by neighbors, by pissed-off ex-spouses! Some allegations are genuine and some are not — or, at least, not sufficiently investigated. These are presumptive reasons to separate children from parents. So the system errs on the side of caution! Add to that, a growing demand for adoptive children by affluent parents who are more than willing to pay all those professional and agency fees. So what do you think happens?"

"Some kids get taken away from their parents by mistake?"

Jeremy gave Evan a clear-eyed stare as if the preacher were a jury foreman and the prosecutor was bearing down on him, delivering the undeniable truth: "The victims, no surprise, are the people who can't buy their way out of the system that entraps them. What we have in this country today, my friend, is government-subsidized kidnapping."

By now, they'd had three rounds, and Evan could tell Jeremy was getting sleepy. But the preacher didn't hold back. "So, will you help?"

"Who's the client? Can't be Shackleton. Even if he didn't make it happen, those two children are right where he wants them."

"Loretta Benton, Melissa's sister. Age twenty-one. They're orphans. It's an open question whether Loretta ever filed for custody of her sister."

"And Loretta? Got any money? Family estate? Cash in a shoebox? Lottery tickets?"

"Cocktail waitress at the Twin Dragons."

"Oh, goody," Jeremy sighed, downing the rest of his cocktail. "If only I needed the write-off. This will be a whopper. Better tell the wife we'll be taking it easy at Christmas."

～

As Evan headed south out of Butler on I-49, he saw a purplish-gray bank of clouds to the west rolling rapidly this way across the plains of Kansas. He had the car windows down, and the air was tinged with ozone. His farm-boy sense told him they were in for a drenching downpour.

SOMEWHERE ON SR 52 OUTSIDE APPLETON CITY

SATURDAY AFTERNOON

*N*o sooner had Evan turned off the interstate than the skies opened up. It was an angry storm with a high westerly wind. The abundant rain was coming down in sheets, driven so hard the droplets chased the eastbound car horizontally like slicing knives.

Visibility was chaotic and blurred. The two-lane highway hadn't been washed down for weeks. The fresh slurry of grime and engine oil on its surface made traction uncertain for the lightweight Fiat. Evan had to wrestle with the steering wheel to keep the car tracking closely to the centerline. Inevitably, he ended up behind a semi that was doing decent speed, but the height of the trailer and the spume flung up from its tires totally obscured Evan's view of the road ahead. Any attempt at pulling out to pass would have been a blind maneuver. Evan decided to slow down even more from his already prudent speed and thus drop back farther behind the truck so he'd at least have a wider field of vision. He estimated he was just five miles from town, so he figured he'd just poke along several car-lengths behind the truck and try to be patient.

Just as he could see around to catch a glimpse of the roadside about fifty yards ahead, an erect figure appeared, standing on the shoulder. The man's hooded poncho concealed any identifiable aspects of his appearance. As the man saw the headlights of Evan's coupe approaching, he thrust out his right arm with thumb up in the hitchhiker's unmistakable appeal.

Even though otherwise inclined to act the Good Samaritan, Evan was cautious as anyone these days about offering rides to strangers on the road. As he stopped the car on the shoulder just past where the man was standing, Evan was wondering whether his car jack would work on anything as large as a farmer's pickup truck, then realized there was no disabled vehicle to be seen. If the fellow's conveyance had slid off into the ditch, the best Evan could do would be to either call for a tow truck or give the fellow a lift to the nearest gas station.

Just as soon as Evan brought the Cinquecento to a halt, the passenger door opened and the soaked wayfarer jumped in, tossing a rucksack on the back seat.

As he lowered the dripping rain hood and ran his palm over his bald pate, he revealed a massive crop of scraggly graying hair over his ears, a bushy beard, and fogged, wire-rimmed glasses. He flicked his fingers as windshield wipers to clear the lenses. At first, Evan thought it might be old Arthur Redwine, who prided himself on looking like a bedraggled mountain man. This guy could have been a frozen hippie, a recently thawed incarnation of the poet Allen Ginsberg at the peak of his hirsute looks.

"Why, thank you!" the fellow beamed, finally turning his head to face his host. "I was afraid no one would stop."

"Where's your car? How'd you get here?" Evan asked, hoping he didn't sound offensively suspicious or paranoid.

"This is where my last ride dropped me, and I didn't mind the breather. Not everyone bothers to use deodorant, know what I mean? But then all of a sudden this torrential wrath of God was upon us!"

Evan was tempted to correct the man's impression that weather has anything to do with the divine spirit's mood, or whether it can be said that spirit even has moods, but instead he simply observed, "At least you were dressed for it." Then he felt compelled to add, "And I doubt God is upset with either of us."

The angry God of the Old Testament is so yesterday.

The fellow chuckled good-naturedly and extended a wet hand, "Leon Weiss, and I'm sure that's true."

It was as if a bolt of lightning shot through Evan's body. Whether the overload in his nervous system coincided with an actual electrical discharge outside, he never remembered.

He couldn't help exclaiming, "Holy shit!"

The old hippie laughed. "I confess I've never been greeted that way before. I'm hardly famous, not even notorious!"

Evan stared into Leon's eyes for a long moment, wondering now whether this presence was composed of solid flesh. Then he said softly, "You're Naomi's brother."

Leon Weiss looked only mildly surprised, grew serious, then admitted, "Yes, I am. And the only soul in these parts who would know that obscure fact would be none other than Evan Jerome Wycliff."

The men sat in silence for another long moment as the rain pounded the metal roof of the Cinquecento like a thousand crazed steel drummers.

Then Evan let him know, "She said she was going to send someone to help me."

Now it was Leon's turn to look mystified. "When would that have been, exactly? I would expect you know she died. It's been three years."

"Yes, I learned about it a couple of weeks after it happened. But why would you have come here if she didn't send you?"

He shrugged. "If she's an angel now, I have no experience of it. The last time I had a message from her was an email a week before that fateful rocket attack. I'd wanted to meet this mystery man she was dating since long before then. But she always kept you to herself. Then, as fortuitous events tend to unfold, last week I retired from my job, and I said to myself it's a perfect time to go in search of this guy who must have meant so much to my sister."

Evan insisted earnestly, "But after I got the news, I tried to find you. I mean, I tried everything I could think of short of hiring an investigator."

He gave a wry smile and said, "Wouldn't have done any good. I had the kind of job where I wasn't supposed to be found."

LUKE WAS in the timeout room, sitting in his underwear on the bare concrete floor. He'd ripped his T-shirt in a fit of anger, which is what had put him in here. So they'd literally taken the shirt off his back. He didn't know how they could make it colder in here, but he was shivering.

His sense that Melissa was in anguish had instilled the same emotion in him — misery. But he knew how to fight back with fury. He feared she was too sweet to do the same. She'd think she could flirt and talk her way out of it. He especially loved her when she was like that.

And the voice came:

I have her now. She is mine to direct, and she will soon do so happily.

This revelation brought tears. Luke tried to turn the voice's anger back on itself, to defy its commanding presence, but he feared the sender was surrounded by a forcefield too powerful to breach.

Luke had no idea what time it was. Clint came on at three, and he'd usually be the one to let him out. The guy acted tough, but he was all right.

EVAN HAD INTENDED to drive to Myerson in the hope of getting closer to Luke and, if possible, having a long talk with him, especially if the boy could pick up anything more about Melissa's whereabouts and welfare. But his long tutorial on children's rights with Jeremy, along with the rigors of their aborted round of golf in the summer heat, had left Evan exhausted. To top it off, the emotional strain of encountering Leon Weiss had sapped what was left of Evan's energy.

Leon confessed he hadn't yet arranged for a place to stay. So Evan drove them back to his trailer, where he was encouraged to find that Leon was a kindred spirit, at least in terms of his love of Tennessee sour-mash whiskey.

Leon was an attentive listener. But he didn't seem inclined to share anything about himself.

Nevertheless, assuming Leon was the helper Naomi had promised, Evan didn't hold back on the facts of his current predicament. Luke Shackleton was probably suffering from schizophrenia and hearing ethereal voices. He might or might not be the father of Melissa Benton's baby Buzz. Luke was under care, but in a private clinic where the management might be motivated more by profit than by competent psychiatry. Melissa and her baby had been extracted forcefully from her sister Loretta's home. Now the girl was in the process of being placed in a new foster family, and the baby was supposedly in the beneficent hands of anonymous adoptive parents. All thanks to Catholic charities working in concert with the state child welfare system — and somehow with Bernice Richards at the Myerson Clinic.

In trying to sort through the whys and the wherefores, when Evan asked himself who benefits, the answer in all cases came up Stu Shackleton — who, if the man had been a human being of only moderate compassion, might have wanted it all to go the other way.

Maybe he doesn't believe Buzz is his grandchild. Or maybe he does, and the child of a mentally impaired son might be the fruit of a poisoned tree.

Evan and Leon were both about four drinks in and getting to the bottom of the bottle when Evan got around to describing the roles and the foibles of the usual suspects at Myerson — Bernice Richards, Clint Everly, and Dr. Dudley Wilmer. Leon didn't express an agenda of his own, still wouldn't offer any details about his own life story, and seemed not at all surprised or reluctant to be drafted as an ally into Evan's struggles. Then, evidently having heard enough, Leon announced he had a plan. But he reminded Evan they couldn't achieve any of it on empty stomachs.

This guy is a mysterious moocher. But why should I care? Angel or demon or spook, I'll assume he's here to help until he proves otherwise.

As the sun was going down, Evan realized it was about time for Loretta to be going off to work. He phoned her to confirm that his close and trusted friend, the family-law attorney Jeremy Bailey, had agreed to assist them *pro bono* for the purpose, at the very least, of ascertaining the specific whereabouts and wellbeing of Melissa and Buzz, and hopefully eventually overturning existing custodial orders in favor of Loretta. Despite what Evan judged to be good news, Loretta sounded distant, as if numb from the punishing events of the previous day. When he told her his plan was to make inquiries at Myerson again tomorrow, she made him promise he'd come by afterward to share with her everything he'd learned so far.

Evan then took Leon to the Cork & Keg, where the preacher spent the last of his recent repo commission money on a couple of thick sirloins with twice-baked potatoes, fresh green salad, and of course more whiskey.

Leon didn't seem terribly surprised when Evan said he'd be skipping church the next morning. Leon admitted he hadn't been in temple for years. Sunday would be the expected visitors' day at Myerson, and that's where the two of them would be putting Leon's plan into effect, even though Leon hadn't yet told Evan what exactly he intended to do.

Leon said he'd be perfectly comfortable curling up on the floor of the trailer, and he was doubly grateful when Evan provided him with a sleeping bag.

Drunk as Evan got, he never confessed to his not-quite-brother-in-law that Naomi visited him frequently, nor that her persistent appearances were having a dampening effect on whatever love life he might otherwise be seeking.

IT TURNED out that Leon was not without funds, and the following morning he treated Evan to a slap-up breakfast at the C'mon Inn. They sat at the counter, and Evan introduced his new friend to Cora. Evan couldn't help noticing both the gleam in Leon's eye and Cora's reserved delight for the attention.

And after the previous evening's excesses, it took several syrupy cups of coffee to clear Evan's head. As for Leon, he reported he'd been up with the chickens and jogged two miles while Evan slept.

MYERSON CLINIC

SUNDAY MORNING

*I*n the reception area at the clinic, a young woman Evan hadn't met who was at the desk reported that Ms. Richards wasn't on the premises today and couldn't be reached. Dr. Wilmer wasn't present either but was expected later. Evan had been sure to bring his letter of authorization from Shackleton, so after a cursory inspection, he was granted a visitor's pass. But Leon had no such credential, and despite Evan's vouching for him as a trusted associate, the receptionist wasn't about to make that leap of faith. (Leon's scruffy appearance probably didn't help.) Evan offered Leon the car keys so he could run errands, especially since the preacher's pantry was bare. Leon accepted them and mumbled something about sticking to the plan, offering to wait in the lobby. When the gleam came back to the odd fellow's eyes, Evan realized the look was saying, "Trust me."

All Leon would say was, "Perhaps someone could find me a cup of coffee."

~

EVAN FOUND Luke sitting up in his bed, fully dressed as he had been on their first meeting, his head bobbing to something he was hearing in his earbuds. When Luke looked up, Evan asked, "They let you have a phone?"

Luke removed the earbuds and explained, "It's a phone with no SIM, no Wi-Fi. So no calls. You could smuggle me a chip, but I don't know when I'd use it. They watch me all the time."

"Video?"

Luke nodded as he pointed to a metallic sphere on the ceiling. Then he whispered, "But no audio!"

"How do you know?"

"Clint told me. Some legal thing about not letting staff hear what patients tell their doctors."

"So, can you tell me any more about what's going on with Melissa? Any clues about where she is?"

"No, she's been sleeping for a long time. They probably gave her something. Like they do here when you're not exactly cooperative."

"Ah," Evan replied as he sat on the edge of the bed. "So, did you get a timeout?"

"Yeah," Luke replied, looking puzzled. "I believe they thought it might calm me down. But I don't think they had me in there all that long. Maybe they didn't want to undo the beneficial effect of the treatment you told me I received."

"So far so good?"

Luke managed the hint of a smile. "You mean about pissing myself? Yeah, sure." Then he added, "I thought my father had forgotten about me. I thought he wanted them to just lock me up and watch me all the time in case I tried to hurt myself or someone else."

"Do you have those feelings? Like you want to hurt someone?"

"No," he said simply. "I don't know why they would think that, but they do. Even now, I suppose. I take my meds, you know. I don't have to, but I do. Sometimes I feel dizzy, but that way there's no hassle for them, and there are worse ways to be."

"So you're okay with it?"

Luke winced again, got that screwed-up look on his face signaling the difficulty of expressing himself. "Mellow isn't necessarily happy. It's not anything."

"What do you mean?"

"Without the meds, you have good days and you have bad days. On the really bad days, you go to open a door, and something really ugly is on the other side. It's not real — and you might *know* it's not real — but it's just as disgusting or scary."

"So," Evan asked, "give me an example."

Luke shrugged. "Snakes. Or corpses with their bellies slit, holding their stinking guts in their hands."

"Hmm. Yeah."

"So, yeah, you don't want any more of that."

"And on the good days?"

"On the good days, maybe you can walk on water. The birds are singing opera. Or hip-hop. The angels are throwing you a party."

Maybe this kid plays in the realm of spirit after all.

Now Evan was curious. "Angels? Is that what they are? Wings and halos?"

Luke shook his head. "More like children. They giggle a lot." He took a deep breath, then added, "But the snakes aren't real. And neither are the spirits, I suppose."

"And what happens when you're on your medication?"

"No snakes. No parties. Problem is, the brain doesn't like mellow. It's boring. So maybe you don't take your meds, you take a chance so you can get back to the party. Or — and this is the part that drives the doctors nuts — even if you stay on the meds, the brain eventually psyches out the drug and finds a way to escape out of the chemical prison. That's why they give you a handful of different pills, a drug cocktail. And they have to keep changing up the mix. But, one way or another, you can't stay what they'd call normal for very long."

Evan concluded, "And that's why you have to be in here." Then he asked, "You say you hear voices? Are they angels?"

"I do," the boy said. "But they're not. Not at all."

"Do you mind telling me what they say?"

Luke was reporting as if it had been a normal conversation: "It's a man's voice. He's not kind. Scary, actually. One time he told me not to trust you. He said you're not a man of God. You care only about yourself."

Nailed it? Maybe he's talking to God after all. I'm not an agnostic. Just an I-don't-know-ist a lot of the time.

Evan took a moment to process this. "Anything else?"

"He said I should forget about Melissa. She's gone from me forever. When I was in timeout, he told me now he controls her. But he doesn't know her. That's not possible."

Luke's frankness was surprising. Evan wondered how far he could push the boy's trust. Then he asked, "Do you actually think you're communicating with someone who's holding her?"

"Maybe," Luke said. "But he won't let me tell him anything."

Everyone who cares about Melissa is sharing their intuitions she's in danger. But there's no evidence. She's trapped in the system, but it's a system designed to protect her. And Jeremy seems to think we're stuck, at least for now.

Evan asked the boy, "What happened between you guys?"

"They put her in here a year ago. She was messed up. I didn't talk to her at first. Then my friend Skeeter decided we should be together. He kept pestering me, saying I should tell her she was hot. But I didn't. I mean, she *is* hot, but I wasn't going to go hitting on her just because he told me to. Then he started pestering *her,* teasing her about her boobs, asking how come she doesn't have zits, how can she breathe in those tight jeans. You know, just stuff to piss her off. Well, that's when I had to tell him to cut it out, and I did it in front of her when we were all in the break room. I was trying to read, but Skeeter was being really annoying. So when I told him to back off, she figured I was trying to protect her. She assumed I liked her, which I did — I *do* — and she decided she liked me. That was Skeeter's idea all along — to bring us together, you see?"

"Clever," Evan said. "You didn't mind he was setting you up?"

"Nah, we were all kind of glad the way it worked out. She caught on to what he did, and she decided she liked him too. Not as much as me, of course."

Evan figured it was time to ask the question, "They're saying you… did something… to her. Do you know what they're talking about?"

Reporting frankly again, he replied right away, "We fucked. It was my first time, probably not hers."

Evan was appalled. "But how did that... how *could* that... happen in here? I mean, what about the *video?*"

Luke shrugged. The explanation was easy: "There's a kind of broom closet on this floor. With a printer, a copy machine, and a coffee pot for the staff. They didn't bother to put a camera in there, and everybody knows. Sometimes the staff takes one of us in there. Melissa was their favorite. Like I say, she's hot. Then she says to me it's only fair she and I get to go in there. It was after lights out. In some ways, it was too easy. I've wondered about that." He stared intently at a point in front of him, trying to puzzle it all out. Then he said, "She had a rubber. It slipped off."

Wow. This does not compute at all.

"Do you know who else went in there with Melissa?"

He shrugged. "Take a guess. I don't know."

"Did anyone else take *you* in there?"

Luke chuckled. "Nope. Guess I'm not pretty enough."

Evan wanted to know more, but he was amazed how much Luke had already been willing — and able — to confide in him. He decided he shouldn't push it until he'd had a chance to think through the implications.

Then Luke informed him, "I know I'm going to Hell."

"What makes you say that?"

"I'm a bad person. I must be. That's why they put me in here. That's why the demon speaks to me, because he hopes I can be recruited to do evil."

"Can you?"

"I don't know. I guess it depends on what he asks me to do."

"So, what makes you think you'll be going to Hell?"

"I told you. I'm bad. I don't deserve to live. But I know how to get out of there."

Evan was baffled. "How?"

"I'll just turn myself into a cockroach and crawl out the back when no one is looking."

Unable to think of what else to say, Evan asked Luke, "Shall we pray?"

"Do you think it will do any good?"

"Always," Evan assured him.

"Okay."

"So, let's bow our heads and close our eyes." Evan waited to see that the boy had done so, then he closed his own eyes and affirmed, "Right here and right now, Luke and I find blessed comfort and joy in knowing absolutely that the power and the presence of God *is* — and abides with us always. Amen."

When Evan didn't say anything more, they both opened their eyes, and Luke asked, "That's it? That's all?"

Evan smiled and gave Luke's leg a reassuring pat. "That's more than enough."

As LUKE WAS CONFIDING in Evan, Leon was working his plan.

IN EVAN'S CAR

SUNDAY AFTERNOON

$\mathcal{E}$van had been tempted to tarry at the clinic long enough to confront Doc Wilmer, but he decided he wasn't ready. Jeremy would have to advise him on the next steps first. He thanked the receptionist, whisked Leon out of the lobby, repossessed his keys, and they got into the Fiat for the drive to Loretta's place.

Once in the closed space of the car, Evan caught a strong whiff of whiskey on Leon's breath. His heart sank.

Some plan! I respect that liquor may be a good man's failing, but maybe he's just a useless drunk. Has this been Naomi's cruel idea of a joke?

As they got underway, Evan finally asked, "So that was your plan? A fifth of Early Times?"

I should have known better than to trust this guy. I figured if Naomi sent him, he had to be righteous. But maybe he's another one of her wise-ass jokes.

Leon chuckled mischievously. "Didn't take a fifth. Pint of Old Crow."

Evan fumed, "Some helper you turned out to be."

Leon sighed as if to say, *Oh ye of little faith!*

They rode along in silence for several minutes, then finally Leon announced, "The Sisters of Mercy program strives to give their wayward girls vocational training. Hairdressing, sewing, house clean-ing, hospitality maid service, assembly line, warehouse picking and packing, even in some cases… slaughterhouse."

For the second time that day, Evan was appalled. "And how do you know this?"

"The genius of a penetration plan is you shouldn't overthink how it's going to work. As you left me in the lobby, you recall I asked for a cup of coffee."

"Yes… ?"

"Well, as you might expect, that place is understaffed, especially on a Sunday. So the receptionist — her name is Lucille — won't leave her post and calls back to somewhere to forward my request. About ten minutes later, here comes a brawler bald guy with a steaming cup — real crockery even, not some jive-ass paper or Styrofoam."

"Clint Everly."

"The very man."

"And you said… ?"

"I give him a wink, and I say, 'You wouldn't have something to put in it?' He says, 'Cream, sugar, and pink stuff.' I say, 'I find myself craving something of a more spiritual nature.' Nice touch, right? He gives me this big, sappy grin and says, 'Sorry, brother. I'm fresh out.' So I dangle your keys in his face and I say, 'How about we take a ride to the convenience store?'"

Evan tried unsuccessfully to choke back a laugh. "You silver-tongued, cross-eyed devil!"

"So our boy Clint's on his afternoon break, and we spend a half-hour in the parking lot of the 7-Eleven, not a half-mile down the road, passing the bottle back and forth and getting pleasantly pissed."

"I'm guessing he told you a lot more."

"Melissa was always difficult to manage. Flirted with anyone in pants."

"Luke seems to think he's the one who made her pregnant. They hooked up when they were both at the clinic, in some closet in the middle of the night."

"Not impossible but not too likely unless the security there really sucks," Leon said. "I mean, you'd think keeping teenagers apart after lights out would be kind of a *basic* part of the drill. That and making sure they can't smuggle in drugs or weapons."

"Yeah, Luke said they watch him closely. Video in every room except for some closet. This would have been a huge lapse."

"Suspicious, even. Let's take this apart." Leon thought a moment and then asked, "We can guess how Luke got there. Shackleton's money opens any door. But how does a poor kid like Melissa get admitted to a private clinic like that?"

"Jeremy Bailey explained it to me. She's underage. If she had a brush with the law and the court found her guilty, the judge might send her to the clinic at state expense instead of into juvenile detention."

"Hmm. If that's what happened, there's a case file. It would be sealed because she's a minor, but there would at least be an arrest record. Presumably, her sister would know why and how Melissa got sent to Myerson."

Evan thought back on his conversation with Loretta. "No, from what she told me, it was the Catholic children's home that got Melissa admitted to the clinic. She did say Melissa is a troublemaker. And then there's the girl's epilepsy. Marcus Thurston said that, when he knew the girls, Melissa wasn't having fits. If the onset of the disease was later in her teens, that could explain why maybe the nuns didn't think they could handle her."

"So, maybe there's no case file after all. At least, not in the state's records. And you won't get to see any of the convent's files without a court order."

"I'll have Jeremy research all the angles," Evan said, "but I'm thinking it wasn't some judge who sent Melissa to the clinic."

"Okay, but one way or another, she would be a charity case. And Myerson is a private, for-profit clinic. They *might* take her in if they needed the write-off, but let's assume not. If the state isn't paying the bill, then who is?"

"Wild guess? It's a stretch, and we don't have much evidence."

"Go ahead. I'm already there," Leon said.

Evan picked up on a thought he'd had before, which he'd expressed to Luke's father: "Let's say someone else got her pregnant. Maybe it wasn't Luke. Okay, no doubt she hooked up with the kid, but maybe she was pregnant *before* she was admitted."

Leon agreed, "Might even be the reason she was sent there."

"What do you mean?"

"I can think of several reasons. One, the nuns would want her to keep the baby, probably give it up for adoption. But she's not so happy about it. She lapses into a depression, possibly complicated by epileptic seizures, and there's good reason to have her institutionalized."

Evan nodded and said, "According to Loretta, some of the nuns believe Melissa is possessed by demons. So they might want her out of the convent, but no chance they'd be paying for Myerson, even less that they could get the state to pay without involving child welfare. We're left to guess that the baby's father has the money — and the influence — to get the placement over whatever objections the facility might have. The social worker, Bernice Richards, doesn't approve of Luke's being there. She emphasized to me the place is supposed to be drug rehab, not a mental hospital."

"If this rich guy needs to manage the situation, what about an abortion?"

"For sure, the Sisters of Mercy wouldn't abide it. And these days, in this state, it's getting to be next to impossible unless you have friends and money. They'd have to get Melissa on a waiting list at a clinic in Kansas, drive her over the state line, and put her into a hotel for a week. Getting it done legally would be an expensive chore."

"Difficult to do without people knowing who shouldn't know. Myerson is private. It's not inconceivable they'd do a gray-market abortion for a paying client. But Melissa didn't go along with it. From what you say, Loretta tried to keep track of her little sister. How could she not know how it all went down?"

Evan said, "If Luke isn't the father, whoever got Melissa pregnant wants to control her. But whether he wanted her to keep the baby — or wants it now — that's another question."

Leon nodded. "And this guy has the resources and the pull to get her away from the home and into an expensive clinic."

"And take the opportunity to get her hooked up with Luke? By getting the staff to look the other way? Why?"

"Maybe to throw suspicion on Luke. There could be a rape charge at issue, you realize." Leon turned to Evan to ask him, "Do you figure Shackleton is still your client?"

"Are you thinking he's the one? That he somehow abused Melissa?"

"Well, he has the resources. And the access, with his son there."

Evan thought about it. "Somehow, I don't think he'd be sending me in there if he was the one. I ask too many questions. He did tell me not to ask after Melissa, but I'm still trying to help Luke, who has to be worried about her. And I've been telling myself that Luke's welfare and Melissa's are kind of connected. So I'm kind of ignoring Shackleton's latest instructions."

"Well," Leon said ominously, "if Shackleton isn't the bad guy, he could be a victim."

"Victim? How do you figure?"

"Whoever put Luke and Melissa together may be intending to hold it over Luke's father. The fact that he asked for your help may mean he's already been threatened. Or he's expecting it."

LORETTA'S TRAILER

SUNDAY EVENING

*E*van was about to go up to the door when Leon walked around the car and stopped him. As he held out his hand for the keys, he warned, "Might not be a good idea to have it parked here."

"You've got a point," Evan admitted. "I'll ask her to put on a pot of coffee for us, give her a chance to freshen up. We'll go leave it at my place and walk back."

"Nah," Leon said as he climbed into the driver's side. "She's got to be scared, and she doesn't know me. You have to admit, I don't make a good first impression. But she might just confide in you. I'm sure you've got this covered." Then he added, "Knock first when you come home. I've got the rest of that pint to kill. I'm going to think unclean thoughts and catch a nap."

EVAN'S INTENTION was to comfort her. He wouldn't come on with questions. If eventually she felt like talking, he'd shut up and listen. At this time of day he figured she'd be heading off to work. The casino was likely to be busy on a Sunday night.

On his knock, he heard her muffled cry beckoning him to come in. He found her curled up on her bed on top of the covers, clad in a faded navy sweatsuit. She had a window air conditioner turned up max, and she wore an oversize pair of winter wool socks to keep her feet warm.

He was startled at first because this prostrate form so little resembled the flashy showgirl who had pulled him out of the diner. For a fleeting moment, he thought this might be Melissa, whom he'd never seen. She wore no makeup, and her complexion was pale, even wan as if her worries had drained her vital spirit. Her long, dark hair was unkempt, gathered at the back. Her head rested in the crook of her outstretched arm.

Naomi, minus ten years. This could get complicated.

Her eyes remained closed as she asked weakly, "Is she safe?"

Evan hesitated, then phrased his response carefully: "We have no reason to think she's not."

"And the baby?"

"Likewise. Safe and sound. I'm sure of it."

Another white lie.

"These foster parents, whoever they are, the situation doesn't have to be permanent. As I told you, I have an attorney on it, and he'll be making inquiries first thing in the morning."

He remained standing just inside the door for a long moment, gazing down at her, unsure what she expected him to do since she hadn't moved.

Then she sniffled, opened an eye just enough to find his form, and asked meekly, "Hold me?"

He lay down beside her. She was facing away. His nose was in her hair, one of his arms flung around her waist. The scent of her intoxicating perfume from their first encounter now was replaced with the distinct, fresh odor of Ivory soap.

After a few minutes of silence during which his breaths relaxed and became almost as shallow as hers, he kicked off his shoes. He didn't realize how tired he was, stressed himself by the events of the last three days.

He'd nodded off to sleep when he felt her sweet breath in his face, then her soft lips on his.

"Is this okay?" she whispered.

He didn't know what to say.

Sure. No worries. Happy to oblige.

Instead, he tried to make a joke of it: "I live to serve."

She didn't laugh, but as he peeked, he saw a demure smile. "Hmm," she cooed. Then she said, "We won't do anything that makes you uncomfortable."

He said, "I think that's supposed to be my line." And he kissed her back.

Neither of them said anything for the next half-hour. He could tell she was more experienced than he was, but it wasn't a performance and certainly not a contest. Through it all, there was a lot of tender kissing, and Naomi had done a good job of giving him patient practice in that discipline.

They ended up naked under a light blanket, and they both slept for more than an hour before she stirred, got up, and he heard water running in the bathroom. He roused and started putting his clothes back on.

She came out wearing a terrycloth bathrobe which, like the sweat-suit, looked far from new.

He asked her, "You don't have to work?"

"Too stressed," she said. "Found a sub, figured I'd sleep." Then she quipped, "No great loss on a Sunday night. The vacationers have mostly left, and the place is jammed with locals. They hog the slots." She made a face. "And they don't tip."

After a pause, Evan said sheepishly, "I'd kind of intended to get to know you first."

"Well," she replied as she sighed and sat down beside him, "by now I'd say you know more about me and my family than anyone else in town. What's this lawyer going to do for us?"

"He's going to find out whether you have any legal right to change things."

"And if I don't?"

"You want what's best for Melissa and Buzz. I don't know what that is yet, but my gut is telling me, if we don't push for it, they won't get it."

She ran her fingernails through her hair, which had come undone, falling to her shoulders. She asked, "How about I make you a sandwich?"

She made grilled cheese and tomato in a frypan and accompanied it with chopped cucumber, red onion, and tomato salad. She offered sweet tea and apologized that the fridge wasn't making ice these days. Evan saw no evidence of liquor in her place, and for once he was thankful not to have to decide to turn it down. She'd pried the top off his lust, and this was no time to be guzzling whatever he had left into delirium. As she'd described it, he'd comforted her. She'd made the request and the first move. He wasn't feeling exactly righteous, but he didn't feel sinful either.

As they ate, Loretta gave him some background on the Benton sisters, which fit with what Marcus had already told him.

"So what put you two at Sisters of Mercy?"

"That was, let me see, four years ago. I was seventeen, she was thirteen. Our mom had died of an overdose, and one day our father just didn't come home. We found out later he died in lockup somewhere in Kansas. So we didn't have any folks at all, no extended family. A neighbor looked after us for a few weeks, but she got tired of that right quick, especially with Melissa sassing her back. The convent is the only orphanage around here, so that's where we ended up.

"A year later, after I turned eighteen, they let me leave. Lying that I was older, I got a job as a bartender at a bar and grill on the lake. There I made a friend of Mick Heston, and he set me up with the cocktail waitress job. He manages the casino."

She admitted she'd been intimate with Mick and some of his friends. Now she assured Evan all of that was over, and she'd thought Mick to be a fair boss and a capable businessman. He'd told her the casino venture would have a new development of luxury condos at the marina, and he promised to move her into an entry-level position in sales. She was intending to take extension courses and get a degree.

"Melissa had a rougher time of it. Once I had the job, I moved in with Mick. But Melissa was stuck at the convent.

"They have vocational ed at the convent. Housekeeping or hairdressing. Melissa chose sewing and millinery. At that place, the pretty and the smart ones get attention and privileges. She showed some initiative, and they sent her out for coursework in fashion design, to Jack Nathan's school. They gave her lessons in modeling, and she got to walk the runway at the annual fashion show one time. She got crazy about it. She was going to catch a big break, be a star, the whole hopeless trip. For a while there, I thought she was going to take something seriously."

"I'm guessing that didn't work out."

"There's a gap in her story, and I've never been able to figure out what went on. The same week as the big fashion show, the convent had her transferred to a day-job at the casino — in housekeeping! She was laundering towels and mopping floors in the spa."

"The nuns let her do that — work outside?"

"She was like an intern. They want the girls to become selfsupporting. After all, she was earning some money instead of costing them Nathan's course fees. And maybe it looked like a path to fulltime employment, you know? So when she started working in the spa, she was living in staff quarters at the hotel, rooming with other girls who were in the same situation. Supervised, she told me."

"Were you able to keep track of her over there?"

"That's the thing. For a while, she'd check in with me. She was bummed about having to quit the fashion school for this cruddy job. But then she let it slip that it was Mick — *my* Mick — who got her that job. I mean, him and me were sharing a bed and a fridge — and he neglected to share this little detail? I confronted him that night, and he blew up. Acted like he was some kind of secret saint to unwed mothers, and I had my nerve asking a lot of questions. And we broke up over it. About the same time, Melissa cut me off, wouldn't answer my calls. I was worried she wasn't getting her meds, you know? I asked the convent, they referred me to Father Coyle, and he informed me I'm not Melissa's guardian and I should concentrate on cleaning up my own affairs."

"I've met him. Not someone I'd want as an enemy. You said you were living with Mick. Where'd you go after the breakup?"

She shrugged, "Here. Damnedest thing. I spent one night in a motel, and then Mick called me, all apologizing. He agreed we should stay split, but he said I'm a good employee, he would move me up to cocktail waitress on the evening shift, and he gave me the keys to the rented trailer home and the Buick. And a gas card. I wanted to know about Melissa. He gave me this excuse that they have this work program going with the convent. Father Coyle has warned him he has to respect their privacy for legal reasons. Well, I wasn't about to turn the deal down. It was a good job, and it got better. But I didn't hear from Melissa until they put her into Myerson."

"So, yeah, there's a gap here — how long?"

"Three months."

"And do you know what got her sent to the clinic?"

"She'd been working at the spa a couple of months. She went off her meds and had fits, then she pulled this suicide attempt. She gulped down a whole bottle of aspirin. Somebody should tell kids that never works. The ambulance took her to the clinic, they pumped her stomach, and they kept her there on seventy-two-hour watch. Then she was admitted. She didn't go back to the home until it was time to have her baby."

"Myerson is private. Who was paying for her care?"

"No idea. I assumed the nuns had a fund or something. I didn't have any say in where they put her."

"Is that where she got pregnant, at the clinic?"

"That's what everybody thought. But she let me think she was doing a lot more than folding towels at the spa."

As he finished his sandwich, Evan confessed, "I have a houseguest, the brother of a friend of mine. He's kind of passing through. I don't know him all that well. And as near as I can tell, he has a background in… investigative work. He's been helping me. I hope you don't mind. I want you to meet him. His name is Leon."

She cocked her head and sipped her tea. "Brother of… a lady friend?"

"She died. It's been three years."

"Wow. I apologize. It was a wild guess. I haven't earned the right to be jealous."

You've made a helluva start, though.

"I wanted to give you a heads up because he's not a... conventional... person. His personal habits are untidy, and you could mistake him for homeless."

"But you trust him."

"I do. He showed up yesterday morning, and already he's helped me dig deeper than I thought possible." Evan didn't think it was the time for a lengthy interview, but he had to ask: "Did you know Melissa hooked up with a young man at the clinic? I mean... they were intimate?"

Loretta nodded. "Luke. She said he was her best friend. And Melissa has a way of leading men friends astray. So, no surprise. Is that how she got pregnant? She wouldn't tell me."

"The doctors think he has schizophrenia. He claims he hears voices. And, yes, he also thinks he's the father of Buzz."

"Hmm" was all she said.

"Let me ask you. Do you think Melissa was already pregnant when she was admitted to Myerson? I mean, was that why she had the breakdown, the reason for the suicide attempt? And who do you think got her admitted?"

"Like I said, I could never get her to tell me who the father is. And, to tell you the truth, I'm not sure exactly when it happened. As for putting her in Myerson, no one asked me about whether to keep her there long-term. I'm guessing it would have been Father Coyle at the convent. Everyone there acts like he makes all the decisions."

"Here's the thing," Evan said. "Leon and I both think it shouldn't have been so easy for two kids at that clinic to shack up in a closet. We're thinking maybe someone let it happen."

"And that's why you're wondering whether she might have already been pregnant?"

"It could explain why she tried to kill herself. She never gave you any reasons?"

"Whenever she does something defiant or crazy or stupid, when I call her on it, she acts like it never happened. She reminds me I'm her sister, not her mother. So you're wondering whether some guy hit on her at the spa?"

"Pretty, underage girl who has a job inside a casino? What are the odds?"

"Mick's a straight shooter. Or I thought he was. They're tight-assed about everything on the job. They give us wait staff monthly lie-detector tests to make sure we're not skimming."

"Luke's father is a rich and powerful man. I've had dealings with him. I suspect — and I know it's a long shot — someone who is also in his world, someone who knew about the pregnancy or maybe even caused it — could want to embarrass the guy, maybe even blackmail him. Or use it as leverage in some deal."

"Well," Loretta huffed, "if there's trouble brewing anywhere, our Melissa will find it."

"Do you think Mick Heston will talk to me?"

She actually batted her eyelashes. "Don't go telling him we had a thing."

"Is that what we have?"

"We could," she said.

"I'd better go," he said and kissed her.

He was almost out the door when he thought to ask, "Do you have a picture of your sister?"

Loretta brought up a photo on her phone. It was a shot of Melissa on the runway of the fashion show.

Evan took the phone, stared at it, then swiped to enlarge the view so he could get a good look at her face. "And she was *fifteen?*"

As he forwarded the image to his own phone, Loretta sighed. "I know. I'm gorgeous, but she's drop-dead gorgeous." She took her phone from him and added, "No one bothered to tell her models can't have boobs that big."

EVAN RETURNED to his trailer just after nine that evening. He found Leon awake. Since they'd each slept through some of the day, neither felt like turning in. So they talked into the early hours.

Evan shared that Loretta had asked him to comfort her, and it had soon progressed much further. Leon didn't seem surprised.

In fact, he doesn't seem surprised at all.

They needed whatever Doc Wilmer would be willing to tell them. And there were two new potential interview subjects — fashion instructor Jack Nathan and casino manager Mick Heston. Evan also wondered whether they would be able to get anything more from Clint Everly and — perhaps more importantly — whether he'd been complicit in the hookups in the utility room at Myerson.

"Clint's not the brightest fellow," Leon offered. "But he seems a decent sort, not the kind of person who'd be capable of deception."

Evan agreed. "I doubt Cora would be tracking with him if he was a bad guy. But from what he said to you, he was aware of the abuse and didn't report it. And if they order a timeout for Luke, Clint would have to enforce it."

"Cowardice in the face of overwhelming force would be under-standable if not entirely forgivable," Leon said.

"So, where do we go from here?" Evan asked.

"It doesn't sound like Melissa accused anyone of rape, but you can ask your buddy the sheriff whether anyone reported instances of abuse at the clinic. Then you can find out what this Dr. Wilmer has to say for himself."

"And I'll check in with Jeremy Bailey. He's supposed to figure the family-law angles and tell us how to get some leverage so we can locate Melissa and her baby. How about you? Are you still all in for this?"

Leon chuckled. "Oh, yeah. If you suspect I have my own agenda, you're not wrong. But I assure you I'm here to help. I'll do some back-ground investigations on Nathan and Heston. I have some former partners in crime who still owe me."

"Crime?"

"Criminal investigations and prosecutions. Traditionally, govern-ment agencies don't readily share information, but since the Patriot Act, we pretend to be friends."

"*We?*"

"Believe it or not, some G-men still wear white hats." Then he added, "G-*persons,* excuse me." When Evan was about to ask further, Leon stopped him with, "I'm supposed to be retired. And you don't get to ask."

EVAN'S TRAILER

MONDAY 2 AM

*A*t about two in the morning, Evan's eyes were starting to glaze over. Leon was already curled up on the floor, snoring to raise the roof. Evan opened his laptop and was about to do a last-minute check on family law when he saw a new email from Jeremy. The lawyer had spent all Sunday afternoon doing his own online researches.

Evan,

Here's what I've found so far in Missouri family law. You probably know better than I do what the practical implications might be.

When a child has no living parents, the court will consider first the child's preference for a guardian or else any "suitable" person who can petition the court for custody and guardianship. But in the case of a child who is a ward of the state, the court typically appoints a guardian, usually the official who is responsible for the facility or the institution in which the child is housed. In Melissa's case, when she lived at Sisters of Mercy, Fr. Michael Coyle was her guardian of record. But when she was institutionalized at Myerson, Dr. Dudley Wilmer became her guardian. Since her recent transfer — presumably back to Sisters of Mercy — the guardianship might need to change again. But if she's headed into a foster family, that determination might still be in process and not yet be formalized.

I believe Loretta could petition the court for guardianship and custody of Melissa, on the grounds that Melissa prefers to live with her sister, and Loretta's of age.

Then again, when Melissa turns eighteen (in six months, as I learned), she comes of age herself, and any guardianship terminates automatically. All the above could be moot if we can't get the process halted because Loretta's petition could take that long — or longer — in the courts, especially if some interested party raises objections.

However (and I know I'm starting to sound like the double-talking counsel here), in the event the girl is not considered mentally competent — which is a possibility considering her recent treatment at Myerson — guardianship could be asserted indefinitely. Which would give ample time for a foster parent to assert guardianship as soon as possible — and keep it for a very long time.

From what you're telling me, if Wilmer is a bad actor in all this, I'm betting as of this moment he has custody and control of Melissa. And I'd venture a further guess that he's about to send the court his considered medical opinion that a) Melissa is not presently of sound mind, b) is therefore incapable of expressing a rational or credible opinion about who should be her guardian, and c) the court-appointed guardianship should therefore not be terminated automatically at her age of majority or in the event she might petition for emancipation.

As for her baby, I haven't found any pending filings, but that process typically takes a while. The adoptive parents would have provisional custody until the adoption could be reviewed by the authorities and formalized. That could take months — or more. I'll keep digging.

Your pro for everything bono,

Jeremy

C'MON INN

MONDAY MORNING

The diner had been full since early morning with crewmembers clad in safety-chartreuse jackets. Nearly every seat was filled. Most of the patrons kept their hard hats on their heads to make room on the scant tabletops for mountainous platefuls of flapjacks. Evan learned from a too-talkative mate seated next to him at the counter that this crew was the cleanup and restoration gang tasked with refurbishing the football field of Appleton City High School. In ordinary circumstances, the crew would be much smaller and could thus stretch out the manhours for weeks. But the field had been the scene on the previous evening of the St. Clair County Truck and Tractor Pull. Now, you might think hosting all those vehicles in a schoolyard would be massively destructive of manicured turf, and summer scrimmages were about to start. But the City Council in its wisdom had promised to plow back the venue-rental fees into an immediate project to grade and then re-sod the football field, a previously unfunded but long overdue budget item. The crew would be contending with some waist-deep ruts. But the morning had been clear and dry, so at least they wouldn't be coping with mud.

However, the workers were all here leisurely chowing down, lingering past the time they were supposed to report onsite because the

146

convoy of flatbeds carrying their heavy equipment had been stalled on the interstate.

Murphy's Law! What can go wrong will go wrong. Should have been a Bible verse. The Eleventh Commandment: Thou shalt not bank on thine expectations!

Evan was trying to keep the seat on his other side open for Leon, who had lit out of the car an hour ago saying he had errands.

The loud buzz in the diner was convenient cover for a confidential question. Evan asked Cora, "Clint Everly. Is he a stand-up guy?"

She made a face. "Don't tell me you're jealous."

"Seriously. I'm learning Myerson might not be a safe place."

"I wouldn't know about that," she replied. "But if you came to church more often, you'd know I'm in Clint's Bible-study class. He's a widower with a Downs daughter, and he works two jobs. So — stand-up? Yeah, I'd say he's on his feet way too much." And she walked away.

Struck a nerve there. Maybe Leon can have another heart-to-heart with Clint. The guy probably knows more than he's said.

As Cora came back to dispense a coffee refill, she teased, "Are you sure your imaginary friend doesn't want something?"

For a moment here, I'm worried she knows about Naomi's visits. But how could she guess? I never told her. She's just upset there's an empty seat.

"He's not imaginary in the least," Evan insisted. "Just delayed. And I should assure you, before you lay eyes on him, he's not a vagrant, just a bit eccentric."

As Evan was saying this, he hadn't noticed the door chime nor the approach of the slender middle-aged fellow who breezed in and helped himself to the coveted seat.

Cora could see this guy looked like an accountant, maybe an insurance salesman. Gray suit, white shirt, conservative navy tie. Close-cropped graying hair. Bald on top.

Evan was sipping his coffee. When he did look up, he said, "I'm sorry. I'm expecting a friend."

To which Leon replied with amusement, "And I assure you I *am* a friend. But I take exception at the characterization of eccentric!"

Now here is a transformation! Who is the real Leon Weiss?

"You said you had errands," Evan said, appraising this stranger with the familiar voice. "You visit your fairy godmother?"

Leon beckoned to Cora, "Coffee, black, please," Then he confided to Evan, "It always amazes me the quality of merchandise one can find at the Salvation Army. I mean, this is a Brooks Brothers suit!"

"Not to mention the fit. You must be a forty regular. How about the haircut?"

"There was no waiting at the barber's this morning. And they even took my credit card."

"I'm not going to say the change is undesirable, but I was kind of getting used to you. I'm sure you're going to tell me why it's necessary."

Leon gulped his coffee greedily and then said, "I *will* tell you what's necessary for you to know. But first, why don't you have a second breakfast while I find out what's so hot about these hotcakes everybody seems to want?"

LEON WOULDN'T SAY MORE until they were back in Evan's car, parked at the curb down the block, with the windows rolled up, air on high, and the radio playing country-and-western full blast. Then he confessed: "Surely I don't have to tell you what a G-man looks like. Seriously, it's an hour later in DC, so in the time between the clothing change and the haircut, I've been on the phone."

Stunned, Evan asked, "So you're — what? — FBI?"

"Suffice it to say, I didn't exactly retire. And from which agency I'm not at liberty to disclose just now. Been on leave, more like. In point of fact, between you and me, they wanted me to see a shrink. You see, I got pretty upset the way Naomi laid down her life for her country. Or was it for Israel? Or for the Saudis? Or the military-industrial complex? What, I ask you, was the divine fucking plan? I assume you believe there's a God — you haven't actually said — but maybe you've figured something out? I sure as hell haven't. Then I had some other life reversals that had me thinking I was in the wrong line of work. At the same time, for their own reasons, my superiors started to think I might not be right for the job either."

"But, judging from appearances, you're back in the game."

"Let's just say you've presented me with a situation that requires me to earn my way back into the game. And regardless of how I might feel about my career personally or the wisdom of my masters, there's a moral imperative here. Wrong has been done, and — if you and I don't take the initiative — much, much worse will follow."

"I don't know about you, but all I hoped to achieve was help Loretta get custody of Melissa and Buzz and make sure Luke is getting the right treatment from the right people." Evan hadn't yet had a chance to tell Leon about Jeremy's email. So he continued, "Jeremy Bailey sent me an email last night, and he's saying it's legally possible for Loretta to petition for custody, but Melissa turns eighteen in six months, and the process could take at least that long. Once she's of age, normally she could decide for herself. But there's the glitch that some shrink could assert she's not competent. Then they — or someone they serve — could keep control of the girl indefinitely."

Leon mused, "Evan, you have a habit of helping people and finding trouble. Well, this time you've stumbled into a cave full of bad guys, and you're going to need help from official quarters. I assure you the situation is a lot worse than you've guessed so far."

How much worse could it be?

Evan asked him, "What all did Clint tell you? By the way — Cora vouches for the guy, so I'm wondering whether the abuse might have happened on someone else's shift. I'm guessing he's heard things, but maybe he's not either a participant or a witness."

"Could very well be true, my friend. But you're staring at trees, and you don't realize you've stumbled into the Dark Wood of Error." Leon put a hand on Evan's arm and went on, "Background checks don't take long these days. At least not inside the Beltway. The head of the fashion school has a rap sheet as long as your arm. But no convictions. Nothing special on the casino manager Heston, but both the school and the casino — through a myriad of front businesses — are controlled by the same holding company. And those guys are not the sweetest Russians you would ever want to meet."

"Whoa," Evan said. "And I thought the Family Welfare Agency was the monster in the room."

"Oh, they're caught up in it. But I wouldn't assume the whole department is corrupt. Let's just say some individuals in that organization are likely to be bent. Before Jack Nathan started the fashion school, he ran massage parlors. All presumably legitimate operations. No citations, but that's living on the gray fringes of the law. Lots of imported help from Thailand, that kind of thing. If I had to guess, I'd say, in his current role, he's what people in the trade would call a *talent spotter.*"

"For what? Modeling agencies?"

"My hunch is he sends the most attractive underage girls to work in the spa at the hotel. Case in point, your Melissa. Loretta told you Melissa was folding laundry, and you wondered why she'd go from modeling into a low-level grunt job with no hope of glamor. Now, since she's underage, she can't be a showgirl or a waitress because of the liquor laws. But a presumably part-time job in the kitchen or in the laundry would put her and her pretty classmates inside the casino. Those girls might even punch a clock along with the backroom workers. But then they'd report to a suite of apartments upstairs, where there would be a 'house mother' and closets full of designer dresses."

"But Coyle said she was being placed with a foster family."

"Sugar daddy, more like. And that's where your custody questions become important. If Myerson is somehow part of the scheme, they could, by declaring Melissa incompetent, make it possible for her to be someone's prisoner for life. Your lawyer buddy got that correct."

"How do we take her away from them?"

"Let's theorize that the Feds are watching the holding company, waiting for them to screw up, probably even laying some traps. I can't muck with an ongoing investigation. I'm not even supposed to know about it, much less you. But that's not any help to Melissa. She'd be just another in a long list of victims by the time my partners in crime-stopping have enough evidence to bring indictments."

"We can't just sit around waiting for a break."

"We're guessing Doc Wilmer is still her guardian. And you still have authorization from Shackleton to pester him. So go ahead."

"I was planning to go to Myerson this morning, unannounced. With Jeremy to back me up, maybe I can get more out of Doc

Wilmer. And I can talk it up with Clint and see what more Luke is willing to share with me. And you?"

Leon replied, "Me, I'll be starting with Jack Nathan."

"So — that's why the suit? Are you planning to tell him you're FBI?"

"Nossir. I'm strictly under the radar, unofficial, unsanctioned, deniable, and freelance. So I get to choose, and I'm going in as his worst nightmare."

"What's worse?"

"I-fucking-R-S!"

TWIN DRAGONS RESORT

MONDAY MORNING

*M*ick Heston was busy inspecting the housekeeping in the Prince Calaf Suite when Jack Nathan barged in on him.

"Mick! I'm being fucking *audited!*"

These rooms were decorated in the motif of an ancient Chinese palace. Heston was examining a cloisonné knickknack he'd lifted from an ornately carved coffee table.

Ignoring Nathan's outburst, the hotel manager looked up at him quizzically. "Corporate is sending *me* a brand manager! Can you imagine that? There had better not be a stick of Early American mixed in with this Oriental stuff, the monograms on *all* the towels must be the *new* chain logo, and no *bent tines* on the forks. If we don't pass inspection, I could lose my bonus. And I can't afford to lose my bonus. It's already spent on a Bugatti Divo. Lightly used, of course." As he delicately set a ceramic bowl back on the glossy surface, he added, "Why are you here? If that's the news, you could've sent me a text."

"I'm sorry if I'm out of line. Your assistant told me you'd be up here. What am I going to *do?*"

"Are you sure this is legit? They usually, I believe, send a letter first.

Then you make an appointment, far enough ahead you have time to collect your records."

"This guy just showed up at the office. He had a *badge!*"

Heston mocked, "Oh, a badge. That's impressive."

"Mick…"

"Jack, did you look *closely* at the badge? Did you *read* what it says on his ID?"

"Hey, I was too freaked to think straight, Mick. It looked official enough. I wasn't about to push back on the guy."

"So what did he want?"

"He said most of their examination has already been done. They call it doing *tests of transactions*. All by computer. I didn't know they could *see* our transactions, but they can. If your amounts seem reasonable compared to similar types of business, they don't question and they don't ask for backup. Maybe you never know they even looked. But if any items are unusual, they want answers."

"So, what are they curious about?"

"Placement fees."

"Ah. And what makes those look wrong?"

"He said the amounts are ten to twenty times what they'd expect. For a school of our size, they figure we'd be finding employment for maybe a half-dozen graduates. Instead it looks like we're staffing a small army. He wanted names and dates. Name of employer, job description, starting salary, name of supervisor, full or part-time…"

"Which you *didn't give him*, I hope, and you want me to *gin up*, which I won't?"

"No, I told him what I remembered. Eight girls. All placed here."

"Oh, goody. And, pray tell, why were those receipts classified in that way? Tuition fees would be larger. Why didn't you just stick it in with those?"

"New bookkeeper. I told her I wanted to keep that money separate. And I wasn't paying close attention. She asked what the check was for, since there was no invoice. So I told her and didn't think much about it at the time. You see, she's not a, uh, creative type like the old gal was. If it walks like a duck, well, you know."

"And just what am I supposed to do about this royal cockup of yours?"

In a low voice, Nathan muttered, "I'm figuring, here on out, it might be a good idea to make those payments in cash. Like for the one the end of this month."

Heston gritted his teeth and growled back, "Let's take this outside."

WHEN THEY WERE poolside with no one in earshot, Heston went on, "Jack, this is an international chain. We don't *do* cash. We don't launder money. We are a one-hundred percent legit business." Then he huffed, "You might as well ask to be paid in cocaine!"

"That's not a possibility, is it?"

"Are you paying attention at all?"

"What about special services? How do the clients pay for the girls?"

Heston hissed, "They *don't.*"

"What do you mean?"

"Oh, they pay for their spa treatments. Goes on their bill. But we tell them *tipping is not allowed.* Anything that happens in their room is strictly private, between practitioner and customer. There's no video in the rooms. And our regulars know they're not to pay for anything that's not on their bill."

"I don't understand."

"This is a *casino,* if you haven't noticed. A *legal* gaming establishment. Our luxury suites — and our premium services — are strictly for high rollers who are repeat customers. We tell them — and we're straight-up about it when they check in, but this part isn't written down — they must understand they don't get the platinum treatment — with all the goodies — if they don't play the high-stakes tables. And play a *lot.*"

"But what if they lose?"

"They *will lose,* genius! The games aren't rigged, they can't cheat, or we'll catch them, and the math decreed since the beginning of the universe says, most of the time, they'll lose — and lose *big.*"

"So why do they come back?"

"*One*, because they're addicts and egomaniacs. And *two*, because if they add up the value of *all* the services they receive, they realize they're getting the best of everything by doing nothing more than indulging habits they can't or won't kick."

"What about when one of these rich guys decides to run off with his favorite therapist?"

"We have a strict rule. No member of our staff can date or be entertained by a customer — in our facility or elsewhere. Grounds for dismissal."

"And you stick to that?"

"Hey, people fall in love. Happens every day. They ditch their wives, run off, get married, shack up, take a cruise, hit the shops on Rodeo Drive and the Champs Elysées, live out their golden years. If the woman is no longer an employee, we can't tell her who to hang with."

"And in those cases, there's no… consideration?"

"Corporate funds a charitable foundation for unwed mothers. In turn, the foundation funds some of the institutions that place students at your school. And those outfits pay *you* their tuition. If a high-net-worth donor is moved to make a gift, we put them in touch with corporate. As to the details, I'm not in the loop. I don't participate in that cash flow." Then he emphasized, "But *you do*. I would strongly suspect, although I don't know for sure, that our foundation writes substantial checks to Sisters of Mercy, for example. And your buddy Father Coyle is fully aware. So I hope you're done asking questions. My suggestion, tell the IRS that you and the bookkeeper both got it wrong. You don't get placement fees. The check from us was for tuition reimbursement as part of our new employee scholarship program. We might have overpaid, but we wanted to do our bit to keep the voc ed schools solvent. When they come asking me, I'll send them to corporate, and the suits will run them around until they get tired."

Jack Nathan's mouth had literally fallen open. Just to make sure he got the point, Heston added, "Get your books clean, no more talk about cash, and you appreciate it could be bad for your health to share a word I've told you."

MYERSON CLINIC

MONDAY MORNING

On the way to Myerson, Evan phoned Jeremy to follow up on his diligent research. The lawyer then gave him a magic incantation in legalese to deliver to Wilmer and Richards that might coax them into sharing more about Melissa and Luke.

When he was seated across from Wilmer in the administrator's private office, Evan recited: "We'll be filing suit against the clinic on behalf of Loretta Benton and initiating discovery. There have been rumors of sexual abuse of patients, in some instances by staff. Do you want to tell me now or wait to put it all into the public record?"

From Wilmer's blank expression, it looked as though he hadn't heard. "Are you sure you don't want coffee?" he asked with a polite smile. "As I recall, caffeine was one of your drugs of choice. I confess a fondness for it myself."

"I'll also admit to sugar and whiskey," Evan informed him. "But, as I believe you know, the opioid thing was never a dependency with me. And as far as your hospitality was concerned, I was happy not to over-stay my welcome when I was in your care."

Wilmer actually chuckled. "Your discharge — or shall we call it *escape?* — was something out of the movies, from what I heard. I wish I'd been here to see it." Then he laid on the sincerity when he added,

"You know, none of us wished you harm. We were simply misinformed as to the reasons for your admission and your condition at the time. If you came here seeking an apology, you have it."

"What's past is past, Dudley, if I may be so familiar. Griggs reminded me you guys thought I was addicted to opioids. I hope by now you realize you got it wrong. We know each other well enough. How about you answer my original question?"

"We don't have anything to hide. And if by sharing information with you now, that might prevent unnecessary legal action, by all means, let's be frank and forthright with each other. This institution has no agenda other than improving the health, welfare, and quality of life of our patients — or clients, if you will. That was equally true when we had you here."

"Can we stop rehashing my past? What happened with Luke and Melissa? And where is she now, and what's being done for him? And where is her baby, if you know?"

The doctor folded his hands thoughtfully in front of him. "It seems you have several separate issues all tangled up there. Let's start with Melissa and these rumors of abuse."

"Yes, let's."

"Melissa came to us a year ago. The first week in June, as I recall. She'd shown repeated fits of temper and refusals to follow directions at Sisters of Mercy. To top it off, she was prone to unpredictable epileptic fits of varying severity. The condition can often be managed with routine drug administration, but in her case, her rebelliousness made everyone worry whether she'd cooperate with the course of treatment. Father Coyle judged her depressed, uncontrollable, and perhaps a danger to herself. There had been a suicide attempt, and that incident put her here — first on seventy-two-hour watch, then for admission after our evaluation confirmed she was at risk."

"Was she pregnant at that time?"

Wilmer hesitated as if asking himself which response would implicate him less. Then he admitted softly, "She may have been. You'd think we'd do pregnancy tests on admission, but we don't."

"Do you know by whom and the circumstances?"

"No," he said emphatically. "Nothing at all."

"Was she aware? Did she accuse anyone?"

"Oh, she was aware from the start. Presumably, it motivated the suicide attempt. She came in here on emergency, and we pumped her stomach." Then he said, "When she'd recovered and after her admission, her therapist encouraged her to share more about it, but Melissa was not forthcoming. She flatly refused to talk about it. She did seem traumatized."

"Who was the therapist?"

"Dr. Louise Stratton. No longer here. We have her writeups."

"She left on what terms? You were the administrator then?"

"I believe the doctor's severance was voluntary, but Dr. Arnold Terry was administrator at that time, and he's no longer with us either."

"Severance also voluntary?"

Wilmer's face went grim and he shook his head. "No. The board terminated his contract after the alleged incident."

"Reported to the authorities?"

He shook his head again. *"Rumored abuse.* No substantiation, but the board wasn't in a mood to take chances. One might quarrel with how they handled it, but this was all before my time."

"And this was the incident involving Luke and Melissa?"

"Yes."

"And have there been any such incidents on your watch?"

"Certainly not," Wilmer insisted.

"You're sure?"

He raised an eyebrow. "Have you heard otherwise?"

I'm not about to make allegations or tell Wilmer who told us staff has been messing with patients.

Evan asked, "What about DNA testing on the child?"

"It wasn't feasible to do until after the baby was born. But she gave birth at Sisters of Mercy, so we weren't involved. She flat out refuses to say who the father is, and they didn't pursue it. The whole matter was more their remit than ours, to tell you the truth. They have a prenatal clinic and midwives on staff. I believe they often admit unwed mothers when they are still expecting. They forbid abortions and promote adoptions — with a preference for Catholic families so the child will be raised in the Church."

"You discharged Melissa when — and why?"

"By April, she'd been responding to therapy, and she seemed manageable. Despite her prior attempt to end her life, she'd never suggested she wouldn't carry the baby to term, and the Sisters counseled her to go through with it. So we discharged her about a week before she was due, and I'm given to understand the birth at the home was uneventful. And, fortunately, the baby is healthy, no consequences of the mother's prior toxic intake."

"When did the alleged incident of abuse with Luke occur?"

"She'd been here just a few weeks. They bonded very quickly. Clients are permitted to have platonic relationships. We want them to develop emotionally, after all. But no holding hands, no kissing."

"Are you still Melissa's guardian?"

The doctor hesitated. Then he said, "I was, but no more."

"Because she's been returned to Sisters of Mercy?"

"No, because she has a new foster parent."

"And who might that be?"

"It's been handled through the Sisters, and I don't have the details." He smiled, and added, "But I believe she's very fortunate."

"Why is that?"

"Older fellow, a widower. Educated and wealthy. She'll be an only child, and she'll lack for nothing."

"Except she won't have her son, who I understand is being adopted by someone else."

"That's right. A well-to-do family, a good home. Catholic, like I said. You have to admit, she might not be the best mother."

"And why would that be?"

Wilmer grew sheepish. "It's not a clinical diagnosis, but the girl is something of a nymphomaniac."

"Because someone made her pregnant?"

"Do you know her?"

"Never saw her."

"I observed her behavior for some months. She's spirited is all I'll say."

I wonder how many other teenagers he knows.

Realizing there wasn't much more to be said about Melissa's character, Evan asked, "No further information on her or her baby?"

"None that I know of, I'm afraid. You might direct your inquiries to Father Coyle."

I'll have to let Jeremy deal with that guy.

"The priest and I are not on the best of terms these days. But I'll give it a try. What about Luke? What's being done for him?"

"As for Luke, we must make a distinction. If you want medical information, you'll have to speak with his father, but all he gets are summary reports. Case files remain confidential, and only clinicians with a need to know get access. But if you wish to continue to visit the boy, I believe Mr. Shackleton is pleased to have your help. You've had a salutary influence on Luke's attitude and behavior. He's cooperating, and that's a decided improvement."

"Yes, I want to see Luke." Before he got up to leave, Evan had to ask, "Do you have any information at all about where Melissa and her baby might be at the moment?"

Wilmer shrugged innocently. "None at all. Again, a question for Father Coyle."

"And this new guardian of hers? Anything more on him? Like where he lives?"

"They told me he's Armenian." Again, the smile. As if it couldn't be better news. "I'm told he has a rather grand spread somewhere in Europe."

MOMENTS AFTER EVAN had left Wilmer, the doctor received a call on his personal phone from Nurse Crandall at Sisters of Mercy. She informed him flatly that Father Coyle had died peacefully in his office, apparently of a heart attack. Wilmer asked her if she'd called 911, and she said no. There was no pulse, she said, and Sister Margaret had only found him just now, but the body was already cold. Not wishing to raise a stir, the Reverend Mother had instructed them to call Wilmer and not the authorities.

Wilmer knew this nurse was competent enough to know whether the priest was beyond help. Still, he wondered why EMS hadn't been called. At this point, he wasn't about to do it.

As both the convent's physician and St. Clair County's medical examiner, Wilmer knew it was his duty to respond promptly. But he knew enough about Coyle's dealings with his clinic, as well as with person or persons unknown, to want more information before informing Sheriff Otis.

SISTERS OF MERCY

MONDAY NOON

*W*ilmer pulled his Elantra into the driveway of the convent just eight minutes after the nurse's call. A weepy Sister Margaret showed him into Coyle's office, then quietly withdrew.

Wilmer was alone with the dead man. The administrator of Flat Branch Catholic Charities still sat diligently at his desk with his hands stretched out on the leatherette writing pad. An uncapped fountain pen lay near his left hand, and Wilmer recalled the fellow was a leftie. Only the sideward slouch of the torso suggested the body was lifeless. Also in front of him on the desk was an overturned bottle of angina tablets, amlodipine, its contents strewn across the surface as if the priest had groped for them in a sudden attack.

Wilmer donned a pair of nitrile exam gloves from his medical kit, then pushed back on the chest of the corpse to make it sit erect in the chair. With his right finger, he lifted the chin so the death mask of the face looked up at him. There was a glazed look in the partially open eyes and a somewhat stunned expression. Death must have been within the last hour or two because the muscles were still flexible and compliant. Rigor mortis had not yet set in. The pallor of the skin was pale and bluish. Nothing remarkable. There was a faint odor of feces, suggesting the muscles of the rectum had relaxed to release some of the bowel contents. Also not remarkable.

Wilmer cataloged these facts as evidence of a routine episode resulting in death by natural causes. This was the finding he dearly hoped he could assert. But he was surely in denial because the obvious exception was staring right at him, had been there at first glance. The sign was just too outlandish to register at first in his cursory examination.

On the priest's forehead, just above the bridge of the nose and between the eyebrows, was an ashen smudge. Two smudges, actually. The sign of the cross. But Ash Wednesday had been two months ago.

More disturbing — and this was the real shocker — were the marks on the forehead. A more inexperienced practitioner might have missed it, but a forensic man doing the autopsy would certainly remark on it.

Wilmer didn't need any more evidence that his worst fears were surely the cause of Coyle's demise. He was thankful that his medical kit included a blank Certificate of Death form. Using the priest's fountain pen, he completed it hastily, listing *myocardial infarction resulting in cardiopulmonary arrest* as the cause of death. He indicated via a simple checkbox that an autopsy was neither required nor suggested. He then phoned the ambulance — not the county EMS but the private service contracted to Myerson — and ordered the body transported to the nearest crematorium, which was in Butler. They would have no reason not to follow his instructions, but to make sure, he phoned Griggs, told him why they should both be worried, and advised him to escort the EMS team from the convent to the crematorium. The news of Coyle's presumed murder predictably upset the deputy, who asked the doctor whether he should inform Shackleton. Wilmer didn't offer an opinion, telling Griggs that now it was every man for himself.

Wilmer well knew that cremation was against Catholic doctrine. But as he left to get back in his car, he told Sister Margaret what he'd done and gave the excuse he had an urgent call back at the clinic.

He had three credit cards, two ATM cards, and his IDs in his wallet. He could get cash on the way, drive all night to put some distance behind him, then buy whatever clothes and toiletries he needed miles further down the road. He'd planned to go fishing for Walleye in Minnesota soon anyway, and Canada wasn't much farther. These days they could track a person, he knew, but if he ditched the car and was holed up in a cabin in the woods, just maybe they'd give up trying to find him. If he were going to stay away and avoid arrest, he'd need a better plan. But this way he'd have plenty of time to think.

After he set out, he called the Reverend Mother. He expressed his condolences to Bernadette, who had known about the father's condition and seemed sad but hardly surprised. When she predictably objected to his directive for cremation, he explained that this alternative, while perhaps not ideal, would save the convent at least two thousand dollars. Her silence told him he'd overcome her objections.

Having made the call and gone scarcely a mile, he pulled over to the side of the road, got out, slipped his phone under the left front tire, got back in, and drove over it. He got out again to throw the shards of the crushed phone into the ditch by the shoulder. When he was back behind the wheel, he took a deep breath, which came with a shudder, turned off the car's GPS, and headed toward the interstate.

GRIGGS KNEW ENOUGH about what was going on to be afraid for himself, but not much more. He knew that Coyle was involved with Wilmer and Bernice. And somehow it had to do with child custody, the Family Welfare Agency, and for-fee adoptions with kickbacks. Maybe even gray-market abortions, but he didn't know that for a fact. Nothing he'd done personally was illegal, he thought. And he suspected Shackleton was aware, if not involved, because there was not a pie in this county in which the banker didn't have one or more fingers.

But as for the deputy's boss, the sheriff, he was another guy who always found out what's what, at least eventually. There would be no keeping the circumstances of Coyle's demise from Otis, even if, as Wilmer must have intended, the incident got filed as a garden-variety heart attack.

Most importantly, Wilmer hadn't shared with him why he suspected foul play. And the deputy didn't want to know.

Griggs didn't plan to lose his job over this, and he didn't want to run. He knew enough about law enforcement's capabilities to appreciate that running was not an option. (He'd give Wilmer a week, if that.) So he calculated that he should go to the scene and handle the matter as routine. While the paramedics loaded the body into the van, he'd conduct a cursory interview of the witnesses. He'd then call Otis, brief the sheriff, and explain he'd be following the ambulance to the crematorium to make arrangements on behalf of the Sisters.

He'd have to call Richards to let her know they were blown. He didn't care for the woman, but he'd best tell her because she knew he was involved, and he could suggest she take a cruise or something.

He'd decide what to tell Shackleton, if anything, after he got the story at the convent. He'd collect the death certificate Wilmer said he'd left on the priest's desk, and he'd follow procedure on getting it recorded.

It made him uneasy that, in his bolstering the heart-attack story as cover, when and if the truth eventually came out, he could be charged as an accessory to murder. But his ignorance of the facts — including who was behind it and why — would be his defense. He was just a cop trying to do his job. If people had lied to him, well, it was an honest man's failure that he tended to believe the best in a person.

If he'd known the Feds were on the case, he would have realized there was nowhere for any of them to run.

But, worst-case scenario, he'd cop a plea and snitch.

A half-hour after leaving Myerson, Evan was about to call Sheriff Otis when his own inspirational ringtone sounded and he saw Chet was calling *him.*

The sheriff was furious. "Do I get clued in *now?* When did I *ever* say you could keep me in the dark until you felt like sharing?"

"I was just about to call you and —"

"And let me know what? That Father Coyle is dead?"

Evan couldn't get the words out. "Chet! What? How?"

Otis growled, "The nuns are saying he had a heart attack. But Wilmer was there *and the bastard left!* He's not at the clinic, and I'm thinking something he saw freaked him out. He summoned Griggs to the scene, don't ask me why. So, what am I, in the dark because I blend in? Meet me at the convent ASAP because I need to know every scrap of crap you've been hiding from me about this godawful shitshow!"

And that was the end of the stunning communication.

ON THE WAY TO OSCEOLA

MONDAY NOON

*E*van called Leon to tell him about Coyle and then picked him up in town, where he'd been using the Wi-Fi at the library.

Evan said, "Wilmer not only runs the clinic, but he's also the county coroner. And if he's freaking out, it's probably because he thinks Coyle didn't die of natural causes."

Leon thought a moment, then said, "And you told me you think Wilmer's implicated. Involved in the guardianship paperwork, maybe even with hospitalizing girls who get into trouble."

"That's right. And he said he didn't know the foster father, but he'd heard the guy has a villa in Europe. He wouldn't tell me more."

"No doubt in a country that doesn't extradite," Leon said. "Armenia, maybe Belarus. I've heard the coast of Montenegro is particularly nice. Somewhere a Russian might want to retire."

"Russian? That's a big jump — from the thugs who ran Melissa at the casino to some guy who wants to *adopt* her?"

Leon said quietly, "If the priest was murdered, that tells us a lot. Not only about who he was and what he was doing, but also about who wanted him dead and what's likely to happen next."

At a time when Evan was thrilled to be picking up pieces of the puzzle, Leon seemed to already have the whole picture.

What does he know that I don't?

"Are you telling me you've suddenly figured it all out? All on your own?"

Leon sighed and smiled. "I guess I better start by telling you who I am."

"Yes, I'd say it's time you stopped changing your story."

"I've told you the truth! I'm *not* FBI. I'm Treasury ATF — Alcohol, Tobacco, and Firearms. Where I was less than forthcoming was about the circumstances of our meeting."

"You tracked me down. Simple enough."

"No, I didn't. That's the miraculous part. I was never retired. I was on assignment to an ongoing investigation of ACH, which is a major offshore investor in the chain that owns the Twin Dragons Casino and Resort. Dmitri Churpov is the big boss of the holding company. The front organization claims to be Armenian, but those guys are ethnic Russians — mafia. Some of them were mustered out of the army, the goons who took back Chechnya and massacred civilians. They're not only cold-blooded murderers but also trained torturers. For their part, the Chechnyan separatists aren't angels, but as far as we know, their hoods are not playing games in your backyard."

"What does the ATF have on those Russians?"

"This is where our lines of inquiry converge, yours and mine. My partners in crime at the FBI have been onto Churpov for a while. As they do, they've been building a case, waiting to grab him for something they can prove in court that will send him away for a very long time. What none of us knew about until you dug it up was this local sex ring, which might look small-time but could be going on at every hotel in the chain. Now, it's a matter of which agency gets them first. You name it, these bad guys are in it. Money laundering, drugs, human trafficking. Any piece of it would be enough to throw whoever we can grab into Leavenworth and throw away the key. But the nastiness that has Treasury's panties in a twist is traffic in small arms to unauthorized buyers. I mean, messing with our money and corrupting our youth is one thing, but you go funding insurgencies and terrorists, we really get mad."

"So that's why you're here? And then, what, we met by accident?"

"Helluva thing. I knew you were in the area, and I had intended to look in on you. But when you picked me up in that rainstorm — brother, it was pure happenstance!"

"Or fate or karma or something."

Leon chuckled. "You'd know more about that kind of thing than I would. Call it angelic intervention, since you seem to think Naomi is still trying to tell you what to do."

"I don't doubt it. She planned to be a wife and mother. And she was going to start by being *my* mother."

Leon sighed, "If only." They exchanged a look.

Then Evan asked him, "This Churpov. What have you got on him?"

"We want him on the gun-running charges, not only to nail his ass for good but also to bust his supply chain, get as many of his vendors and his customers as we can. But it's hard to prove. The guy's a wiz at money laundering, and that's a coverup for all their sins. But now his involvement in the sex trade makes it all urgent. Who'd think we'd get him on child endangerment?"

"So it's not just that Melissa got caught up in that racket — *this creep is her new guardian?*"

"I told you I was going to pay a visit to Jack Nathan, pretend I'm an auditor. The guy has the spine of a noodle, and he caved right away. He didn't even check my credentials. I got a list of the students he placed in entry-level jobs at the casino. Including Melissa. He's getting an outsized placement fee from the hotel, and you can bet it's not because they need help in the laundry."

Child endangerment doesn't begin to describe…!

A shiver went through Evan's body. For a moment, he was having trouble keeping the car on the road. He flashed on the hands of some ugly criminal at Melissa's throat. He tried to banish the thought by asking, "And what about Mick Heston?"

"He'll be sharper than Nathan, a lot sharper. If they quit the sex trade at the hotel, as I suspect they will immediately now that they've been exposed, the place will probably look totally clean in every respect."

"So if they killed Coyle, does that mean he was involved somehow?"

"If the priest was murdered by those hoods, we can bet he was in on the trafficking. Whether he made it happen or simply allowed it — that's an open question. Maybe they killed him to silence him. Or he was standing in their way. Or he screwed up somehow." Leon took a deep breath and said, "Let me tell you about Dmitri Churpov."

Leon had been briefed on the contents of an FBI case file. When Evan heard the story, he could appreciate why his friend had warned him he was in over his head.

Here is evil. And he has a name. Every one of us, whether saint or sinner, caregiver or murderer, believes in our heart our actions are justified. We tell ourselves useful lies — fibs, white lies, partial truths, denials, heuristic fictions. It's the only way a human can survive from one day to the next without God's mercy.

ALDY, CHECHNYA

FEBRUARY 5, 2000

On this eventful date, Russian special forces based in St. Petersburg massacred more than sixty civilians and raped six women in the city of Aldy, a suburb of Grozny and the seat of the separatist government. Civilian houses were burned and looted. The atrocity, which Putin's government has never admitted was a war crime, became known as the Novye Aldi Massacre. During this campaign, Russians recaptured the city of Grozny, and the Chechen separatist Ichkerian regime fell.

The Russians' tactical decision to storm Aldy was largely symbolic, a message of brutality and oppression to come. Fleeing the destruction that had taken place during the Second Chechen War, most of the town's population of 27,000 had abandoned their homes. The remaining citizens numbered about two thousand, mostly old people who were too infirm or too stubborn to go. In the case of the Churpovs, being in the small number of the ethnic Russian minority, they may have risked staying because they thought the invasion would bring more settlers of their faith. They had always been on good terms with their Muslim neighbors, and they saw no reason to expect they wouldn't be able to seek new relationships in church.

Dmitri Churpov was twenty-two, in his last year of undergraduate studies in economics at Chechnyan State University in Grozny. Dmitri lived with his parents and three sisters in Aldy and rode the bus into town to attend school. This day was Saturday. The air was frigid. Rooftops of the town were covered with snow, the streets with ice. Early that morning, Dmitri's father Sergei had left the house before his children were up. He hadn't told any of them where he was going. His wife Marta asked why he was in a hurry to leave as she poured his morning coffee for him. He simply replied he had urgent business to discuss with the elders.

Since dawn, the sounds of exploding mortar shells had drawn closer and closer. Everyone knew the Russians were encamped around the perimeter, and shelling, although fearsome, had become more or less routine in recent weeks. The town's Muslims, which made up most of its population, had celebrated their holy day yesterday. The devout Eastern Orthodox, including the Churpovs, would be attending mass tomorrow. Today would have been a day for people to run their weekly errands in the marketplace, gossip with one another in the tea shops, or rest at home.

That morning, Dmitri intended to walk to the vegetable stalls in the central market with his youngest sister Eva, but even though the bombardment sounded far away, they stayed locked and hunkered down in their cottage. At the same time, about an hour after dawn, their father was planning to confront the invaders, hoping to tell them the war was over and his neighbors would be offering no resistance.

Sergei led a small band of elders toward the Russian gun emplacements atop a hill in the nearby Chernorechie district. Each of the two-dozen elders carried a white flag, really just a handkerchief or a scrap of towel. They waved their flags vigorously over their heads as they climbed resolutely up the hill.

As the rag-tag group was partway up the hill — about fifty yards from the soldiers' battery emplacement — a voice from the top commanded, "Halt!"

The elders immediately fell to their knees, heads down, almost as if they were kneeling in prayer. They huddled, shivering, wrapped in their warmest clothes, panting in the cold air next to the wet ground. These old men were pathetic, miserable, and already disheartened.

Sergei alone remained standing. He called up, "We come in peace! We are elders of Aldy! We come to tell you there is no armed resistance in our town! You are shelling our houses — killing innocents! This crime must stop! See our flags? We offer no resistance! The city is yours!"

The voice from the hill called back, "Come no farther! You've been warned!"

Low voices buzzed behind Sergei, pleading with him to retreat. Some of them began to crawl back down.

He turned around and beckoned to them: "Stand up! Stand up! Wave your flags high! If they can see, they won't dare shoot!"

Some held their flags up, but cautiously. Still, the soldiers must have seen them.

When Sergei turned around, as he took his first step toward the crest, an army marksman felled him with a carbine bullet to his chest. His countrymen, all observant Muslims who nevertheless respected this Christian — a Russian, no less! — pivoted, dropped their flags, and scurried back down the hill, keeping their heads low.

GROZNY

FIVE YEARS LATER

*A*fter his father's murder, now being the head of the family, Dmitri moved his mother and three sisters to Grozny, where there were more commercial business opportunities for him. He got a job as a teller in an international bank, and he settled the family together in an apartment downtown. His mother took a job as a cook in the ethnic Russian school her daughters attended.

Chechen separatists, refusing to accept a Russian dictatorship, were now conducting terrorist actions in Moscow, including placing bombs in the subway. Meanwhile, the Russian army was continuing its atrocities in Chechnya. The cessation of hostilities that Sergei had envisioned, along with any stability that might have come under Russian rule, never materialized.

On September 1, 2004, a gang of Chechen separatists armed with military weapons invaded the school, taking a thousand ethnic Russians hostage. They demanded that Putin order the withdrawal of Russian troops from a disputed region of their country. It was the first day of school, and the hostages included not only students and faculty but also proud parents who had come to celebrate the beginning of the new academic year.

The occupation of the school dragged on for three days, during which more than three hundred of the hostages — half of them children — were killed.

Among the victims were Dmitri's mother and all three of his sisters.

Dmitri was now entirely on his own. He didn't even have any extended family in the region, and he decided there was nothing for him in Chechnya. He emigrated to Armenia, where there was a large ethnic Russian population in an alliance with Putin's government.

Although far from a pacifist — and, by now, a cold pragmatist — Dmitri fiercely refused to take sides politically. Either way, he'd have to commit to life as a murderer. He was well aware that taking lives is a mortal sin, but seeing the pointlessness of his father's sacrifice and the senselessness of the slaughter at the school, he saw morality as a useless virtue. If the way of the world was murder, one might as well profit by it. He got a job as a financial analyst in Yerevan and worked his way up to portfolio manager for the wealthiest patrons, many of whom were mobsters. From that position, he was approached and recruited into the Russian mafia. His talent for manipulating banking transfers and currency trades had been noticed, and he became an expert in the practice of money laundering.

WHEN HE WAS A BOY, Dmitri had been an altar server in the church. Each Sunday mass, he'd wear the sticharion and assist the priest, a doddering old fool but harmless. Dmitri was even training to be a reader, which greatly pleased his mother, a point of pride she'd share with any neighbor who would listen.

In his training, he'd learned how to pray, after a fashion. He never felt the presence of the divine, and he could never point to any earthly result from his frail pleadings. But after his father died, Dmitri concluded that prayer was useless. And after his mother and sisters were killed, he abandoned worship altogether.

That is, he abandoned the church but not his faith. He was sure that God refused to hear him, but he never doubted the existence of the spiritual realm and its ghostly influence. He had personal proof that evil pervaded human affairs, and after the tragedies he'd experienced, he acknowledged its invincible power.

And, like the most superstitious peasants in his village, he believed that demons — the agents of Satan — were everywhere, all the time, exploiting every opportunity to lie, to conceal, to confuse, to embitter.

One night, a voice came to him:

You are mine. Serve me and you will lack for nothing. You will be invincible. When you die, you will rule at my side. But betray me, and I will strike you dead instantly and cast you into the Lake of Fire.

Thus, Dmitri Churpov made his deal with the devil. If he could not vanquish evil, he would submit to its domination, offer himself for employment, and delight in its works and worldly benefits.

Yes, there was an Evil Eye. It would be *his*.

ON THE ROAD TO OSCEOLA

MONDAY AFTERNOON

When he'd finished telling Evan about Churpov, Leon mused, "I wonder how unusual that story is. How many Russian hoods have become so cynical they have absolutely no morals, no sense of shame?"

Evan replied soberly, "And then here was a Catholic priest who was hardly a saint. But how about you and me? You've got to believe we share wounds with him. We lost Naomi. How did Coyle suffer? Who did he lose? And what special credential does our hurt give us? Are we wronged but righteous human beings? How are you and I different from Coyle or Churpov or from anybody else?"

Leon grumbled, "You and I think we know right from wrong. If we find ourselves in a gray area, there's the law. Okay, maybe you'd say the Bible. Even gang members have a code of conduct. It's how civilization works, how we manage in groups. Dare we say you and I are special because we still have some notion of justice?"

"This Churpov. Do you have any recent information on him?"

Leon pulled up a photo on his phone and handed it to Evan.

Evan studied the photo — a glamorous couple in formal dress at what looked like a gala social event. The guy was middle-aged, slender, and handsome in his tux. The beautiful trophy escort on his arm in a satin gown with gloves to her elbows was — *Melissa?*

"This guy is *him?* What's he doing with *her?*"

Leon nodded and answered, "That's his wife. Estranged."

"Wife? That's *Melissa!"*

Now it was Leon who looked totally confused. "What are you saying? That can't be Melissa."

"I've never met her, and I realize neither have you. But Loretta showed me a shot of her at the school fashion show. She was fifteen then. It's only been a couple of years. When was this taken? She certainly looks older here."

Leon was stunned. "I was showing you this because I'm sure this is Churpov and a woman by the name of Tatyana Bulganin, whom he married four years ago in Armenia."

Evan felt his stomach knotting up. "Wow. The resemblance is incredible."

"This was taken two years ago in Nashville. Since then, the wife up and left him. And she disappeared. Whether he had her killed or she ran away, we don't know."

"Is he… delusional? Surely he can't think he's *found* her?"

"No, I doubt he's unhinged enough to confuse one for the other. He couldn't keep control of those operations for long if he was wacko. His bosses would take him out. But now we know why he's got to have Melissa. She's the next best thing. Either he wants her for his bed — or to make her life miserable. Or maybe both."

"Torture?"

"Think about it. A guy like that is a sociopath. He can't punish his wife. But he could hurt Melissa, and it would feel a lot like revenge."

"Maybe we don't have to think the worst of Coyle. Maybe, like you said, he found out how sick this guy is and stood in their way."

"In the world of hoods, when they kill one of their own, it sends a message. It's a lesson to other insiders about the price of disloyalty. Or incompetence."

"So, are we sure Coyle had to be *in* on it?"

"They don't do that to outsiders. And they don't make mistakes. No matter what the medical examiner finds, Coyle's accomplices will assume it's murder. This was meant to be loud and clear. Like a public hanging. As if to say, 'This guy fucked up, and we're taking his whole operation down.' They'd know the Feds would understand the message too, which means whatever network the priest was involved in is blown. Like I say, there won't be any sex workers at the hotel. These guys won't be sticking around."

"Network?"

"Here's how I'd guess it worked: Coyle was selling girls into prostitution at the casino, by way of Jack Nathan and Mick Heston. When there were mishaps like drug overdoses or pregnancies, Bernice Richards got involved. They'd shove the girl into rehab or send her back to the midwives at the convent, then work with the Family Welfare Agency to get custodial rights and adoptions done quickly — and legally. After all that, if the girl cooperates, she could be back in the trade. When she's older, she could be a house mother. But if at any point she won't go along, she might have an unfortunate accident — another overdose, say."

"But Melissa got special treatment."

"All because she has the misfortune to bear a strong resemblance to Mrs. Churpov."

"She has to be in danger, and we have to find them!"

"Danger, certainly. I expect she's alive, perhaps even being treated well. But if she doesn't cooperate — if she's as rebellious as they say she was — she'll come to wish she were dead."

A squad car was parked in the convent driveway. Evan knew Wilmer drove a new Elantra, but it was nowhere to be seen, nor was there a van for removal of the corpse. As they got out of the Fiat, Leon said, "For now, when we're in there, introduce me as your friend."

TWIN DRAGONS RESORT

A YEAR AGO

ne morning at 11 a.m. — it was the Fourth of July — Melissa received a text from Natasha:

Prince Calaf top flr 1 pm on time is late early is on time

This had to be Vasili! She'd been waiting for more than a month. And having been off her pills for most of that time, she was still on the upward spiral of a manic phase. Now she was exhilarated.

Her dreams would come true now!

She showered, perfumed, and powdered. As she put on her face in the mirror, she turned the thermostat down so she wouldn't sweat. She was careful not to go too heavy with any of it. Hers was a natural beauty after all. She might be mistaken for his mistress, but never a hooker.

At half-past noon, Stan, the security muscle who often carried her massage table, gave a polite knock on her door. She opened cautiously, leaving the chain on. He simply asked if she'd be ready and told her to meet him at the elevator on this floor in twenty minutes.

She dressed in her most ravishing silk sheath with pale, sheer stockings. So she wouldn't be conspicuous on her short journey upstairs, she wrapped herself in her plush bathrobe with the entwined dragons crest on the pocket. She slipped her feet into her trainers. She packed a gym bag with her heels, makeup kit, and even some lightly scented lube. She had a last-minute pang of regret about not packing condoms, but she didn't hold onto the thought.

Stan was powerfully built with bronzed skin and jet-black hair. As she approached him standing dutifully with the folded massage table at the elevator, she wondered why she'd never asked him to coach her in the gym. He must work out.

As they waited for the car, she asked him, "Are you an Indian?"

He laughed, "Like from Mumbai or from Standing Rock?"

"Sorry," she said. "I guess I should know more about you by now. You're, what — Osceola?"

It stood to reason. Osceola was the name of this little town where the Twin Dragons had been erected on land adjoining what used to be the only boat ramp for miles around. Truman Lake would need to attract a whole lot more customers in the years ahead to catch up to the Lake of the Ozarks, now booming with its retiree residents and weekend tourists. And both destinations weren't nearly as developed as Branson — or Vegas. (She'd skip over all that — straight to Hollywood!) Still, on this national holiday, the marina was jammed with overpowered cigarette boats leased by rich party animals from Up North.

She was glad she'd thought of the robe. The elevators might be jammed. But no one else would be headed for the penthouse.

Stan laughed again. His low voice was commanding, but not at all resentful: "Melissa, there's a hole in your high-school education. Osceola isn't a tribe. He was a person, a Seminole in Florida. Before the Civil War, the locals here renamed their town for him because they thought he was a hero. The newspapers told how he stood up to the government, and they were Rebel whites who vowed to do the same. Me and my people, the NiuKonska, are what's left of the Great Osage Nation — the People of the Middle Waters. All the land in these parts used to be ours."

She bowed her head and admitted softly, "I'm sorry. I got a D in world history. U.S. would have been the next year, but I had to drop out."

He smiled. "It's okay. Just having fun."

She was trying to make a joke when she replied, "No, I'm glad you're on my side. Do you have any idea who this guy is?"

"Nope. Just that he's a big boss and you do what he says." Then he turned to her and added, "But if he tries to hurt you — if you get so much as a hint it'll go wrong — you got your pager?"

She nodded, a bit freaked that he thought it might be necessary.

"You hit that button, I won't be far away."

The elevator door opened on a housekeeper, who was wheeling a bin of fresh towels. They were glad to ride up with a member of the staff.

VASILI WAS STRIKINGLY HANDSOME, just as she'd expected. Custom-made black serge suit, white silk shirt with diamond-studded cuff-links, and shiny Ferragamo slip-on loafers with black silk hose. On one wrist, a Rolex. On the other, a bracelet of amber worry beads. He was seated at an ornate cocktail table near an expansive window that looked out onto the marina and the Osage River. He was sipping from what looked like a glass of ice water, but later, when Melissa caught a whiff of his breath, she would realize it was vodka or a vodka martini.

His hair was dark, his face lined and chiseled — but not with age. Perhaps with care or hardship. Perhaps with cruelty. His features tended toward that perpetual sneer of Natasha's — as if he were reacting to a bad joke or an unpleasant smell.

But his voice didn't have a trace of an accent. Or anger. He spoke like someone on TV. His instructions were not requests or questions, he recited facts. But she'd seen so many movies and scanned enough fan pages to know he wasn't some big star. He might be corporate or a gangster or both.

"Please, sit," he said to her and gestured to the chair across the small table from him. It was a deep, resonant voice — like Stan's, but without the kindness.

Stan was standing just inside the door, still holding the folded massage table. "Set it up?" he asked the boss.

Vasili shook his head and waved Stan out of the room. He left immediately, taking the table.

Melissa set down her gym bag. Before she sat, she took off the bathrobe, laid it over the back of her chair, and slipped out of her trainers.

She pointed to the bag. "I brought heels," she explained.

He gave her a sardonic smile. "For dancing, maybe? Not today."

He gulped the rest of his vodka. "You want a drink?"

There wasn't a bottle on the table or even a glass. "No," she said. "It's okay." Then she wondered whether this was his first instruction and she'd failed to comply.

"Pretty dress," he said, wiping his mouth. "Please, stand."

She stood up, pushing back the chair.

He got up and walked slowly around her. It was an appraisal, not unlike the way Oleg had looked at her.

"Amazing," he muttered. "Remarkable."

She smiled back at him, thinking it was a compliment.

Then he said, "Allow me." And he stood at her back, unfastened the dress, pulled on the spaghetti shoulder straps, and let it slip down over her ankles. She was wearing lacy, crotchless panties and no bra.

He ran his hands over the tops of her shoulders and along her sides. She had a few beauty marks on her back, and he touched each with the tip of his finger as if noting its size and location. Then he glided both hands over her hips. He grabbed her upper arms gently and turned her around. Looking intently at her body and never in her eyes, he cupped her breasts — a judgment of size and shape — and lightly pinched the body fat around her middle.

There was nothing sensual in his touch. He was assessing merchandise.

In fact, she couldn't know but had an inkling, he was comparing the warm reality of her with the cold memory of someone else.

When he took her, the experience was brief and passionless. He bent her over the back of an upholstered chair. His thrusting was mechanical. He might have been inspecting an automobile. Was the upholstery supple? The sizing of the bore well-matched to the length and girth of the shaft? The fit tight but not restrictive? The lubrication automatic but not so fluid as to inhibit a desirable degree of friction?

He took a minute, maybe two. He didn't want more. She got no pleasure from it.

Through it all, he hadn't undressed. He zipped as he stood up and offered, "Use the bathroom if you like."

She didn't bother. She didn't have to be told he didn't want her to stay. She avoided looking at him as she tied her bathrobe, picked up her bag, and walked out the door of the sumptuous Prince Calaf Suite.

She didn't start to cry until she saw Stan waiting for her at the elevator.

SISTERS OF MERCY

MONDAY AFTERNOON

A deputy Evan didn't recognize stood at the portal of the convent. He stopped Evan and Leon with a wave of the hand.

Evan explained, "I'm Reverend Wycliff. The sheriff asked me to meet him."

"The sheriff is on his way," the officer said. "You'll have to wait for him out here."

"How about Deputy Griggs? Is he inside?"

"Come and gone."

"And Dr. Wilmer?"

"Here earlier. Called back to the clinic, they say."

The deputy turned to Leon. "And who would you be?"

Leon reverted to his mild-mannered insurance-man persona and simply stated, "Designated driver. I was almost his brother-in-law. Long story."

The cop was not amused.

Leon turned back to Evan and confided, "For now, I'll just hang around outside. If you can find the Mother Superior, now might be a good time. I'll catch up with you later, and we can tell the sheriff why it's urgent he help us find Melissa."

Evan turned to the deputy and asked, "Perhaps I could have a word with Reverend Mother Bernadette?"

The deputy waved him in, saying, "Second floor to the left. The other rooms are off-limits, you understand? If you weren't who you are, no way I'd be letting you in."

Who does he think I am? A man of the cloth? A friend of the sheriff? The local guy who can work miracles?

Leon asked the deputy, "You wouldn't have a smoke?"

Leon will open this guy up like a can of beans.

EVAN WAS WEARING his coat and tie, which he hoped would be sufficient credentials for the preoccupied nuns to assume he should be there. In the reception area and in the hallways, he walked past several of the sisters, mostly middle-aged and wearing traditional black-and-white habits. In recent times when other orders were seen more often in street clothes, he'd heard the Carmelites wore their habits faithfully. They called their manner of uniform dress their *eschatological witness,* meaning it advertised their mission in the world and their role in it. Today, these nuns walked swiftly and quietly with their heads down. Evan wasn't sure whether this behavior was the norm for their order — or whether the shock and grief of the fateful morning had them longing to be not only meek but also invisible.

He found the Reverend Mother in her office on the second floor. Hers was an unremarkable cinder-block cell with the same institutional austerity as the Myerson counseling room. Bernadette's head was bowed, and he could see that her Bible was open on the desk in front of her. Her habit was distinctive, slightly more ornate than the others, but just as austere. She had a lined face and pale gray eyes framed by those wire-rimmed glasses so characteristic of yesteryear's school matrons.

Hmm. Whatever passage she's reading is in the very back of the book.

As Evan appeared in her open door, she adjusted her glasses as she looked up from her reading. She didn't open her mouth. She just folded her hands in front of her and stared at him. Her look was neither pleading nor threatening. It was a sincere, questioning look — as though she expected Evan had answers rather than questions of his own.

"Sister, I'm Reverend Wycliff — a friend of Loretta Benton and the Shackletons. May I come in?"

The open expression on her face didn't change as she beckoned for him to sit down. She requested, "Please close the door," and he did. Then Evan smiled nervously as he eased himself into a chair.

Unsure whether it was appropriate, he offered, "My condolences."

Hmm. No reaction.

"Some people call me Preacher," he explained, "but —"

Now her eyebrows rose slightly. "You're the one who was inquiring about Melissa Benton. And the word around town is you're a faith healer." She was stating a fact, not a judgment.

"Gossip has a way of distorting the truth way out of recognition. I don't claim to work miracles. Of any kind."

"Would that you could." She bowed her head and spoke quietly to her hands, "You know they took Melissa. I assume that's why you've come." She looked up at him and added, "With what's happened, there's no reason not to be forthright. I apologize if I seemed evasive on the phone. As I told you, the Father managed our business affairs."

I'm going to take a chance here.

"The sheriff told me to meet him here. I don't know whether I should be saying this, but I believe he has some suspicions about how Father Coyle died."

"It wasn't his heart." This was a statement, not a question.

"Perhaps not. I suspect there will be an investigation. Sheriff Otis is on his way here."

She pursed her lips, not as though she were annoyed. More like she was disappointed. She said, "I realize now I should have been more attentive to everything Father did."

"How do you mean?"

"I'm sure I don't know all of it. But I was aware that he knew how Melissa Benton had gotten into trouble. Yesterday — actually, while you were here meeting with him — a man named Oleg Olachek came here with a power of attorney and custody papers, and he took Melissa. She had just suffered an episode, and I was concerned she was leaving us too soon, before we were sure she was stabilized."

That ambulance! What an idiot I am!

"Where did he take her?"

"I don't know." Then she said meaningfully, "Very likely Father Coyle knew." She sighed. "There isn't much to say about what happened this morning. It was all over so quickly. I've already told Deputy Griggs."

"Would you mind telling me? Perhaps we can be... forthright?"

She didn't mind the implication. "I was here in this room after I'd had my morning cup of tea. Sister Margaret was sitting at reception. What I know I got from her. Father told her he was expecting a courier, and sure enough, a fellow walked in with a briefcase. He was in Father's office a very short time, no more than a few minutes, and he left abruptly, carrying the bag. Father's door remained closed, and when he didn't come out for lunch, Sister knocked, got no answer, and went in and found him." She looked up almost apologetically and added, "They say we must have security, but we don't. Father wouldn't have it. But whoever could imagine something like this?"

"So you don't think he had a heart attack?"

"No. No, I don't. Oh, I suppose the fellow could have upset him. But Father was not easily provoked. He did have heart trouble, though. Those men, those evil men. Surely they knew, and they have their ways."

I'm sure they do. Which is why Wilmer freaked.

"So did you tell Griggs you think it was murder? What did Wilmer say?"

"No," she said reluctantly. "I haven't shared my suspicions until now. I didn't speak with the doctor when he was here, and I understand he had to hurry back to the clinic. I'm grateful to have this opportunity to speak frankly to you. At first, I didn't want to assume there was a connection. But if the people who killed Father are the ones who've taken Melissa, I'm so afraid for her. You see, I believe the courier had come to take the executed copies of Melissa's guardianship papers. Father had been fretting about them. He actually refused to sign them when Mr. Olachek was here. It was something to do with our expenses not having yet been reimbursed. But, you see, all this is only a guess on my part. I usually don't concern myself with such matters." Then she added, "I trusted Michael — Father Coyle," and the tautness of her lips told Evan she knew she'd made a mistake.

Evan tried to keep the emotion out of his voice when he said, "I think we can assume Melissa is in some danger now."

The Reverend Mother nodded soberly and said, "We sent her away with the phenobarbital Dr. Wilmer prescribed. She'd calmed down, and she went with Mr. Olachek without assistance."

Where did she think she was going? Did she know the guy?

Evan was anxious to tell the sheriff, but another question had been dogging him.

Do these nuns believe Melissa is possessed by the devil? And if they do, is that why her baby was taken from her?

But he didn't want it to sound like an accusation. Instead, he began by asking, "Were you in charge of Melissa's care when she lived here?"

She nodded. "The dormitory has a house mother, Sister Monica, and she reports to me. And we have a private-duty nurse on staff, a layperson, Elvira Crandall."

Evan confessed, "I've never met Melissa, but her sister Loretta has been worried sick, even before today. You may know that both mother and baby were extracted by force on Friday morning from Loretta's home by child welfare. I was told they brought Melissa back here, but I haven't been able to learn where they took the baby."

Bernadette spread her hands, indicating she didn't know either. She sighed, "I try to know all our girls — as well as they will let me. Melissa has always been a troubled soul, as I'm sure you know. Father Coyle saw to the baby's adoption, and he didn't share his reasons or any of it with me."

"Do you think his decision had to do with Melissa's epilepsy?"

"No."

PREACHER FAKES A MIRACLE

"Her sister seems to think some of the nuns here believe the girl is possessed by demons."

"Reverend Wycliff —"

"It's just Evan."

"Mr. Wycliff, then. I'm acquainted with Reverend Thurston — not well, mind you. But I know him to be a decent man and a God-fearing pastor. But I wouldn't expect either of you to know anything about Church doctrine on the subject of demonic possession or evil."

"So, please. Help me out. Could that be why they took Melissa's baby from her?"

Marking her place with the black ribbon bound into its leather cover, she closed the Bible meticulously as if she were about to begin an academic lesson. She looked Evan in the eye, perhaps wondering whether his request was sincere. Then she said, "It's wrong to assume that we're horrified of Satan and his familiars — or that we condemn the unfortunate people who are possessed. The patristic scholars, including St. John Chrysostom, drew a sharp distinction between possession by evil spirits and the deliberate choice to do evil."

"Which would you say is true of Melissa?"

"Both, sadly."

"I'm not at all sure what you mean or how it might affect how you'd... care for her."

"Contrary to what laypeople and even some parishioners might think, a person who is possessed by demons — mentally ill, if you will — can't help being so afflicted. Traditionally, the Church has taken these people in, ministered to them, and even admired them."

"Admired? How so?"

"Because — and this is not only in the patristic literature but also borne out by my limited experience — the afflicted often bear their infirmities with grace. Even cheerfulness. What's more, they don't blame God for their fate. Oh, they may curse their caregivers, if they do at all, only rarely, when in extremis. In short, we have to admire how they bear their crosses."

"Do they then deserve their afflictions?"

"That is not for any of us earthly beings to know."

"So I believe you're saying Melissa's epilepsy is an affliction not of her choice. And you don't think it makes her evil?"

"Her fits are evidence of the presence of evil. But, no, any wrong she might do as a result would not be deliberate."

"You realize, she was under medication. And that epilepsy is a clinical condition having something to do with an imbalance of chemicals in the brain."

"What you have described, which I don't doubt, is simply the mechanism by which the person is possessed — a symptom, not a cause. It might be desirable and beneficial to treat symptoms with drugs. But doing so will not remove the cause."

"You said Melissa has both — an affliction and, what, a choice?"

"She often chose not to take her medication but to lie and say she did. And she ran away. More than once. She didn't choose to go work at the hotel, but she may have allowed herself to be abused there."

"You *knew* about that?"

"I *suspected*. As you can imagine, I fear the worst now."

"Are you're saying those are the acts of a sinner? Not of an insane person?"

"Mr. Wycliff, those of us who are not saints are *all* insane. We make terrible choices time and again, thinking we can improve our lot on our own by the effort of our human will. I do this. Repeatedly. So do you. So did Melissa. 'For all have sinned and come short of the glory of God.' You know it."

"I assume she showed no desire to repent."

"We prayed for her. And we prayed with her, when she would stand for it. Hours and hours. Day after day. But the poor girl is a slave to her passions. That part of her is an evildoer."

"I see. You said you don't know where the baby might be. Do you have even a wild guess about where Melissa might be? When I leave you, I'll work with the sheriff, and now we'll get some action."

"Sadly, I don't know. I pray for her return to our care, perhaps to the clinic, if need be. I pray for her repentance and for relief from her suffering. Believe me when I tell you, I wish we could have done more."

"Sister, I appreciate your candor. And I know you must have tried everything you could to help Melissa." Evan feared he'd overstayed. He really needed to get downstairs and confront Otis. He hesitated, then said, "But as long as we're being frank, I'll ask something more."

"You understand Sister Margaret is the only one of us who actually witnessed anything. I don't know why Deputy Griggs had to be here. Dr. Wilmer had to rush away, and I believe the deputy is helping by handling the arrangements."

None of that makes sense, but first things first.

"What I want to know is more… personal."

"I'll try to answer. But you must know our personal lives are totally unremarkable."

"When I came in, your eyes were dry. They are still. I met with Father Coyle that time, but only once. His manner didn't exude compassion, as I must say you do. In fact, he seemed hard-hearted. You must have worked closely with him, and I'm sure you're in shock. But you're not grieving."

She sniffed. "He's with God now. As I said, 'For all have sinned.' To which we must affirm, 'Judge not that ye be not judged.'"

Evan decided to proceed cautiously but went on to ask her, "This gangster who did this, or had it done. And who's taken Melissa. The authorities think they know who he is. And one of their rackets may prove to be forcing some of your girls into prostitution."

Okay, we're not hinting around about it anymore.

"I preferred to think Melissa and some of the others found a wayward path on their own. Being in denial is another sinful choice we all make. But this crime confirms the worst."

She'd already said as much. Evan didn't expect to hear more. He was about to get up to leave when she added, "I suppose the reason I refused to face the truth was because I feared the state would close us down. If it's as you say, it will be a despicable scandal, and historically the Church has not provided adequate financial support when convents are closed and nuns are forced into retirement."

Evan got up slowly, hoping it seemed respectful.

I doubt if she's told anyone what she just admitted to me.

He gave her a courteous nod as he said, "Now I'll let you go back to reading the Book of Revelation."

She looked mildly surprised, seeing him with new respect. "You may know, for centuries the Church fathers didn't know what to make of it. They were not at all sure that it should be included in the Holy Bible, very much doubting such phantasmal writing could be the word of God."

"Yes, I do know. That book and Dante's poem were the subjects of my doctoral studies in divinity school."

She smiled. "Do you preach fire and brimstone?"

"I preach that God is all that there is. And I believe — if only as a practical matter — that Revelation is best regarded as metaphorical poetry. May I ask why you're reading it now?"

"I suppose the same reason some people listen to the blues when they're already sad. It reminds me how little we understand, how much will be revealed, of the worlds beyond this one."

Then he asked her, "Do you think Melissa will need an exorcism?"

She shook her head. "No, not at all. That's another popular misunderstanding. I suppose they get it from the movies. Invoking the name of God at any time, by anyone, banishes demons. It's the word that terrifies the ugly guest, not the speaker. Anyone with fervent belief can do it. We tried repeatedly with Melissa. But, you see, the trouble comes when the afflicted person welcomes them back. That's the element of choice and sin. She has to *want* to be rid of them. Do you see?"

"I believe I understand what you're telling me, although I'm not sure I agree."

"Perhaps you're a healer after all," she said demurely. Her look was sober, but her tone was ironic when she asked, "Evan, are you partial to gospel music?"

He replied, "I confess I'm obsessed with Roy Orbison, but for sure gospel is on my playlist. Especially on those Sundays when I miss church."

She smiled back and said, "I sometimes listen to a gospel-hour broadcast on the radio on Sunday mornings. The host is gone to her rest now, but Edna Tatum used to sign off with, 'You pray for me and I'll pray for you — because that's what God's people do.'"

He nodded gratefully and said, "Amen," as he slipped away.

~

SHERIFF CHESTER OTIS insisted on wearing his Stetson even in the heat. He'd taken it off and was mopping the sweat from his close-cropped steel-wool hair when Evan and Leon were escorted into the room. The administrator's office was just as the administrator had left it — except for the body of the administrator, which Sister Margaret told them had already been removed from the premises by Deputy Griggs and some ambulance drivers.

Otis nodded in the direction of Evan's escort, the deputy they'd met on the porch, and the fellow retreated dutifully back out of the room to resume his post at the front door. The sheriff mumbled, "I didn't like the man. But I didn't *dislike* him this much. Helluva thing."

"They said he had a heart condition," Evan offered. "You're thinking it was something else?"

Otis mumbled dismissively, "Might could be. But I got no evidence but this crick in my neck." Then, annoyed, he asked Evan, "And why is it once again you're the center of my attention?"

Evan replied, "Because Stuart Shackleton asked me to counsel Luke, and then Loretta Benton asked me to find her sister Melissa and her baby. Both of them were taken into state custody last Friday morning without due process. That's the errand your boy Griggs was on when he lied to you he was helping me. Now Melissa's been given over — from here, I'm told — to a foster father who just may be the gangster who wanted Coyle dead."

"Cripes, you have a talent, Reverend," Otis said. "And who's this guy?"

Evan replied, "My friend Leon Weiss."

Leon grinned, nodded sheepishly, and muttered, "That would be *Special Agent* Weiss."

Otis cocked an eyebrow. "Friend? So you're tight with a G-man? Now, I know I'm late to the party, but will somebody tell me why you're suddenly all chummy with the federal government?"

Leon said to Otis, "We're pretty sure we know who did this — that is, had it done — and he's a person of interest in an ongoing federal investigation. This murder of course falls under your jurisdiction. But you may not know that there's also an urgent matter of child endangerment."

"Oh," Otis mocked. "Did I say Coyle was murdered? We got angina pills on the desk. And he had a condition." Then he growled, "But the sister out front says he was fretting about some delivery. Courier comes and goes, nobody stirs. Next thing you know, they go in and find him cold. Then that lying sonofabitch Wilmer shows up, glances at the body, scratches out some bullshit death certificate, lights outta here like his ass is on fire, and my deputy scarfs up the paper. Then Griggs is gone like some scared perp, chasing the wagon taking the dead priest — to the fucking *crematorium?*"

"Not exactly kosher for a Catholic," Evan said.

The sheriff offered, "I'm Seventh Day Adventist a coupla times a year, and even I know that ain't right. And what was Wilmer thinking? They don't just burn a body without the paperwork. Even if the priest had no next of kin. So that's another reason I'm thinking the doc was in a big damn hurry. It just doesn't smell right. I ordered Griggs back to the barn where I intend to horsewhip him, and I turned that meat wagon around and told 'em to grab a coffee because they're hauling ass to Columbia where we can get a for-real autopsy." Otis harrumphed, "Evan, you know how I hate being the part of the horse goes over the fence last. You best tell me what you guys know, and damn quick."

Evan said, "The gangster who killed this priest is responsible for taking Melissa Benton out of this place yesterday under false pretenses. It was supposed to be a new, legal guardianship by a foster father, but Leon here and ATF have been tracking the guy, and his intentions are nasty. He's a Russian hood named Dmitri Churpov, he owns Twin Dragons, and he thinks Melissa is a ringer for the ex-wife he'd like to strangle."

Otis went wide-eyed, took a deep breath, then wanted to know, "Is *that* all?"

Evan quickly added, "Churpov's operation has been doing sex trafficking at the resort with the girls in work-study who were placed there from this convent by way of Mick Heston and Jack Nathan's fashion school. Father Coyle ran this end —"

Otis blurted, "Fuck, *no!*"

Evan went on, "And they probably took him out because he wanted his money or to shut him up. Bernice Richards and Dr. Wilmer at Myerson are also implicated because they dealt with the girls like Melissa who got into trouble."

The sheriff sat down hard, set his hat delicately in his lap, and mopped his brow again with his handkerchief. Then he huffed, "What's next? What else is going on in my little backyard while I'm all fat, dumb, and happy?"

Evan said, "I believe Stuart Shackleton is tied up in this somehow, and Griggs is running errands, but he might not be fully aware."

"Oh, shit," Otis spewed. "Some mornings it just don't pay to get outta bed." He stared up at them. "Well, where do we go grab this guy? If you're tracking him, I assume you know where he is."

Leon answered, "He operates out of Nashville. We know his man Oleg Olachek was here with a power of attorney to take the girl. They have a habit of making everything they do look like legitimate transactions. But they've all gone off the grid. That's not easy for anyone to do these days, but they've vanished. In fact, we can expect they've all gone to ground. Richards, Wilmer, Nathan, Heston — they're not pros, and we'll find them sooner or later. But in the meanwhile, there's the question of where they've taken the girl and can we get to her before she comes to harm."

Leon went on, "An assassination like this sends a message. The rats jump ship. It also tells us they're not worried about us. They must have an escape route, and you can bet they're on it. The good news for you, sheriff, is they'll be rolling up their network. The casino will go clean."

"I'll take care of Griggs. What about Shackleton?"

Evan pulled out his phone and called the banker.

Amazingly, the man answered.

All Evan said to the banker was, "Meet me at the clinic. It's kind of an emergency."

Shackleton asked, "Luke's had some fit? Is he in trouble?"

"He's in safe hands, they can handle it, but Wilmer's not there, and they need your authorization."

Another white lie!

"Dammit, I'm at least a half-hour away! Tell me what's going on!"

"Look, my battery's crapping out. I'll get there before you do. Just hurry."

Evan ended the call and refused to pick up when Shackleton rang back.

Evan remarked to Leon and Otis, "If he knows about Coyle, I didn't ask, and he's not saying."

MYERSON CLINIC

MONDAY NIGHT

*E*van ran back into the Myerson reception area, telling Lucille he must have left his phone in there somewhere.

This fibbing is getting to be a habit.

He wasn't about to tell anyone that he was sure Melissa had been abducted. Nor was he going to inform them that Wilmer and Richards were presumed missing, all because Father Coyle had just died under suspicious circumstances.

EVAN WAS on his own now at the clinic. Leon had left the convent with the sheriff. They'd be cooperating with FBI and ATF. If there was an action to be taken, they'd have to figure out where the gangster was holding Melissa. Even though Luke couldn't be specific about the location, Evan hoped that the boy might be able to give him enough clues to make a good guess.

Leon believed that Churpov wouldn't be waiting around for Olachek to bring Melissa to him in Nashville. And, if he was in the area, he might not simply jet off to Europe with her. Leon had told them, "Russians are chess players. It's all about strategy. It's all about not only what's your strategy, but what does your opponent *think* your strategy is? The second possibility is they want us to think they're desperate to get their boss and his — what is she, trophy daughter? — somewhere safe offshore. But what if they're not? With Feds watching, any form of aviation will be impossible. They'd love for us to waste time and personnel blocking roads, searching airports, grounding choppers and Gulfstreams. But maybe they have her stashed somewhere in plain sight — somewhere around here?"

"And why would he do that?" Evan asked.

"It would give Dmitri one last chance to check the goods before he buys. I suppose the original plan was for a legal adoption. But now that the casino operation is exposed, he'll be leaving, and soon. But I bet they lay low with her somewhere — somewhere we wouldn't think to look — and they keep her there long enough for the panic to die down. Maybe they even fake an extraction to make us think they're already home and dry. Then they slip out quietly in a week or two."

ON THE WAY to Luke's room in the adolescent residence wing, Evan found Clint escorting the sullen boy down the hallway. As the preacher approached them, Clint held up a hand and warned, "Bernice says you're not to see him. Maybe you can get her to change her mind, but I can't. She's not around, and neither is the doctor."

Evan came close, gave Luke a reassuring look, and asked the orderly softly, "Could I just have a word with him? It's kind of urgent."

Clint took a look around, then muttered, "Two minutes," and stepped away a few paces to give them privacy. But he kept an eye on them.

Evan asked the boy, "Luke, you thought Melissa felt she was floating. I was thinking they'd drugged her. But I wonder, what if she's on a boat? You know, the marina, the lake?"

"Yeah, a boat," Luke said drowsily.

They've given him something to mellow him out.

"That give you any ideas?"

"Sure," Luke said, then seemed to let it go.

"Like where? Where could she be?"

He said it as though the answer was obvious, "My dad has a boat. Fancy yacht. On Truman Lake."

"Maybe *he* took her there to keep her safe?"

Luke thought for a moment, then he said, "He didn't take her. The voice said he owns her now."

Clint came back and shoved them apart. "That's enough."

Evan called out, "Clint!"

"Not now. You wanna get me fired? Trust me, you need a friend on the inside. I'm just trying to do my job."

Evan shot back, "And is there a way of doing it without hurting people?"

Clint was serious and sincere when he replied in a low voice, "Preacher, believe me, I try every day."

As Clint was leading Luke off, Evan called after them, "Luke! Tell her we're coming!"

Clint shouted back, "The boy can't tell anybody anything!" And they turned a corner, out of sight.

He senses her feelings. But he didn't say whether he could pick up on her thoughts.

EVAN CAUGHT up with Stu Shackleton in the parking lot of the clinic. However, he didn't recognize the banker at first. The fellow rode in on a gleaming black motorcycle. He was dressed head-to-toe in black, from the Tony Lama lizard boots, distressed black Levis that stopped short of being ripped, and a leather bomber jacket with epaulets, topped with a full-face helmet covered by a dark-smoke shield that permitted no view whatever of the man's face. As Shackleton dismounted and strode over to Evan, the preacher felt he was being approached by some extraterrestrial stormtrooper.

As he drew near, the man pulled off the helmet to reveal a crop of sand-colored, tousled and sweaty hair. He must have gone without shaving since their last meeting, the stubble giving him a youthful, rakish look that complemented his athletic build.

"You do like your toys," Evan observed.

Shackleton cocked his head toward the bike and said, "Ducati Superleggera V-Four. Expensive as bikes go, but a fraction of the price of a decent sports car. And just about the only way I get my thrills these days. Edie won't ride with me, and if I'd let her have her way, she wouldn't let me ride either."

Pretty brash bragging about dating Bob Taggart's widow. Especially since you were doing her for years before he was dead. But now you know everybody knows, so you can be shameless throwing it up at me.

But all Evan said was, "How is she these days?"

"You know, after the memorial service, she went to her sister's in Arizona. Needed some time to herself, she said, and since you were handling the estate, she felt she had no reason to stay. She's back in her house now, and we intend to pursue the matter in the courts as far as it goes. We don't expect to prevail, but even so, she can expect a considerable benefit."

Backed by the banker and hoping to leverage her inheritance into one of his land-development deals, Edie was contesting the terms of Bob's will, to which Evan's deceased friend had made him executor, presumably because he didn't trust his wife.

"Just so," Evan agreed. "It's more or less out of our hands now, isn't it?"

"Good way to look at it," Shackleton said with a lame grin. "Let's have our talk in your car and crank up the air." As he unzipped his jacket, he added, "I'm sweating like a pig in this get-up."

"You don't want to go in?" Evan asked him. "Luke's been sedated. Evidently, the crisis is past."

It was a good guess, what I told him. It's just coincidence now I'm telling him the truth.

"I think not," the banker said. "What do you have to tell me, and what's so urgent you needed to go back in there today?"

So they walked over to the robin's-egg Cinquecento and got in. Evan started it up and switched the air on full. Then he said, "I was really hoping you'd come in with me. I think he'd want that."

"I doubt he knows what he wants. Or whether he's ready. I'm not.

If they don't need me in there, I'm not going in. I have a tendency to upset him."

Do I tell him I know about the boat? How can I get him to tell me whether he knows for sure that's where they're holding Melissa?

Evan decided he wasn't quite ready to share the news about Coyle or challenge Shackleton about the abduction or the boat. Instead, he led off with, "I'm beginning to think Luke has a serious emotional attachment to Melissa Benton. A lot more adult than a crush."

Shackleton looked irritated. "I told you, in his state, he can't possibly know what he wants, what he needs, or *who* he needs. The goal has to be for him to get stable. Find the right drugs, the right dosages. Then maybe he can maintain. I don't intend for him to be at Myerson forever. But I can't care for him now. With the right help, maybe someday. Then, there's my own situation. I have to get stable myself. There's too much uncertainty in my world just now. Stress. Risk. People who, if things go the wrong way, could be… dangerous. I can't involve Luke in any of that."

"Dangerous business partners? Are you talking about Dmitri Churpov?"

Shackleton gave Evan a long, appraising look. It was as if they'd just met and the banker were deciding whether having this guy's shaky business was worth the huge risk. Then he said, "You've gone way beyond the scope of your inquiry. There are schemes here you can't begin to understand, and it's not just that it's none of your business. You'd be better off not even knowing the name. You're getting in so deep I won't be able to help you if they decide you're a threat to them. Hell, I'm not sure I can help myself."

"Melissa's baby could be your grandson. Do you care at all?"

"What if he ends up like Luke? Or like her? Afflicted, cursed! All the money in the world won't make that hurt go away. I'm a man of faith, or I used to be, but it pains me to say she should have had it aborted."

Evan confided softly, "I don't pretend to have all the answers. And my life is no model. But I do believe all things happen for a reason. Pain and suffering — intense and awful as the experience might be at the time — is a wink, no more than a breath, in the drama. And death is no relief. It's we the living, breathing humans who have emotions and regrets — and the ability to act in the physical world. The angels envy us! We can *do* things! For all of Luke's suffering and supposed shortcomings, he has perceptions and spiritual gifts I'm only beginning to appreciate. I think he has a lot to give — to you, me, everybody."

"You're overthinking all of this, Evan. There are bad people who do bad things. And there's no one to stop them, no divine justice. Yeah, things happen for a reason. And the reason is that there has always been evil loose in the world, and you'll never be able to control it."

"I believe Father Coyle placed baby Buzz with adoptive parents. Did you have anything to do with that?"

"It seemed to be the best thing. You know they don't share that information."

He knows more than he's telling. But I have to believe the baby isn't in any danger just now.

"And I heard Melissa's being given over to a guardian. Churpov?"

"That's why there's no hope of her ever being with Luke. Even if they could both find ways to maintain. She's bought and sold. And there's nothing anyone can do about it."

Bought and sold? Just who was the broker? Coyle, probably. But who else? You?

"Do you feel any sense of responsibility? I haven't even met her, but whatever Luke has found in her, I imagine she's an exceptional being too. Worth caring about."

"I don't know her at all. It will break his heart, and that's a bitter pill."

If he knew about Coyle, he'd have said something by now. Maybe his partners in crime wanted him to be the last to know.

Evan took a deep breath, looked Shackleton square in the eyes, and announced, "Father Coyle is dead. Heart attack this morning, only the sheriff doesn't buy it. Could have been a murder, an assassination. Somehow the priest crossed Churpov. Now Wilmer has fled, probably Richards has too. Griggs might not know enough to be scared, but the sheriff plans to squeeze him dry. Now, I have to ask you whose side are you on? I think you know, at this minute, Churpov is holding Melissa — on your boat."

"Sorry about Coyle," he muttered. "Something of a shock. A rotten apple, that guy." He said this without emotion, but then his expression grew dark when he added, "They commandeered my boat, and it's a fucking outrage. Churpov has legal custody of her by now, and I had nothing to say about that. But with all that's happened, with the authorities involved now, I won't cover for him. And I have to admit you're right to be worried about the girl."

He told Evan about the *Namouna,* the extra security he thought they had, and where the boat was moored.

ON THE NAMOUNA

MONDAY NIGHT

*T*he guy in the suit had ice water for blood. Melissa guessed there was going to be a lot of talk before he subjected her to whatever came next. She still hoped it was a game. The guy wanted a mind fuck. Then maybe the other kind. Okay, as long as it didn't involve touching her with cigarettes or ice cubes. Or tweezers or pliers. Or sharps.

But he was certainly taking his time. He'd done hardly anything yet except sit at the edge of her bed and pose these riddles. By now, she knew she'd been onboard since Friday night, and she'd slept here — unmolested, so far. She wasn't tied down anymore, but she was being watched. And she was careful to cooperate. A guy they called Skip brought her meals to the room at first. Then they let her step out the door to take a seat at a table, where she dined alone. That's when she knew for sure she was on a boat, and a classy one, at that.

So here he was sitting at her side again. The sun was just going down. She was sitting up in the bed, wearing the clothes she'd arrived in, as he coached her. It was as if she was in the clinic again and here was a visitor like those doctors who did nothing but ask questions and take notes.

"I asked you *why*," the man repeated, drawing out his words, "and you refuse to tell me. But excuse me for beginning at the end. We shall start again. What is your name?"

"What is *your* name? They called you Vasili. Maybe that's not your real name. And maybe I should care. You could be the father of my baby. You must know about Buzz. And where is *he?* Where have you taken him?"

He was irritated again. "Would you not try my patience and answer *my* question?"

That voice. The Russian name, but the flat tone of a newscaster. Is this role-playing? Does she get to pick? No, better play it straight until she knows that's not how he wants it. "Melissa," she admitted quietly.

"No!" he growled. "Try again." His anger signaled she wouldn't get more chances to get it right.

She had a good guess what to say next. "I can be whoever you want me to be."

He calmed down. "Just so."

When he didn't say more, she gave her voice an edge. "Don't make me guess. You and I both know you're the boss."

"Tatyana. Your name is Tatyana."

"Wife or mistress?"

He didn't answer.

She guessed again. "Wife, then. I cheated and left. Or left and cheated. Which?"

"You lied. No one *lies* to me!"

"If I said I loved you, I probably did. At the time."

"Now I'm hearing something like the truth."

"So, what's going on here? And when are you going to give my baby back to me? Or is he *our* baby? Did *she* give you a baby, or was that another disappointment?"

He had to think about this. Then he said, "I have to decide whether you're worth keeping."

Melissa was desperate to know where this was going. Keeping both of us? Keeping for keeps? Or just keeping alive?

She had to believe Buzz would be no use to them dead.

Unless he decided to kill her first.

TAGGART HOME, STOCKTON

MONDAY AFTERNOON

*E*die greeted Shackleton with a kiss, but it was little more than a peck. "You told me this would be temporary," she said, too quietly.

Thinking her unusual subtlety sounded like either alarm or annoyance, the banker asked, "What's wrong?"

"He's sleeping!" she said in a hush. "He eats, he poops, he sleeps. It took me a while to get the formula so he wouldn't spit it up. Breastfeeding isn't exactly a possibility, you know."

Shackleton gave her a look as if to say, *Is that all?* Adding, "Can I at least come in?"

Bob Taggart's widow kept the stonework ranch home on Stockton Lake meticulously, as she did everything. But caring for a newborn had seriously disrupted this middle-aged woman's orderly routine.

"You'll have to make yourself comfortable in the kitchen," she said. "I put the cradle in the living room so I could keep an eye on him. But it's hardly necessary since he wakes every two hours and wails until he gets his bottle."

The granite-topped kitchen island with its premium Perigold fixtures was just off the wood-paneled, plush-carpeted living room area, and because Edie was usually cooking when she wasn't cleaning, she spent most of her day there. Some people find it tedious to cook for one, but she was sufficiently self-absorbed to take pleasure in it. She'd always make larger portions on the chance Stu would take time to stop by, but often the extra languished in the freezer until there was an evening when she was too exhausted to fire up anything but the microwave.

Stu sat, and she brought him black coffee right away, the sweetener already stirred in the way he liked it. Softening, she eased onto the stool beside him, setting her mug down on the counter in front of her. The cup bore the emblem ROUND TUIT in red block letters.

"I've always meant to ask you," he said, taking a gulp and indicating her mug, "what that means."

She glanced at the cup, not fondly but as though it were the only souvenir of a barely memorable vacation. "I gave it to Bob as a joke gift one summer. We were having the house redone. I had a long list of honey-dos for him, things he refused to pay the contractor for. He kept saying the usual, you know, "When I get around to it." So I shoved the mug at him on a Saturday evening after dinner, making sure I'd spiked the coffee with a double shot of his sour mash. He frowned at me, and I just shrugged and told him now he was out of excuses." She smirked, "It actually took him a minute to get the joke."

"Or maybe he just didn't think it was all that funny." Shackleton remembered how his Ann had hectored him, but sweetly, in her way, until she simply didn't know what day it was or what this man was doing in her house.

"For a long time there, when he was fretting over his aunt's will, he didn't think anything was funny. But he'd get with his pals, and they'd be yucking it up." She sighed. "Let's not speak ill of him. The plan was to get through the court case, then somehow you were going to put over some big deal, and we'd live happily ever after. But now you've parked the kid here, and all you've told me is it's some unfit mother who's over there with Father Coyle and we have to help them out. Okay, for how long? Stu, you're not giving me the whole story, and maybe you'll say that I don't want to know, but I do. This is over and above. The baby is adorable and all, but you and I both know I was never cut out for this."

Shackleton needed to change the subject, and, as much as the news was grim, he realized there would be no better time to tell her. "Father Coyle passed away this morning. Heart attack."

"Oh my," she said without emotion. "He wasn't a warm person, but I believe you respected him." She thought a moment, then added, "And he's the one who stuck me with Buzz. What happens now?"

"It's more like I volunteered you. And it actually changes a lot," Shackleton said reluctantly, setting his cup down and pushing it away to make the point. "Coyle was in over his head in a debt situation. And you know the Church doesn't give them all that much to keep the place running."

Edie began to realize the news about Coyle was the opener, not the story. She asked cautiously, "But how does this affect us?"

"I cosigned for the loans. Then unbeknownst to me, he refinanced them with some shady outfit. Now that he's gone, they'll be coming after me for it. I can't put that much together just now, but they're not the kind that listens to reason."

Shackleton must have figured it was close enough to the truth that his conscience wouldn't be bothering him, especially if he could convince her of his plan to keep her and the baby safe.

She was stunned. No one these days thought priests or bankers were saints, but she hadn't expected Stu would be involved with anything so foolish. "You mean crooks? Mob people?"

"Coyle might not have understood, but it's the gang with controlling interest in the hotel chain that runs Twin Dragons. And, yeah, Russian mafia."

She stared at him. "How could you let that happen? Coyle might have been clueless, but you're not. What do we do?"

"I'm invested heavily here. I'm a local boy, people trust me, trust the bank. We're involved up to our eyeballs in the hotel, the casino, and the marina. And the development plans we had for the area around your farm. Branson Two, you might say. I don't know if that can still happen. It was supposed to be our ticket to the big dance. But what I do know is there's no way out for me. I have to stand my ground. Here. There's nowhere for me to run."

"You know you're telling me — you're actually admitting for the first time — that you're as corrupt as they are. I always suspected you had some deals in the gray market, but I never thought you'd get in deep enough some thugs could order you around."

"These days it's a global financial system, all interconnected. Wall Street and the politicians and the sheiks and the mandarins and the African princes. You need a billion, you all have to draw from the same pools — the Great Lakes, the Black Sea. You turn on the tap, and the money flows. No telling who put it there, where else it's going. It's a resource. You don't ask questions until you begin to think it's poisoned. Then it's too late."

"Pardon me if I change the channel, but none of this relates. Why are you here, and what do you expect me to do?"

"I think it might be wise for you and the baby to go away for a while."

Edie gave Stu a hard look. "Back to my sister's in Arizona? I kind of wore out my welcome there after Bob died. I only came back because I still believed you were going to get the estate matters settled so we could go ahead with everything we planned."

He shook his head. "They'd find you right away at your sister's. I want to be absolutely sure you're safe. A friend of mine has a place in the Caymans. Gated compound, armed guards. It's beautiful there, white sand beach, crystal water, fully staffed. And there's a yacht. A sailboat so big you can land a chopper on it. Either all this will blow over and you can come back, or I'll find a way to join you there."

"What about *your* boat? Who would think to look for me there? We could sail away."

"There's no outlet from the lake. Anyhow, it's kind of in drydock," he fibbed. "And too close to home."

"This is serious," she said, this time without sarcasm. "And what's so special about Baby Buzz? When were you going to tell me I have to step up to this? As if I have a choice. You never told me his birth name."

He gave her a weak smile, "It's Robert. Bob."

"Oh, give me a break!"

"It's on the birth certificate. I didn't believe it, so I had it checked out. I had them run the DNA. He's Luke's son. Bob Shackleton. So both of his parents are… unfit."

She looked over at the crib and sighed. "So this is Bob. If my dead husband is watching us, he has a sense of humor after all."

WITH EVAN AND LEON

MONDAY NIGHT

"So, what's the next move?" Evan asked his friend. "If they're on the boat, you guys just go and arrest him, right?"

"The agencies agree now is the time to grab him. A team came in from KC last night. Problem is, it's two nasty situations combined — barricaded, armed suspect *and* a hostage situation. Procedure would be for the SWAT team to surround him, we establish communication — cell phone or bullhorn if there's no other way — and we have an ace negotiator sing him a song. We have a helicopter waiting onshore for evac, emergency or otherwise. We have rescue boats and divers in case anyone ends up in the water. It's all in that course 'Taking Out Bad Guys on a Boat One-oh-one.' But you have to be prepared to take losses, and the outcome will be by no means certain."

"And what if he refuses to deal?"

"We act as if he will, but we have to assume that he won't. Remember, we don't want him dead. We want him to spill his guts about his operations. But if we go in, someone's sure to get hurt. We have to make sure it's not Melissa, and that's where he's got us."

"When do you go?"

"You'd think nighttime, the cover of darkness, would favor us, especially with all our high-tech toys. Right now, we've learned he's out there adrift at anchor in the middle of the channel, and he has a three-sixty unobstructed view. He's got his own toys for seeing and hearing, and his protectors no doubt have high-powered automatic weapons. Maybe even a SCUD that could bring down a chopper. No, given that the first round is talk therapy, it might as well be daylight so we can see each other clearly. So we go in at dawn, just like some ancient battle plan, and at the end of the day, as the sun's going down, we make the decision whether to close in on him before it gets dark — even though it won't be a surprise."

"How do you think it will go?"

"The guy is arrogant and rich as anyone could hope to be. He's made himself a sitting duck, not to hide, but to put distance between us, give himself decision time. He might as well say, 'Come and get me.' Now, a guy like that will have an army of lawyers. So if we couldn't nail him on a crime of violence directly, the smart move would be to cave, let himself be taken, and let the attorneys find a way for him to wriggle out of it or skip. But with child endangerment, possibly even rape of a minor, he won't have an argument. International flight risk, no bail."

"Meaning he'll fight back?"

"I don't know. That's what has me puzzled. Why would he put himself out on that lake, hiding in plain sight, knowing when we show up his options are go to jail or take a bullet or drown?"

"Would he destroy himself rather than give up? Like some terrorist?"

"Nah, what would he be dying for? Freedom for Russians to pursue capitalist greed in the good old U.S. of A.? It's more like he thinks we won't dare touch him. And what has me worried is how he could be so sure."

"What are you thinking?"

"I hate to say this, but it wouldn't be the first time DOJ told us to back off a righteous case for reasons that made no sense. These guys have influence in the corridors of power. A sign of the times, I'm afraid."

"What if I could think of another way?"

Leon scoffed, "Are you going to pray us out of this? Work another miracle?"

Evan was serious. "Maybe. But I'll need help."

When Evan told Leon his plan, the man muttered, "Now that's one helluva Hail Mary."

LEON TOLD Evan he thought the plan was wacko, and he was strongly against the preacher going anywhere near the scene of the raid. But he admitted that the psychological insight on Churpov was an angle none of the Feds would understand or know how to exploit. Evan explained he needed to have a close estimate of the time when the gangster would know he was under attack — and where on the shore Evan should be so the amphibious team could pick him up.

Leon agreed but urged Evan to carry a sidearm, offering his own from the shoulder holster under his coat, which the preacher took reluctantly but had no intention of using.

As the light was fading on the day, Evan drove Leon to a pickup point where a Fed was waiting for him in an anonymous-looking sedan. Leon said he would be conferring with his fellow wizards, and no, he would not be the one to negotiate with Churpov. He admitted it would be a cute trick for him to convince the expert negotiator to hold off and react to unfolding circumstances, but he said his approach would be to simply stall any overt moves, which was to be their plan anyway.

For the first time in their relationship, Leon asked for the preacher's prayers. On the curb outside Taggart's Pharmacy, Leon stepped out of Evan's car and into the night.

Then Evan drove to Myerson.

ONCE AGAIN, Evan had to talk his way past Lucille at reception and then Clint at the nurse's station. He had an excuse about urgency, the need being all too real, but its description being another white lie.

Would that I could go to confession. It's getting to be a recurring vice.

Evan found Luke lying stretched out on his bed, staring at the ceiling. The boy didn't stir as the preacher entered the room and closed the door behind him. He drew up a chair, sat slowly, and leaned over until his face was so close to Luke's he could feel the boy's breath on his cheeks.

"Luke," he said softly, "can you hear me?"

"Sure" was the reply, but from a fog. Luke's eyes were glassy and remained focused on some distant point as if seeing through the roof and into the cosmos.

Is he drugged? What if I can't get through to him?

"Do you know who I am?"

"Sure." A minimal reaction.

"Do you trust me?"

"Sure."

"You know Melissa is in trouble."

Now with a blink, Luke was present in the room. "Yes, I've been telling you. She's upset, she's worried, she's cold."

Good, he's with me.

"I know a way you can help her," Evan said.

Luke pleaded, "I send her loving thoughts, but it's not enough."

"Let me ask you. When you link with her mind, you say you can feel what she's feeling. Can she also hear your thoughts? Can you send her a message?"

"I don't know. I can try. I tell her I love her, and I think she knows. But I'm not sure what she hears."

"Tell her now I'm coming to help her. In the morning. Close your eyes and clear your mind and take as much time as you need. Do it now."

Luke glanced up at Evan, seeing him clearly for the first time. It was a doubtful, worried look.

"Trust me," Evan said. "This is going to work. But I can't do it without you. And if she can't get the message, we're done."

Luke tried to smile, then closed his eyes. He remained that way for minutes in silence. In a short while, the boy's breathing became steady and calm. Then the orbs of his eyes gyrated beneath his lids.

Luke's eyes popped open wide.

"She's happy! She knows you're coming!"

No one is going to believe this, but I must!

"That's all for now," Evan explained carefully. "When I leave now, you can say your private things to her. Sleep tight, sweet dreams, sing her a lullaby. Tell her to trust, remain calm until daybreak. It would be good if she can get some rest."

"Okay," Luke said. "I feel so close to her. Thank you."

"Here's what else you must do," Evan told him. "Clint will wake you in the morning. Watch the clock in the hallway. When it's six-thirty, send her this message. Say exactly what I'm going to tell you. I'll be right there, where she is. And I'll handle the rest."

They were alone together in the room with the door closed, and they'd been speaking in low tones, but nevertheless, Evan leaned in and imparted the message in a whisper.

Some more drama won't hurt. He needs to know this is powerful magic, our secret.

As he left the clinic, Evan asked Clint to give Luke a wake-up call at six.

He explained they'd planned a sunrise meditation with the First Baptist teens.

Addicted to lying? Hey, I can stop whenever I want.

EVAN ASSUMED Loretta would be beginning her shift at Twin Dragons, but when he called her, she informed him she was at home.

"They fired me," she said. "It was some new asshole from corporate. Mick's gone, so I'm guessing they shit-canned him too."

"I've got a lot to tell you," he said, and she invited him over.

Leon won't let me tell her what's going down. But I have to assure her I'm doing all I can, that if this works Melissa will be out of danger very soon. Then we just have to find Buzz.

Then he thought, *Either this works, or it's on to the next life. I'm such a fixer here, my next assignment might be as an angel. Now, that sounds like hard work!*

~

EDIE HAD WANTED Stu to stay over that night, but he begged off, lying that he had a board meeting in the morning and needed sound sleep. True enough, he knew the baby's cries would wake him with infuriating frequency. He'd almost forgotten what it was like. Luke had been an only child, and Ann was his caregiver. When their son was a fitful newborn, she never once made Stu get up. But Edie would not be so generous. She would remind him sternly that taking on this responsibility had been his idea, so she'd insist he do his share.

But not tonight. He'd ride the Ducati to Osage Bluff Marina, where he'd rented a houseboat. He'd already cached everything he would need on board.

Griggs had tipped him off but said he wouldn't be any help. This friendly advice was as far as the deputy could go, and from then on, the banker would be on his own. But Shackleton didn't want or need the deputy's help, nor did he want the guy to have the slightest suspicion of what he intended.

This was something he had to do alone.

ON TRUMAN LAKE

TUESDAY DAWN

*J*ust before dawn, Melissa was roused from a dream.

The gentle voice called to her, and she knew it was Luke's. It was familiar and comforting by now because he'd been communicating with her last night as she was falling asleep. He'd made a promise, and now he was telling her what she must do.

She was surprised she hadn't thought of it before.

GRIGGS HAD TIPPED off Shackleton about the raid and its timing. The deputy was sufficiently embedded in the business of the sheriff's office — and, so far, sufficiently isolated from complicity in any crime — to know the Feds were planning to move on Churpov. They typically disdained local help, but prior notification was in order, not least because yesterday's preliminary autopsy results on Coyle's body suggested foul play, and the crime of murder would ordinarily fall to the county sheriff to investigate. Churpov was presumed to have ordered the hit.

The Byzantine relationships among the federal authorities were complicated in themselves. Having built the Truman Dam and Reservoir, the U.S. Army Corps of Engineers still controlled land use onshore. But it was the U.S. Coast Guard Sector Upper Mississippi River that handled federal law enforcement on the water — going back to the days of barge traffic on the inland waters before the erection of the two dams cut it off. And in the Churpov matter, the FBI, an agency of the Department of Justice, and ATF, an agency of Treasury, were no doubt having heated discussions about who wanted the gangster more. But for either of those white hats to approach within hailing distance of the *Namouna,* they'd have to hitch rides on USCG patrol boats.

Shackleton had an app on his phone that tracked the location of his yacht. Churpov couldn't very well order the crew to shut down the GPS or transponders. Doing so, especially on such a large and prominent vessel, would have the effect of summoning the Coast Guard. No, the Russian wasn't exactly hiding. Whether in Nashville or visiting his holdings elsewhere, he must know his movements would be tracked. And as far as having the Benton girl onboard, he'd contend his position was perfectly legal. By the sponsorship of Father Coyle and with the cooperation of Dr. Wilmer, Churpov would soon have the paperwork to attest to his legal guardianship. Sadly, he wasn't capable of caring for Melissa's child, and the unavoidable separation had been traumatic for her. By taking her on the yacht, he was offering her time to recover, making sure she was appropriately medicated and giving her the royal treatment she'd someday come to expect. And soon they'd be beyond the reach of all these persistent hounds.

The complication for Churpov, which Shackleton and Griggs appreciated, was the fact of Coyle's murder. By this time, the gangster must know that the priest was dead. And he would assume, wrongly, that the authorities believed the cause of death had been a heart attack, not an assassination. But the banker and the deputy knew the truth, for different reasons.

MELISSA HAD ALWAYS HAD warm feelings for Luke, and she thought of him often. She worried she'd never been able to do enough for him, and even though his caring could calm her worries, she had no idea what she could ever do or say to relieve his distress. She knew he had an inherited disease, as she did, and she knew those clinical names. There were medicines, and there were hovering doctors. But she knew as Luke did that the best medicines were like Band-Aids, covering the wounds but doing nothing to heal them.

She only had her intuition, but she was sure Buzz was Luke's. The lady shrink at Myerson informed her that on admission she'd had what they called a phantom pregnancy, *pseudocyesis*. The shrink explained it might have been because Melissa was carrying guilt about her encounter with Vasili (whom she didn't dare name) and feelings of shame about rape. She didn't dare let on to Vasili he hadn't made her pregnant that one time, although he might not care. But being possessive about Buzz might be one more reason he was keeping her alive, so she'd best shut up until she knew more about his motives.

Vasili knew enough about her, including the fact that she'd given birth. Here on the boat, they had her medicine and encouraged her to take it. They were actually caring for her rather nicely. They'd provided her with some clothes — smart sportswear in her size and deck shoes, along with toiletries and makeup, a French perfume, lace underthings, several silk camisoles and negligees, a couple of scanty bikinis, a floppy straw sunhat, a plush robe, and flip-flops. The man they called Skip, who piloted the boat, was also the cook, and he was happy to serve her whenever she liked. Vasili didn't always join her at the table. In fact, he kept to himself a lot of the time. She could hear him and Oleg speaking in muffled tones behind doors, and they must do a lot of drinking because she saw bottles on the wet bar, mostly vodka with a Russian label, along with the fine wines and liqueurs they had at the dinners they shared with Oleg.

This morning she was alone in the bed in the master cabin where she'd been kept all along. Vasili never slept beside her, thank God. Once he'd sensed she was playing his game and wouldn't make a fuss, she was free to get up and walk around on this luxurious yacht, within limits. Oleg had explained she could use the flybridge and the salon, which were on separate decks like a two-story apartment, and she could stretch out in the sun on the forward deck. Meals were served mostly at the dinner table in the salon, which was decorated like an elegant living room, but she could always request a sandwich or a snack as she lounged on the flybridge or afterdeck. She was surprised how well she picked up the nautical jargon. Oleg was proud he knew it, proud to coach her. He was actually a rather jolly fellow, clad like a tourist in his oversize Hawaiian shirts and shorts, but she knew she would be wise to fear him, especially if she took it in her head not to cooperate.

She was amazed the boat never seemed to move. They were stuck in the middle of the lake somewhere. The water was calm, disturbed from time to time with gentle rocking from the wave of a passing speedboat, some towing skiers, others tearing past full throttle to thrill their drunken, screaming passengers.

It seemed a languid life that could go on indefinitely. She could stand it if she had her baby and if Vasili wasn't so fearsome. They were adrift in a big puddle, a watery prison.

She couldn't imagine what Vasili intended to do.

SHACKLETON HAD A PLAN, but he knew it was by no means flawless. The outcomes hinged on how events transpired. He refused to allow Churpov to pull him down. And commandeering his boat had been the ultimate humiliation. All he could do now was be smart and play the odds.

Around five in the morning, he parked the Ducati in the lot at the marina. He shucked his bomber jacket, tucked it with his helmet into a carryall, and looked unremarkable in a T-shirt, KC Royals ball cap, and black jeans. Only the cowboy boots said he was a landlubber. He had to sign out the boat with the harbormaster on duty, and he bowed his head in cursory greeting to a couple of fishermen on the dock who were loading up their outboard for a day of trolling along the shoals.

He boarded the houseboat alone.

If he were to encounter any of the Coast Guard vessels out on the water, they'd surely order him to turn back. They'd allow no civilian boats anywhere near the action. Shackleton reasoned that they'd come in several patrol boats and set up a perimeter some way off from the *Namouna*. He guessed 100 – 200 yards, close enough to hail the yacht over loudspeakers yet keeping a cautious distance because they'd assume the target would repel any boarding attempt. Weapons on both sides would be well within range at that distance, however.

Shackleton had his deer rifle. The Ruger American .308 with Nikon scope had a maximum range of more than 600 yards, but accuracy at that distance would be nearly impossible. He wouldn't get many chances, and the rifle only held four rounds. He figured if he could get within 300 – 400 yards, he'd be close enough for a kill shot. So he'd try to approach as close as he dared. When they hailed him, he'd come about in compliance, making his way slowly toward shore.

Then he'd go dead in the water long enough to take his shot. Choppy water might frustrate his aim, but he figured he could cope with the slight bobbing of the houseboat on the usually calm lake. If he could assume a firing position before the engagement with the Coast Guard began, he might have a chance of sighting and dropping Churpov. In any case, he'd have to take the chance both sides would assume they were being fired upon, and a firefight would ensue. There would be casualties and his lovely boat would be torn up, but at least the disgusting gangster would not have the option of peaceful surrender.

Besides, his friend in the Caymans owned the bigger boat he coveted.

If the girl were killed, her life would be a sacrifice, collateral damage. Holding her hostage, after all, was the one way Churpov might be able to spare himself. She was not for Luke, and Luke was not for anyone. The boy would get over it, as he was sure to face an inevitable lifetime of hurt, and guilt for her death would haunt Shackleton forever.

Coyle had deserved his fate. So would Churpov.

Shackleton was not about to let the Russian live.

～

Melissa knew that Vasili had the VIP cabin to himself, and the guest cabin was for Oleg and Skip. Those were the only other staterooms onboard. Three other crew, all of them men, slept on the couches on the flybridge, and two more huddled in the small "beach club," a closet-sized cabin with benches off the engine room where bathers could dress and egress the boat at the stern.

After he'd made sure she understood she was to answer to the name Tatyana, Vasili's questions of her had stopped, along with whatever game he'd been playing. So far, he hadn't touched her, which made her alternately relieved and apprehensive. To make sure they wouldn't harm her baby, she was prepared to go along with the game. But either this Russian boss was planning some exquisite torture or he'd already lost interest in her. If he'd decided the game was over, he'd either put her ashore or kill her.

But for now, it was all too pleasant.

At 5:45 in the morning, just at daybreak, four U.S. Coast Guard patrol boats set off from the west banks of Warsaw, Missouri, on the Truman Reservoir side of the dam, and headed south and upstream along the Pomme de Terre arm toward the location of the *Namouna,* which was drifting at anchor in the deepest water of the fork at the mouth of the Osage Arm, about 28 miles downstream of the yacht's home marina slip in Osceola. Those boats carried a contingent of 24 federal officers in total, comprising a SWAT team with high-powered rifles and body armor, as well as divers with rubber rafts. A helicopter dispatched by U.S. Treasury ATF set down on a rise near Osage Bluff, the closest onshore rendezvous point and less than a half-mile from the marina from which Shackleton had set out this morning.

Shackleton had succeeded in navigating within 200 yards of the yacht when the patrol boats overtook him. The lead boat sounded a claxon, and an anonymous voice commanded, "Come about and head to shore!" Shackleton complied, proceeded under power for a few minutes until all the boats had passed him, then cut the engine and started to drift.

The patrol boats diverged to encircle the *Namouna,* giving her a wide berth of about 100 yards in each direction, just as the banker had guessed.

Second mate Kiril had the con on the yacht, saw the approach on the monitors, and alerted Skip and the others. They were already dressed, having slept in their clothes, except for Vasili, who pulled on his pants in a sour mood because he was unused to being awakened at such an early hour. All of the men, including Skip, donned sidearms, and the security crew also took up Kalashnikov assault rifles.

All this activity took place around Melissa, who, having been awakened by the voice in her head, was sitting demurely at breakfast in her bathrobe on the afterdeck of the flybridge. Skip had been on duty at first light, and she'd prevailed on him to serve up generous portions of scrambled eggs, toast with marmalade, and orange juice.

Decked out in a wetsuit over which he wore Kevlar body armor, Evan steadied himself at the railing on the deck of the *USCGC Milton* flanked by two scuba divers. Beside him stood Leon and Special Agent Arlen Brinkman, the hostage negotiator, who had the mic to the ship's hailing bullhorn at the ready.

Technicians on all ships had binoculars and acoustic surveillance dishes trained on the yacht. The audio was fed to comms receivers in their earpieces so all the officers could hear whatever transpired at the target.

Brinkman cast glances at his colleagues, finally resting on Leon, making sure all of them were ready and alert.

SHACKLETON LAY prone on the aft deck of the houseboat, the butt of the Ruger pressed to his shoulder. The surface of the lake had remained calm, allowing him to use the railing of the boat as a stable turret. He'd draped a blanket over his head and the rifle so that only the tip of the barrel stuck out. After taking a deep breath and holding it, he had the afterdeck of the *Namouna* squarely in his sights. He fingered the trigger nervously.

He'd have a clear shot at anyone who ventured out on the afterdeck. When inside the flybridge, they'd be surrounded by smoked glass, presenting a more challenging target.

He was doing this for Luke and for this little forgotten corner of the country he loved. He no longer thought the Church could stand for righteousness, not after what Coyle had done. Big, corrupt offshore money was buying up everything, and it wouldn't be long before real Americans would be taking orders from the likes of Churpov and his bosses.

⁓

BRINKMAN BEGAN to raise the bullhorn mic to his mouth.

⁓

SHACKLETON COULD SIGHT Melissa sitting at the table on the afterdeck. There was no sign of Churpov. Time was running out. If he took his shot now, if he killed her instead of her captor, his purpose could be served. Each side would think the other had fired upon them, and the Feds would prevail.

He would hate himself for the rest of his life, but he couldn't catch a glimpse of Churpov, the girl was expendable.

⁓

ON THE *NAMOUNA,* the crewmen were assuming prone positions with their weapons around the railings of the yacht as Vasili barked orders to them in Russian from the captain's chair, which was forward, well within the interior and surrounded by dark glass. Oleg stood alongside him arguing, perhaps urging there was no reason to start shooting.

⁓

EVEN VETERAN FEDERAL agents were unnerved when the fury of hell exploded in their earpieces.

~

THAT'S when Melissa's body went rigid as if she'd touched a high-tension wire. As she sat bolt upright, she flung both arms open violently, flinging dishware, silver, and glasses from the table. The chaotic clatter jangled already frayed nerves, confusing the bosses and crew. As her jaw clenched and her face turned red, she fell to the deck, kicking violently, making distressed gagging sounds.

Already in a panic, Vasili, Oleg, and Skip shouted at each other in their mysterious mother tongue, and only Oleg rushed to her side.

"She's having a fit!" he exclaimed in Russian as he knelt down next to her. "We must do something! She could choke!"

Vasili, whom the girl had presumed to be the cruel torturer, was suddenly horror-struck. "Don't touch her!" he shouted.

Oleg bent over her writhing body, "But we must help her! She could swallow her tongue!"

"Give her this to bite on!" Skip cried, holding out a wadded-up dishtowel.

Oleg took the cloth and was reaching down to pry her mouth open when Vasili stopped him with the command, "Leave her!" He spat out, "She is possessed!" He drew his pistol, aimed it at his trusted surrogate, and ordered, "Both of you. Back off or the spirits will enter you, and I will have to shoot you all."

"No!" Oleg appealed to his boss. "You can't! You won't! You kill her and the demons won't die. We'll all be doomed. They will overtake you, and you'll die cursed yourself!"

Her kicking suddenly stopped. Her eyes grew wide and wet, her face flushed red with rage. She drew herself up on her knees, splayed now on all fours, facing Vasili like some crouching, snarling dog.

When she opened her mouth, her voice croaked. It was a horrific sound — a rasping, tormented, menacing bellow, as she pronounced, "Dmitri Sergeyvitch Churpov!"

The man they called Vasili stood frozen. His face had suddenly gone white and rigid with fear. His breaths came as gasping wheezes. His inhaler was in the front pocket of his pants, but he couldn't command his muscles to reach in and grasp it.

For the first time in years, Churpov was bewildered and panicked. The old asthma took hold of him. He'd learned it was a passing, if searing, discomfort — if only he could control himself and not fly into a rage. But this time he feared he might not slip so quickly through the vise grip of pain.

This time he might be finished!

"You have betrayed your unholy vow to us," the girl snarled as she rose to her feet, steadying herself on the edge of the table. "You allow yourself to be defeated by these pathetic mortals, to bring us down, to defy our plan. You serve only yourself, and we cast out your worthless soul, into the deepest circle of Hell to suffer in anguish for eternity!"

While the boss stood transfixed, Oleg moved toward Melissa, but the demonic voice stopped him, "Touch her and we cast you immediately into the Lake of Fire to burn forever!"

During her explosive rant, Skip had ducked into the supply cabinet under the wet bar. He emerged with a coiled rope. In a rapid series of moves, he shoved a chair under Melissa from behind. Her knees buckled, and she sat back into the chair. Skip expertly threw one, then two, coils of rope around her body, pulling them tight and lashing her to the chair.

"I didn't touch her," he said breathlessly, his excuse to Churpov.

From across the water came the voice on the bullhorn: "Private vessel *Namouna!* This is the U.S. Coast Guard. We are monitoring your situation. Stand down. We are sending help." Then the voice added, "He is a man of God. An exorcist. Signal you acknowledge."

SHACKLETON LOST HIS NERVE. Events had taken a bizarre twist, and now he judged the moment had passed.

He watched in amazement as the lead cutter pulled up alongside the *Namouna* without firing a shot. And even as the Feds were climbing aboard the yacht from the fantail, Churpov's gunmen and the captain were leaping over the port side into the water, leaving their weapons lying on the deck. Shackleton realized it was the smart move. The scuba team wouldn't hesitate to pull them out.

He shuddered to think what he'd almost done. He was far from blameless, but at least he hadn't taken an innocent life.

He guessed who this miracle worker was, and he was suddenly impressed with the dark humor of the situation. If some higher power were directing Evan Wycliff, perhaps mere mortals had best allow that divine plan to work.

C'MON INN

WEDNESDAY MORNING

*T*he iconic diner was packed and buzzing with excited gossip. You'd think the ghost of Elvis had risen from the dead and was expected at any moment.

Evan and Leon entered to applause, cheers, whistles, and foot-stomping.

As they took the seats Cora had saved for them at the counter, someone yelled, "Let's hear it for the Preacher Man!"

To which Cora yelled back, "Pancakes on the house!"

Evan realized he was expected to say something. He remained seated, raised a hand in modest acknowledgment, and called out, "I don't know what you've heard, but if you want to know what really happened, catch my sermon at First Baptist on Sunday!"

It's worth a try, anyway. I hope Marcus has enough coffee and donuts for fellowship afterward.

Cora was already setting their coffee in front of them when she announced, "Take it easy on the new trainee, you hear?"

Loretta had been working alongside the cook at the griddle in the back. She turned, came forward, and stepped from behind Cora. Without makeup and her hair pulled back, she was much less of a sensation than she'd been in her last appearance here. But her face was glowing, and anyone could see she was about the prettiest young woman in town.

Cora quipped, "I'm jealous as all get-out, but if she can manage on minimum wage and tips, I can sure use the help." She bustled off to pick up four steaming plates of hotcakes from the cook. She juggled them — one in each hand, one on each forearm — as she headed out to deliver them to some hungry farmers in one of the booths.

Loretta smiled and said to Evan, "I haven't had a chance to thank you."

"Happy to provide the job reference, my dear," Evan replied. "At least you can put food on the table when your sister comes back."

At Leon's urging, the Feds had released Melissa into Evan's custody after the rescue, and he'd driven her to Myerson. The new interim director hadn't shown up yet, but Evan made Clint promise she'd get compassionate care until she could get a proper workup and new prescriptions. And supervised visits with Luke. Now that she was out of the clutches of the man she called Vasili, she was obsessed with finding Buzz. Evan promised that reuniting her with her boy would be his next assignment, and perhaps because she realized he'd had a hand in this miracle, she believed he could do it and let herself relax a bit.

I'll have to put Jeremy to work on the custodial issues.

"I mean for what you did," Loretta explained.

"Just what did you do?" Leon teased. "Sure, it was another miracle. But I'm interested in what the magician did behind the curtain."

Evan explained, "You told me Dmitri Churpov had been raised Eastern Orthodox. And I did some research. I also had the benefit of a long talk with Reverend Mother Bernadette about Catholic doctrine on demonic possession. The Eastern Church is more rooted in the past, and particularly in those rural villages, the old superstitions would still be strong. Any mental disability is proof of sinfulness, possession by the devil — period, no question. Then I tried to see into Churpov's soul. I took some wild guesses. You said he'd been an altar boy, may have been devout when he was young. So he felt all the more betrayed when both parents and his sisters met senseless, violent deaths. He was no stranger to evil and evil deeds when he served in the army, and when he got out, maybe he thought he'd made a deal with the devil. Now he must think that worked because he'd become very successful, incredibly wealthy, very fast. The key is, Satan is more real to him, more powerful — and actually more just, in his experience — than God is. Churpov trusted their bargain. Some of the faithful think God protects them, favors them, so they can't come to harm. Maybe that's what Churpov believed when he was a boy, why he felt so betrayed when it all went bad. So then he believed that Satan would protect him the same way. That's why he was so confident no one could touch him on that boat."

Leon mused, "So, Churpov feared the wrath of Satan much more than any earthly punishment the U.S. government could inflict on him. But how did you know Melissa would suffer a fit of epilepsy at just the right moment?"

Evan smiled. "She didn't have a fit, not clinically anyway. She was putting on an incredible show. She really has some acting chops after all."

"You were able to communicate with her? What did you do, smuggle a cell phone in there?"

"That was another guess. Luke said he could get into her mind, pick up her feelings. He claims he hears voices. So I wondered if it could work the other way. I asked him if he could send her messages. So right after sunup, when the raid was going down, right on cue, she gave the performance that saved her life."

Leon turned to Evan with a sardonic smile and said, "You were so busy hovering over Melissa, you missed the collar. Brinkman and I took two of the guys to search the lower decks. We figured Churpov was still armed, and very possibly panicked. He wasn't on the bridge, and at first we thought he'd gone over the side with the others. Then we found him curled up on the deck of the little cabin, not much bigger than a closet, next to the engine room. His guy Oleg was standing over him holding an asthma inhaler. Between wheezes, all the guy could manage to say was, 'Take her. Get her off. And don't let that priest come near me.'"

"Melissa obviously didn't need an exorcism. I simply reminded her God is always with us, and she didn't mind hearing it just then."

Leon teased, "So, Preacher, tell us. I get that you believe in God, despite your professed doubts. But after all this, don't tell me you believe in Satan."

You're not catching me on this one!

"All I can say for sure is that Dmitri Churpov believes fervently in Satan. And that's what brought him down."

SHERIFF'S OFFICE

WEDNESDAY NOON

The sheriff was not amused. "Wycliff, how about you move to some other jurisdiction and shake them up? This stunt you pulled might've turned out all sweet and nice, but it could just as easily have gone to hell and back."

"I'm just following where spirit leads, sheriff," Evan offered lamely.

"Damn nice piece of work," Leon put in helpfully.

"Hmph," Otis grunted. He shoved a file folder across the desk at the preacher. "You mind telling me what I'm lookin' at?"

Evan opened the folder to find three photo blowups — printouts from the Coyle autopsy. These were extreme close shots of the face and forehead. "Oh, now I'm a forensics expert?" He passed the photos to Leon so he could also have a look.

"They got their opinions," Otis said. "But something tells me there's a religious significance, and these days you-da-man in that regard."

The first view showed an ashen cross painted on the forehead, just above and between the eyebrows. In another shot, the cross filled the frame, and at this magnification, two puncture marks could be seen in the center of the cross. The marks were separated by about four centimeters, as though the priest had been stabbed with a barbeque fork. The third shot had been taken at even greater magnification, and the soot had been cleaned off. In the areas around the puncture lesions, the skin was reddish-brown and swollen.

"Well, first I'd say, you probably want my opinion as a farm boy and not a preacher," Evan began.

"Pray tell?"

"Burn marks. From a cattle prod," Evan said. To Leon, he asked, "Is that a Russian assassination device?"

"Nah," Leon replied as he frowned over the curious markings. "If Russians want to kill you in private, they shoot you in the face. As a lesson to others. If they want to off you in public, they stab you with poison or run you over with a car. And if they really want to make their point, they throw you off a building."

"But what about that cross?" Otis demanded.

"It's not just the Christian sign," Evan murmured. "It's covering up the puncture marks, which no examiner could miss. And then there's the location."

"Heh," Otis sighed. "Right between the eyes!"

"In the *third* eye," Evan insisted. Then he added, "You're right. I'd agree it's a message. A rather sophisticated one. Religious, or I'd say esoteric."

"Russians are crafty," Leon put in. "But subtle, they're not."

Evan said, "It's an angry message. In the esoteric tradition, which these days we'd call New Age, the third eye is the portal of insight, the window to the soul. It's where the spiritual light gets in. The killer is telling us Coyle betrayed his calling, corrupted his inner light. And then the cross marking took some trouble to plan and do. Mind you, the stabbing had to be executed swiftly, had to be a surprise. The cross covers the transgression. That is, Coyle used his office and his false piety to cover up his crimes. So he betrayed himself, his religious community, and his holy office."

Otis asked, "So some Catholic killed him?"

"Perhaps, but the message is telling us something else. Let me ask, did Sister Margaret give you a description of the courier? The guy who showed up right before they found Coyle dead?"

Otis shrugged. "Not much help. Rode up on a motorcycle, which she heard but didn't see. He had on a leather jacket, black jeans, and boots. Wearing one of those helmets that cover the whole head. I think they call it Bandit style because the faceplate is all blacked out."

Evan shot a look at Leon, who only knew some of the story. Then the preacher explained, "It's difficult for someone to be both a Mason and a Catholic. Traditionally, going back a few hundred years, the Freemasons were founded to oppose the Church and the king. These days, they are supposed to be nondenominational, and they don't seem to have trouble admitting a Catholic to membership. But the Church still won't condone Masonry. Now, there's nothing about the third eye in Catholic philosophy. In fact, the symbol would probably be regarded as occult and heretical. But to the Masons, the eye represents divine, all-seeing wisdom."

"All this meaning what?" Otis asked, growing impatient.

"Meaning you shouldn't waste any time picking up Lodge Grand Master Stuart Shackleton on suspicion of murder. He just bought a new Ducati, and you just described his motorsports attire."

CORK 'N KEG BAR AND GRILL, APPLETON CITY

FRIDAY NIGHT, ONE WEEK LATER

*E*van was buying Leon a hearty sendoff dinner at the local steakhouse. They'd been through several rounds of Wild Turkey, and Leon's admiration for Evan was positively glowing. Loretta had informed Evan earlier today that the casino — in fact, the entire hotel chain — had been sold to another international hospitality group. Mick Heston had accepted their offer with a transfer to New Zealand, and extradition would be pursued — that is, if he didn't manage to flee somewhere else so he'd be out of reach. The local cops had picked up Jack Nathan and charged him with insurance fraud.

And Bernice Richards must have seen the light on her way to Damascus because she'd called to say she was making a formal recommendation to child welfare that Loretta get at least temporary custody of Melissa once the new doctor at Myerson judged she'd be stable on her cocktail of maintenance drugs. And when Edie learned her lover had been apprehended and charged with felonies, she'd driven over to Loretta's, handed over the squalling Buzz, and informed her she'd be locking up the house in Stockton and taking up permanent residency in Scottsdale.

Leon summarized, "With Coyle dead and if we didn't suspect anyone else had a hand in it, there might not be anyone to link Shackleton to Churpov's sex ring. Could be that Richards and Wilmer suspected, but so far, we can't prove they were witting accomplices." He reflected, then went on, "Otis figured Wilmer hustled the cremation and then promptly skipped out of town. That's what made our clever sheriff suspect it wasn't just a heart attack. No doubt Wilmer couldn't miss the burn marks. Whether he thought he was protecting Shackleton or staying clear of the Russians, we won't know until they pick him up, which should be soon."

Evan agreed and followed with, "And no one can prove Griggs knew enough to implicate him in any crime. He'll say he was just carrying messages — and documents — between responsible parties. If he knew Shackleton and Coyle were in business with Churpov, I doubt he'll admit anything now. But you can bet he'll be playing it straight. And Otis will be keeping an eye on him." Evan took a long pull to drain his drink, looked up wistfully at Leon, and said, "I'm going to miss you, brother."

The G-man chuckled and knocked back his own whiskey. "We better cut ourselves off pretty soon because we're going to have to head out at oh-dark-thirty to catch my flight in Springfield."

"I'd ask you to stay, but it's up to you to wipe out the rest of the sex trade, after all."

Leon grew uncharacteristically serious. "I wish it were so, my friend. You saved a girl's life, we caught some hoods, and we caused a nasty operation to close down. We didn't get everybody, but we never do. But — *wipe out* the sex trade? Never happen in any lifetime. It's not only pushing the world's oldest profession, but it's also one of the world's oldest and largest global enterprises. Slavery has been and will continue to be just one department. Today, all forms of human slavery, including the sex trade, account for more than a hundred and fifty billion dollars a year. And that's a conservative estimate. And why do I think there's no stopping it? The profit margin is around *sixty* percent. The best-run multinational corporation in a good year returns about eleven."

"And the Russians are in charge?"

"You can't say they run it all. It's everywhere, with tentacles into every government and every major business you could name. But these days, Russians have a lot more cash than anybody, simply because oligarchs only pretend to respect the banking laws."

"Wow," Evan said. "You're a real buzzkill."

"Hey," Leon chided. "Why so glum? Look who you've got on your side!"

FIRST BAPTIST

SUNDAY MORNING

*P*astor Thurston was overjoyed for Evan to deliver the guest sermon, doubly pleased because the sanctuary was packed. Birch needed help setting up folding chairs in the aisles and out into the hallway. Even then, some of the men had to stand against the wall in the back.

Loretta sat in the first row, beaming up at the preacher, and there was Bernice Richards nestled cozily beside her.

Some people will rush to the side of the angels, at least when they're winning.

Evan didn't hold back with the facts. The unvarnished truth was juicier than gossip, and that's what most of them were eager to hear. The news that some of their high-school-age girls had been literally sold into slavery went down hard. Appearances, and the otherwise honorable practice of job creation through internship, had been much easier to believe.

"So here we are," he continued, "gathered again as we're confronted with another horrific crime that makes us ask, 'Why is there evil in the world?'

"I'm not sure we can ever know. But we can decide what we intend to do about it.

"Now, I hope you'll agree we can't overcome evil by praying it will go away. We can't ask God for miracles, because on Earth, in this physical world, we humans have to make our own miracles. Let me give you an example. We read in the Gospel of John that, when Jesus attended a wedding at Cana, he turned some water to wine because they were having such a good time they ran short. Now, people point to that and say, 'Why, that was a miracle. No mere mortal could do that.' But I believe God created a physical universe that operates according to physical laws, rules that absolutely can't be violated, not even by this man Jesus when he was flesh and bone and blood.

"I've said many times from this pulpit, and I will remind you today, that taking every word in the Bible literally can get us into a whole lot of trouble. This is my belief, and I know many of you don't share it. But when I was in college, I studied the Bible very closely. I learned the history of how it came to be written. I learned about all the theologians and scholars who've offered interpretations over the centuries. And I've come to believe that there never was what you'd call an Age of Miracles. No, I also studied quantum physics and stellar evolution, and I can state firmly that the laws of the physical universe then and now follow from the same unyielding principles they did right after the creation, fourteen billion years ago.

"What, then, is the Holy Bible? Is it a work of fiction? Mythology? I suggest to you that the inspired word of God is a book of profound wisdom — expressed as poetry and oral history. And the miracle of turning water to wine is a good example.

"You see, Jesus led a group of revolutionaries. The Romans feared those rebels would one day overthrow their empire. And the movement that came to be known as Christianity brought down the Rome Empire eventually, but it took centuries of struggle, and not by the kind of uprising anyone expected.

"The religious order associated with those Jewish rebels was the Essenes, and they lived apart, encamped in the desert outside Jerusalem. Another conservative, traditional faction of the Jews, which included the aristocratic sects called the Sadducees and the Pharisees, taught that, in the temple, men were to be segregated from women. They taught that only the men should conduct the service, read the prayers, and sing the hymns. But the radical Essenes Jesus led believed that women should join in all of it — on an equal footing with the men.

"The ritual drink of the traditional Jews at the time was water. Jesus taught the radicals to use wine instead as a symbol of their faith and their rebellion.

"The story was handed down in coded form — as a parable — because anyone who advocated using wine instead of water in the rituals would be branded a heretic and punished — not by the Romans but by the Jewish establishment. But all the rebels knew what the parable really meant.

"So Jesus made a world-changing miracle — an epic transformation so much more powerful and lasting than providing a few more drinks for a wedding celebration. The poetry and the oral history give us the inspiring news that Jesus turned the water to wine. He welcomed women into the sanctuary as fully empowered worshippers, and the faith of those rebels is our legacy today. And why many of you are sitting where you are in this sanctuary."

Evan ended his message by leading them in prayer. To many, perhaps most, of his listeners, the lesson he'd just given was outrageous blasphemy. But they listened respectfully, and some even considered the possibility that he could be right.

Because no one could deny he was the preacher who had worked miracles.

EPILOGUE

ZED MOTORS, MONDAY MORNING

*E*van didn't blame his employer for being upset with him. His investigations on behalf of the Shackletons and the Bentons had taken him away from his primary responsibilities for more than a week. His list of sixty-plus-day, past-due accounts now had five names on it, and he had no progress to report.

When Evan reported to Zip Zed in the office at the dealership, the man had a scowl on his face. Evan expected a scolding, and he was fully prepared to own up to it and promise heartfelt repentance.

Just because they're saying I can work miracles doesn't mean I can bring all his folks current.

But even before Evan had a chance to sit, Zip surprised him with, "Arthur Redwine was in here, got his tail all in a twist. And you're the only one can do something about it."

Evan sat down hard. Redwine was not on any list of his, and, as far as he knew, the old fellow was a time-honored client of the dealership only because his refurbished Model T roadster was perpetually in need of spare parts that were impossible to find.

Evan was genuinely mystified. "Me? You know I'd do whatever is necessary to please that loveable coot. I can't imagine how I might have offended him."

Zip sat back and put his feet up on his desk. "Well, I confess I'm partially to blame. I'm the one gave you that little Fiat to drive."

"It's a sweet ride. What's Arthur's issue with it?"

"He says it is not suitable transportation for a Man of God to be driving."

Evan chuckled, "Yeah, when I had it stored in his barn he called it 'that infernal Catholic thing.' But what business is it of his?"

Zip broke out in a gleeful smile, "He wants to buy you a new car! And I'm just the deserving vendor to sell it to you."

Oh, Zip. You shameless peddler!

Evan pushed back, "But I like what you gave me. Everybody knows it's me when they see it coming."

Zed spread his hands. "The owner giveth and the owner taketh away."

"For what purpose? Who else wants it?"

"For the purpose of earning me a profit and making you an honest customer, that's for what purpose."

"So, what are my options?"

Now Zip was in his element, the proud pitchman: "I can put you in a new Lincoln Navigator Premier. Color, Infinite Black. All tricked out and prepped. It's on the lot. I'm having it washed as we speak."

"That's a tank! I can't afford the gas! And, besides, that paint job? Infinite Black? For a Man of God? That should tell you something, right there."

"Okay, we can downsize a bit. Lincoln Aviator Grand Touring. Color, Pristine White Metallic. Downright angelic!"

"How can I afford this? Not just the gas, but how about insurance? And what kind of impression would it give? Marcus drives a Focus that's long past its prime. I'm sure you sold it to him. Or maybe your father did."

"We'll title it to the church. Consider it a company car. Arthur can even write it off. He'll love that!"

"Come on, Zip. This just isn't fair."

Now Zip was annoyed. He'd expected the preacher to be grateful. "Would it spoil some vast eternal plan if you were seen driving a Ford product for a change?"

"Besides, I'm not even an employee of the church, as you know."

"We can fix that, I'm told. Marcus wants to retire — as *you* know. I wouldn't mind having you off my payroll anyway."

"I'm not on your payroll. You pay me commission. Or has it been so long you don't remember?" He thought a moment, then suggested, "I wouldn't mind slightly more comfortable living accommodations."

The trailer is even less sumptuous than the car. But the price is right.

Zip pretended to think. "You show some kind of salary, you can take your pick. Edie will be selling the Taggart place on the lake. Shackleton won't need that grand house when he's in jail. And they're going to drag Redwine kicking and screaming into assisted living any day. That farmhouse has a view for miles around, plus those ponds are stocked with smallmouth bass."

"As for the first two, no way I'll live with those memories. And the Redwine place, it may have been charming in its day, but it's a ramshackle dump."

"Nothing that can't be fixed with a stick of dynamite. You can build!"

"Zip, are you serious? Where are you going with all this?"

Zed did get serious when he replied, "I woke up this morning, and I was thinking about the accounts. I love you like a brother, Evan, but you're the wrong guy for the job. Then I'm thinking, *What is Evan suited for? My dear friend, they say he can work miracles, but what can he do in the real world?* Then it hit me. Of course, the pulpit. That part is a no-brainer. But then I'm thinking — and here's the vision that came to me, it just came to me — why don't you propose to that hot Loretta Benton? Now, we both know the Shackleton boy and her sister probably can't make it on their own. Even with the miracles of modern medicine. And then there's the baby. But you guys take a big house, you and Loretta get custody of her sister and the kid, and — it's another goddamn *miracle* — you're one happy family."

"Wow," Evan muttered. "Don't do me any favors."

"And do you know how I know this is the perfect solution?"

"I know you're going to tell me."

"You will absolutely *need* that Navigator!"

∿

EVAN DIDN'T GIVE Zip an answer. Instead, he promised to get to work on his list right away, and he left the office quickly.

Back in his by-now beloved Italian Easter egg, he was hardly shocked when Naomi finally reappeared, sitting demurely in the passenger seat she often occupied.

She's smiling like she won. I hate it when she gloats. And gets all dressed up like it's a party. As if we could ever go.

There was a long pause before he started the car. At last, she asked, "So, what do you think of Mr. Zed's plan?"

I bet I know who put it into his head!

Evan replied submissively, "I told him I'd think about it."

To which Naomi ordered, "Don't think — *pray.* And then honor the answer."

EXPLORE THE SERIES

(YOU NEEDN'T READ THEM IN SEQUENCE)

Preacher Finds a Corpse (#1)

A lapsed divinity student who is fascinated by astrophysics finds his best friend shot dead in a cornfield. It looks like suicide. Having returned to his farm roots near Lake of the Ozarks, Evan works as a skip tracer for the local car dealer. He learns his friend was involved in a dispute over farmland ownership that goes back two centuries - complicated now by plans to make an old weapons facility a tourist attraction.

Paperback · Kindle · EPUB · Audiobook

Preacher Fakes a Miracle (#2)

Evan often gets dragged into dealing with problems others have given up solving. An orphanage serves young women, and some get placed in part-time work at the lakeside resorts. They're supposed to be working in the laundry, but some get recruited as escorts for favored guests. And then one goes missing. Along with related abuses of the child welfare system, Evan uncovers the teen trafficking ring run out of a luxury casino resort by a Russian oligarch.

Paperback · Kindle · EPUB

Preacher Raises the Dead (#3)

A full-time minister now, Evan visits the hospitals. He attends to near-death experience, late-stage dementia, long-term coma, and consequences of the pandemic. His old nemesis investment banker Stuart Shackleton is back — and claims to be converted. Shackleton's money sustains a critical-care medical breakthrough, the building of a new church, and a career boost for Evan as a celebrity evangelist. Has Evan sold his soul?

Paperback · Kindle · EPUB

This Book - Preacher Stalls the Second Coming (#4)

A crazed scientist knocks on Evan's door with a bizarre warning - the Deep State may be planning to fake the Second Coming of Christ with advanced virtual-reality technology. Meanwhile, a faith-healing evangelist is luring poor and homeless people to a religious retreat with promises of ample food, then exhorting them to prepare for the End Times by starving themselves to death. Evan can't ignore these unbelievable stories when a young woman from his church disappears inside the cult leader's farm.

Paperback · Kindle

NOW READ THE SEQUEL

PREACHER RAISES THE DEAD (EVAN WYCLIFF #3) - SAMPLE

Guest preacher and part-time investigator Evan Wycliff reluctantly takes on the role of full-time minister and walks straight into more responsibility and trouble than he can handle. He attends to near-death experience, late-stage dementia, long-term coma, and consequences of the pandemic. His old nemesis investment banker Stuart Shackleton is back — and claims to be converted! Shackleton's money sustains a critical-care medical break-through, the building of a new church, and a career boost for Evan as a celebrity evangelist. Are these thrilling transformations part of a divine plan, or has Evan sold his soul?

CHAPTER 1.

Evan Wycliff didn't consider Stuart Shackleton his personal adver-sary, but the investment banker certainly was his nemesis. Every time the fellow made a request of him, it led the preacher into a nest of snakes. And now, as a result of Evan's curious meddling into matters that needn't concern him, Shackleton was behind bars pending trial on a charge of first-degree murder. If he were convicted, perhaps the consequences of the man's schemes would soon be at an end.

It was the height of the pandemic. The balmy spring weather in southern Missouri at least offered more opportunities for holed-up families to venture outside and greet their neighbors. Here in the courtroom, fewer than half the participants were wearing masks. State government hadn't mandated wearing them, and Evan well knew that whether on or off was pretty much a badge of political affiliation. Predictably, the defendant wasn't masked. He had friends and connections in Jeffersonville. Evan had one on, and his reputation as science apologist to his church congregation required him to set an example. Now that he was pastor, those pressures were wearing him down.

Despite what I think and advise, if all of the folks were wearing masks, it would look like a convocation of the Klan in here.

The alleged murder of Father Michael Coyle of Flat Bank Catholic Charities had occurred more than a year ago. As the pretrial of the case had dragged on, Shackleton was in jail because he was a flight risk. A guy with all that money and access to private jets would have to be.

So it was ironic in the extreme when last evening Shackleton's attorney Bertram Harrison phoned Evan and urged him to pay a compassionate visit to Ann Shackleton because her husband was in lockup.

"She's in a bad way," Harrison had told him, perhaps saying all he knew about it.

Evan had never visited the assisted-living wing of the Myerson Clinic. He'd certainly had enough to do with the adolescent treatment and rehab programs when he'd counseled teenage Luke Shackleton. He was struck by the signage on the building: *Myerson Memory Center.* True, many if not all of its patients were challenged with dementia, but he doubted whether the focus of treatment was improving or even recapturing their memories. Now he was here to see Ann because presumably her husband was worried about her, but the reasons were still unclear. Before erstwhile pastor Rev. Marcus Thurston had retired, regular compassionate visits had been part of his routine. Now Evan realized making those rounds would fall to him.

Thurston had served as the first black minister of a predominantly white congregation in this farmland community. Evan could only imagine how difficult it had been for him, especially in the early days of his service. And as long as Evan had known him, the old pastor had been wise about knowing when to keep his mouth shut. And perhaps fortunately for his sanity, he'd retired before the onset of Covid. On public health policies since that time, he'd expressed no opinions, while agreeing privately with the deacons when they decided worship services should be suspended.

Amid governmental confusion over pandemic policies, local medical facilities and assisted-living centers in this state were still permitting compassionate visits, counseling family members to come less often and to distance themselves when they did. As a member of the clergy, Evan was permitted everywhere except inside an ICU, but he had to wear both a mask and a plastic face shield as well as answer a checklist of health questions to gain admission to each facility.

Before she'd slipped into dementia in recent years, Ann Shackleton had been a devout Catholic. She might not know or care about Evan's denomination, but it baffled him why Stuart Shackleton should be so eager to enlist a Baptist minister — especially Evan — for this personal mission.

What about her home church? Do they even know I'm involved?

When he asked after Ann Shackleton at the desk, Lucille, the receptionist, looked puzzled. The petite girl was so young she might be an intern. Her head was a mass of carrot-colored hair and blue-paper mask, with her eyes just peeking out, so her confusion was a perceptible squint. Rather than waving Evan through, she advised him to go back to Urgent Care and take a seat in the waiting room. After what seemed a long delay there, a registered nurse came out to greet him. Her badge identified her as Ornette Wheeler. She was middle-aged and slender, with a gaunt face the color of cocoa and more than a lifetime's share of worry lines. She'd been sweating so much the perspiration was fogging her face shield.

When he introduced himself, she also looked puzzled, asking, "Reverend, may I ask the purpose of your visit? The priest has only just left, and I must tell you it's been a difficult few hours."

"The priest?"

"Father Vasquez from All Saints," she sighed, adding in a subdued tone, "he'd come to give her the last rites at two this morning, but she went too quick."

"Oh, my," Evan said, regretting right away he hadn't asked more questions of Harrison. "I assume someone has informed her husband."

"The contact information we have at the nursing station is for his lawyer. Last night I let Mr. Harrison know she was having arrhythmia, but she's had those episodes before. Then early in the morning, as I say, she got very much worse, very fast. There's always a priest on-call, but by then all we got for the lawyer at that hour was voicemail."

I doubt you know I'm her son's guardian, but did his mother even know the boy exists?

The situation with Luke would be too complicated to explain just now. All Evan could think to say was, "I wasn't aware of the urgency. I should have come earlier. I've come too late."

"No," Nurse Wheeler assured him, "I wouldn't say that. I wouldn't say that at all."

"I don't follow."

"You see, we thought we'd lost her. Actually, we *did* lose her. She'd been in a-fib through the evening. We medicated — but suddenly, arrest. She coded, the team tried to resuscitate her, but she stayed flat-line. The doctor called it, and the team left the room. I sent a pickup order to the morgue. But evidently miracles do happen. I don't know how, but when they came to get her, she was back! Sitting up and chattering like a jaybird!" The nurse shook her head as if wondering whether she'd imagined it all.

"How is she now?"

"That's the thing. Before this, she was withdrawn. She has hardly said a word to anyone for months. Listless, low appetite. After a serious episode like this, we'd expect to keep her in ICU for a while. But today she's sitting up and running on like a motor mouth! She's not making much sense, which is her way, but she's acting like she's got a new lease on life!" This usually stoic nurse seemed close to grateful tears.

Evan asked cautiously, "May I see her? This may not be the time..."

"She's negative for Covid, so this cardiac episode is unrelated. The night-shift attending has gone home. The resident is here, but he wasn't on the floor when she coded. Me, my shift was over an hour ago, but I really want to be sure she's stabilized. You shouldn't stay long, especially if it makes her more agitated. We'd give her a sedative, but all that adrenalin right now might actually be what's sustaining her. So I'm thinking, if seeing you might help her calm down, it could be just the thing. If it's all right, I can stay in the room — I'll give you a nod if it's not working."

"Actually, she doesn't know me at all, so I don't expect she'll be telling me anything you shouldn't hear. I'm a friend of the family. Her husband is indisposed, which is why you had to go through Mr. Harrison. I want to give Stuart a report, but if this is not the time, I won't stay."

~

It was just past eight in the morning. Ann Shackleton was indeed sitting up in bed in a private room. There were oxygen tubes in her nostrils, and she was hooked up to a heart monitor, which was displaying a steady sinus rhythm.

"Doctor!" she declared as Evan entered the room with Ornette. The patient's cheeks were rosy, her eyes were sparkling blue, and her hair was a mass of white curls. Evan calculated she should be in her mid-fifties, but because of the effects of her long-term illness, he'd always thought she looked much older. But today she seemed vital and didn't look at all like an invalid who had been anywhere near death's door.

"Doctor of Divinity," Evan muttered as he sat. "I'm Reverend Wycliff from Evangel Baptist. Stuart asked me to call on you." Nurse Wheeler stood next to the bed and gently took Ann's arm by the wrist with her gloved hand as if taking her pulse. The monitor's electronics were already doing that, but Evan guessed the nurse thought her touch might be comforting to the patient, and it was her excuse to linger by the bed.

"Stuart. Stuart. Stuart. Stuart," Ann tsked, with a pronounced lisp. "That man will be the death of me. But not yet!"

And of how many others? Wait — innocent until proven guilty!

"He's had some life challenges of his own recently," Evan offered. "I'm sure he'll want to see you as soon as he can put things in order."

"You know, doctor," the woman insisted, "my left arm was hurting s-s-something awful. And pressure on my ches-s-st! But now I'm breathing easier. What did you give me? Must be good s-s-s-tuff!"

Evan realized her hissing lisp was because several of her upper teeth were missing.

Ornette interjected, "We gave you medicine to keep your heart beating steadily. You're doing fine now. But you need your rest. The Reverend can't stay long."

Evan thought to ask Ornette, "Does Mrs. Shackleton perhaps have a denture? She might be more comfortable talking if she can have it."

"Oh, I'm so sorry!" Ornette exclaimed. "In all the excitement last night I forgot where I put it."

She started to open the drawer to the bedside table when Mrs. Shackleton shouted, "Not in there. You put it in my slippers, dear."

Evan looked where Ann was pointing to see a pair of fuzzy pink slippers near his elbow, perched on the radiator. The slippers were monogrammed with the patient's initials, AKS, except the S was larger and in the middle, spelling *ASK*.

Now, there's an omen.

Evan was startled to hear Nurse Wheeler gasp as she rushed over to grab the slippers. She shoved her hand inside to retrieve Ann's dental bridge, removed it from its clear plastic bag, and quickly handed it over. Ann shoved the denture in, and her face lit up in a broad smile. Having all her teeth certainly made her prettier. Also tucked inside one of the slippers was gold jewelry, which Ann clutched at eagerly, perhaps not realizing her watch and wedding rings had also been missing.

"And put those slippers back on me," Ann commanded, this time with no lisp. "My feet are cold."

The nurse turned the covers down, replaced the slippers, and tucked the patient in. Then she turned to Evan and whispered, "Could we have a word outside?"

Ornette looked solemn, and she was shaking. Evan couldn't imagine what had transpired in the last few moments to upset her so.

As Evan got up to follow the nurse out, he said to Ann, "We'll have a longer visit when you're feeling better. Is there anything you'd like me to bring you?"

She flashed him a girlish grin and replied, "You always tell me I already have all that I need, Father."

First I'm the doctor, now I'm the priest. Yet she seems to know her husband's name.

"Wise words," Evan agreed.

She must think I'm her parish priest. I wonder whether he was the one who came to give her the rites.

In the hallway just outside Mrs. Shackleton's room, Nurse Wheeler grabbed Evan's arm as if clutching him for support.

"What's the matter?" he asked her. "Are *you* feeling okay? I suppose it's been an ordeal."

She responded breathlessly, "I removed her slippers, then I removed her denture. And her watch and her rings. I was gathering her personal effects. Procedure is to bag them before they come to take her to the morgue. But I didn't have a bag handy, so I just set them aside."

"What are you trying to tell me?"

"She couldn't have seen me do it! She'd been clinically dead for fourteen minutes!"

ACKNOWLEDGMENTS

I am grateful to my friends and colleagues John Rachel, Morrie Ruvinsky, and David Drum, who read early drafts and gave me insightful notes. Beta readers who helped me with reality checks included Pamela Jaye Smith, Peter Meech, and Marilyn Anderson. Laurie Shiers, Sharon Goldinger, and Desirée Duffy have lent their wise counsel on publishing and promotion. Heartfelt thanks to Emma Graham, who provided a close reading and editorial support. And my wife Georja Umano continues to sustain and inspire me, as well as generously indulge my extended fits of concentration.

Thanks also to the judges of Independent Press Awards and the Eric Hoffer Award for acknowledging the literary merit of *Preacher Finds a Corpse*.

References to the Family Welfare Agency in this book are entirely fictional. There is no government agency by that name in the state of Missouri. In reality, minor children who are wards of any state in the U.S. do not have the same Constitutional rights as convicted adult criminals who are incarcerated. Despite efforts by both lawmakers and child advocates over the years, matters of both family law and mental health deserve higher national priority in our debates about public policy.

I drew the human slavery statistics cited by Leon from *Sex Trafficking: Inside the Business of Modern Slavery* by Siddharth Kara. The figures he cites are dated 2007 and no doubt have not decreased since then.

The recent reinterpretation of the Marriage at Cana miracle when Jesus turned the water into wine is drawn from *Jesus and the Riddle of the Dead Sea Scrolls: Unlocking the Secrets of His Life Story* by Australian theologian Barbara Thiering.

For information and support on health conditions such as epilepsy and schizophrenia, please consult the National Alliance on Mental Illness (nami.org).

- Gerald Everett Jones
  Santa Monica, July 2020

ABOUT THE AUTHOR

GERALD EVERETT JONES is a freelance writer who lives in Santa Monica, California. He has been a longtime board member of the Independent Writers of Southern California (IWOSC) and host of the GetPublished! Radio podcast. He holds a Bachelor of Arts with Honors from the College of Letters, Wesleyan University, where he studied under novelists Peter Boynton *(Stone Island)*, F.D. Reeve *(The Red Machines)*, and Jerzy Kosinski *(The Painted Bird, Being There)*.

Find out more at geraldeverettjones.com, and read his Thinking About Thinking blog posts at geraldeverettjones. substack.com.

ALSO BY GERALD EVERETT JONES

Fiction

Harry Harambee's Kenyan Sundowner: A Novel – Multiple awards in Literary Fiction

Preacher Finds a Corpse (Evan Wycliff #1) – Multiple awards in Mystery

Preacher Fakes a Miracle (Evan Wycliff #2) – NYC Big Book Silver 2020

Preacher Raises the Dead (Evan Wycliff #3) – Multiple awards in Mystery

Preacher Stalls the Second Coming (Evan Wycliff #4)

Mick & Moira & Brad: A Romantic Comedy - Multiple awards in Romantic Comedy

Clifford's Spiral: A Novel – IPA Silver in Literary Fiction 2020

Mr. Ballpoint – Page Turner Award in Fiction Finalist 2022

Christmas Karma – WGA Diversity Award (Screenplay) 2016

Choke Hold: An Eli Wolff Thriller

Bonfire of the Vanderbilts: A Novel / *Bonfire of the Vanderbilts: Scholar's Edition*

My Inflatable Friend (Misadventures of Rollo Hemphill #1)

Rubber Babes (Misadventures of Rollo Hemphill #2)

Farnsworth's Revenge (Misadventures of Rollo Hemphill #3)

Stories and Essay *Boychik Lit*
Nonfiction

How to Lie with Charts - Eric Hoffer Award Finalist in Business 2020

The Death of Hypatia and the End of Fate

The Light in His Soul: Lessons from My Brother's Schizophrenia (with Rebecca Schaper)

Searching for Jonah: Clues in Hebrew and Assyrian History by Don E. Jones (Afterword)

www.ingramcontent.com/pod-product-compliance
Lightning Source LLC
Chambersburg PA
CBHW050403260626
47156CB00003B/846